As the only child of busy parents, Doreen Fellingham used her vivid imagination to go on amazing adventures and build wonderful worlds. Initially the stories were the ones she told herself, but eventually they were even acted out with her friends. In time she started to write these ideas down. Her career in teaching enabled her to finally develop and use many of her ideas, turning them into plays, or stories which she used along with her artwork to entertain, encourage and engage children. Travel had always played an important part in her life, from her early years with her mother and then with her husband. It was on one of these trips that she first saw her leading lady.

For Ian, who puts up with me and for friends, Barbs and Dorothy and others, (you know who you are) who provided much needed encouragement and support. Thank you.

Doreen Fellingham

THE COURIERS

AUSTIN MACAULEY PUBLISHERS®

LONDON * CAMBRIDGE * NEW YORK * SHARJAH

A CIP catalogue record for this title is available from the British Library.

ISBN 9781398462403 (Paperback)
ISBN 9781398462410 (ePub e-book)

www.austinmacauley.com

First Published 2025
Austin Macauley Publishers Ltd®
1 Canada Square
Canary Wharf
London
E14 5AA

Prologue

'Well, it's not here,' Remy Akbari said crossly, as she closed the boot of the car. 'Where did you put it?'

'Me?' Farzad laughed, his smile was both indulgent and mocking.

'I thought you had picked it up. It was on the cupboard by the door and you were the last one out. You always forget stuff. Oh goodness! That means we have left it behind.' Remy sighed and gave her husband an exasperated look. 'We can't go in without the gift, you know Serena would never forgive us.'

Perhaps, she thought, I should volunteer to go back and get it, I could check to see if he is alright, he did look so unwell. She knew her daughter, Alessia, would be home later, but returning would also give her the opportunity to speak to him alone, maybe then she could finally say what she should have said a long time ago.

Her thoughts were interrupted, as she realised that Farzad was already walking back towards the car, saying he would go back, as it wasn't far, and the roads were quiet. She started to say that she would go but was too late, he was almost in the car.

'Look, you go in; I won't be long,' he called.

Watching him go, she realised that maybe now wasn't the right time for such a difficult conversation. She called, 'Don't forget the diversion.' He nodded, there had been a board saying it would be in operation later that day. 'And see if…'

'I know. If he is feeling better, I can bring him back.' He smiled, stopped and called back. 'In case I forgot to say it in the rush, you look particularly beautiful tonight and I love you.' With that, he got in the car, waved and was gone.

Remy sighed, then turned and rang the doorbell.

Walking back to the car, Farzad smiled as his deception had worked, now he would have a chance to talk to his friend alone, to find out the truth, before he decided what to do. He owed him that.

Farzad drove up to the diversion sign and stopped at the red light. When it changed, he started to turn to go around the block. As he did, he briefly caught sight of the truck hurtling towards him. The impact was tremendous, spinning his car, which hit the kerb, and pushed it onto its side.

Across the street in a bar, people came running out at the sound of the crash. Some ran towards the car, but as they got closer, the truck seemed to explode and this set the car alight. As the car's fuel tank exploded, people ran back screaming. There was nothing they could do as the flames quickly engulfed both vehicles.

Standing silently, uncertain what to do, the crowd were amazed to see a fire engine turn the corner further up the road. The crew, returning to the station from another call, immediately sprang into action but although the flames were soon under control, it was already too late for both drivers.

The fire, although fierce, was doused quickly, meaning a crucial piece of evidence was not destroyed. Being small, it was missed by investigators, who gave the wrecks only a cursory inspection and then recorded it as just another tragic accident.

A man in a car at the end of the road picked up his phone and sent a text.

"I am sorry, darling; I have been called into a meeting and I am heading there. See you at home. Fx".

Remy sitting chatting to a friend, felt her phone buzz and picked it up. Reading the text, she was annoyed. Farzad was often called into meetings these days without any warning and she again chided herself for not having talked to him about it.

Angrily, she called Alessia's number, realising she would need a lift home. She was surprised when she heard that her friend had left, leaving a note that said he felt better, so was going home. She was relieved however, to hear that her daughter could pick her up later.

The party was almost finished when the doorbell chimed and Serena, drink in hand, walked to the door, still chatting to Remy over her shoulder.

'Probably your Uber,' she said laughing, barely looking as she opened it, expecting to see Remy's daughter, Alessia.

Turning, she was surprised instead to find herself facing a highway patrol officer and a man in plain clothes.

'Oh sorry, I thought,' she stopped immediately, flustered and suddenly fearful.

The plain clothes man offered his badge and said, 'I believe Mrs Akbari is here. We spoke briefly to her daughter, who is apparently on her way.'

Serena's hand went to her mouth as Remy, still laughing, turned around.

'Serena, are you okay?' Seeing her friend's face, she rushed to her side.

Serena shook her head. 'They are asking for you.'

Remy, a cold chill seeping through her body, faced the officers. She stammered, 'Is everything all right?' But she knew it wasn't, and never would be again.

'Can we go somewhere quiet?' The man asked. Serena nodded and now holding her friend's hand, they walked into the lounge, away from the noise of the celebration.

'I am sorry to have to tell you that your husband has been in an accident and,' he paused, clearly finding it difficult.

'What happened?' She asked, barely able to speak.

'His car was hit by a truck. I am afraid he died instantly at the scene. I am so sorry.' Remy's knees gave way.

Having dropped to the floor, Remy was barely able to get her breath.

Alessia arrived and raced sobbing into her mother's arms. They clung together oblivious of the people quietly leaving and the sudden deep silence that had now descended on the house.

Eventually, Alessia helped Serena get her mother into her car. As she reversed down her drive, they were unaware of the man watching them from a parked car across the road.

He smiled as he watched them go, then called the client's number, and said, 'It is done.' He hung up, started his car, and drove away from the house, whistling along to the radio and thinking of his next job.

The architect and deliverer of the explosion that had killed Remy's husband had been paid well for a relatively easy job. He had simply placed a small incendiary device in the petrol tank of Farzad Akbari's car and a remote-control device in the lorry of the driver, who was already dead and tied upright in his seat. He had taken over control of the traffic lights and set up a simple diversion to ensure he could control the cars that passed the spot where the "accident" would occur.

He knew that when the target's car came into sight, his well-timed and familiar plan would work well, no one would survive. Finally, he then left his calling card, a small metal lighter with the inscription "Love ♥ NY" etched into it, which he tucked under the driver's seat, where it would likely survive the flames that engulfed the car.

Once the Akbaris had left, the man lying on the couch got up and quickly went into Farzad's study. Having searched the room, he finally found the documents he was looking for and smiled. Taking an envelope from his pocket, he left it on the hall table as he left the house. Getting into his car, he threw the file onto the passenger seat and set off towards the airport. His phone rang. He answered it and after the short message, a satisfied smile twisted his lips. The money he had paid to remove one problem, had now almost certainly presented the opportunity to possess something he had long wished for. He was satisfied that the danger the dead man had represented had been dealt with.

Now for the second part of his plan.

Chapter 1

Two years later, sitting in the car on the way to the ship, Remy Akbari was deep in thought. She was recalling the awful night her husband had died. Try as she might, she could barely recall all the events or details of that evening or the next few days, grief seemed to have clouded her memory as if trying to protect her. Now, although her pain was deeply hidden and guarded, memories still returned. She remembered Alessia arriving but not the journey to the hospital, or all the people coming and going. The funeral was still a blur.

Looking out of the window, she remembered how a fire engine returning to its station saw the flames and had rushed to douse the fire, but too late sadly to save the two drivers. There had been only a brief investigation, which determined that it was clearly an "accident" and the case was closed, so some crucial evidence was lost.

Sitting alone in the car, nothing could change the longing and emptiness in her heart. All that she had left of her beautiful Farzad was his ring, his broken watch, and a small inscribed lighter. The ring and the watch were in her safe in New York. However, the lighter, which she had never seen before, was in a box somewhere.

Her limousine manoeuvred its way through the lunchtime traffic in Southampton. Remy sighed and picked up her phone to finish reading the email she had just received. Arriving at the port, if she had looked up, she might have noticed several ships were in the dock, resulting in the area being busier than the last time she was there. The driver carefully picked his way through the lines of assorted vehicles, each containing people clearly excited to see the ships. The scene was as always chaotic. People anxious to start their adventure struggled with luggage, so both they and it were scattered everywhere, making it difficult for cars to move through them.

Some were clearly excited about their impending voyage; some waved and smiled, while others now clearly irritated or frustrated at the mayhem, raised angry voices. It was not a place to linger. However, her car slowly moved well away from others. Preoccupied, she ignored the scene and the pre-arranged baggage collection service that immediately moved forward as the car stopped. They unloaded three large, expensive cases from the car's boot and then disappeared into the building.

Diamond status and those travelling in the Cunard Grill Suites were allowed priority boarding, and for her, the warmest of return greetings. Remy had travelled from New York on the ship just three weeks previously and this would be her third return trip this year. She abhorred flying, so whenever, and wherever possible, she travelled by ship. Now the internet was much improved, it ensured that much of her business could be easily completed using a fast worldwide internet connection, which was a considerable improvement on Queen Mary's previously unreliable service.

She thanked her driver as a uniformed officer from the ship opened the car door and offered his hand. Stepping out, she acknowledged him with a warm smile and a quiet thank you, then followed him through an entrance at the end of the building into the embarkation area.

Entering the cavernous hall, she noted the lines of passengers excitedly, or sometimes angrily, filling in forms, but overall, the buzz of noise and the palpable air of expectation. Remy followed the officer through the dimly lit building and out into the sunlight. As ever, she stopped and looked up at the Queen Mary, admiring her beautiful lines. She truly was an ocean liner in the finest tradition of that designation. Remy loved the mostly blue hull, the distinctive red funnel, and the red flash, below the Plimsoll line. This moment always stirred something in her heart, and she caught her breath, a faint smile played on her lips, so many memories.

Stepping onto the gangway, the smell of sea air was barely detectable but she knew it was there; her mood lightened and she felt herself relax. It had been a trying time as dealing with family matters often were. This time, her niece, Sophia, had caused yet another commotion in the family by marrying for the fourth time, this time to an elderly, titled member of the Royal Family. Remy had to work hard to calm her aunt while fending off the press. Now was not the time to think of these problems. She stepped onto the gangplank.

By now, her elegant, carefully considered appearance had not gone unnoticed by other passengers boarding the ship. As ever, she had paid great attention to the image she presented. She remembered long ago, her mother had said that even on the worst of days, "your appearance is everything". She often chided her daughter for running to meet guests in bare feet and shorts, or an old dress. Consequently, as she grew older, under her mother's watchful eye and guidance, she took great pride in her appearance. By the time she was twelve, she had visited many famous couture houses, and by eighteen, wore creations by Dior, Lanvin or Hermès.

'Come, *Mon chou*, try this on for me. *Tu es si belle, ma chérie.*'

Today, she had chosen a structured black checked Chanel suit, and a small red Balenciaga bag and shoes completed her carefully constructed appearance. Her long grey hair was artfully swept into a chignon, seemingly held in place by a single diamond star. Sunglasses hid her extremely blue eyes and red lipstick completed the look. Her slender body was the perfect frame for such a sharp image. To others, she appeared ageless.

She looked up at the familiar sleek lines of the "Queen", aware of the eyes of others who had waited in line, but she was unconcerned by their appraisal or feigned annoyance. Boarding the ship made her always remember the first time she had sailed on the previous Queen Mary when she was just a young girl. The ship now in Long Beach, California, was a relic of a golden age. She remembered that was why her father had insisted they travel on her, despite having ships of his own.

'Will we see movie stars?' She had asked him, and they had. Audrey Hepburn left a lasting memory and was the one who had most influenced her style. Remy had watched her as others watched her now. The actress had been so beautifully elegant, and Remy had tried to emulate her. Looking at her now, others could not fail but to agree.

Entering the ship, she ignored the glass of cheap fizz offered by a resplendent bell boy; instead leaning in, whispered a request. He hastily departed, quickly returning with another uniformed officer who again greeted her warmly. She slipped her arm into that of the smartly dressed man, who bowed slightly, amused by those trying not to watch. Together, they left the scene, leaving only the scent of Channel No. 5 to show she had arrived.

Having escorted Remy to her suite, the officer inclined his head in a part bow and left. Remy entered and was warmly greeted by the butler, who was busily opening a bottle of champagne. She accepted a glass of Dom Perignon and his offer to unpack. The luggage had already been taken up the curved staircase, so he disappeared, which she was glad of. Although a butler was lovely, she had things to do and didn't really want him fussing around. Remy picked up her phone and settled on the enormous sofa to read through the endless emails, finding nothing urgent to demand her attention. She settled back, enjoying the comfort and familiar surroundings of the large Balmoral suite.

As the time for the ship to depart neared, she went out onto the spacious balcony and gazed out at the scene, of people waving their farewells, highlighted by the late afternoon sunshine. As the ship cast off, she enjoyed the last warmth of the day, and as she relaxed, she felt the tension in her shoulders lift.

Leaning her elbows on the polished wood of the handrail, she watched as the sun glittered on the waves created as the ship churned the water. She thought about how ships always made her think of her childhood. As a little girl, she had followed her Uncle Panas, as he visited his shipyard. Her father was often away and although she loved him, her uncle was always there for her. Even as a small child, he talked to her, almost as if she were a friend, filling her mind with exciting stories and wonderful projects.

She was a quiet studious child, always listening and learning. It had been fascinating to hear him as he talked with designers and craftsmen. But it was when he spoke about his passion for building *kaikia*, handmade wooden masterpieces, that his eyes would shine. He told her how for centuries these small wooden fishing vessels had stood witness to the country's long seafaring tradition. He would quote *Odysseas Elytis*:

'*If you take Greece apart, in the end, you will be left with an olive tree, a vineyard and a boat, which means that with these items you can rebuild Greece…*'

At the thought, she shook her head, smiled and walked back into the cabin.

Remy had been kept busy in London both by family matters and also work plans, however, she had ensured she was in time to board the ship. Seven nights on board would enable her to consider the next, and possibly the most complex operation, she had agreed to consider.

Unlike her many business interests, the idea of brokering different commissions and offering a courier service had come about by chance. She had originally agreed to act on behalf of a friend, negotiating, buying, and then planning for the delivery of a sculpture. It had sounded interesting and it was an obvious business opportunity. Having discussed this idea with friends, it was clear that there was a place for this type of discreet operation. Within the year, the business had already delivered a profit, much to her surprise; but its success meant she could no longer manage it, in its current format, and she would need more staff.

Deals, which she was good at brokering, took time to manage, but she now needed others to ensure everything went to plan and produced successful outcomes. She also needed access to a broader range of contacts and skills, who she could trust and rely on, which had proved difficult.

This brought her back to thinking about the next commission, which she was still unsure about. What the client had asked her to consider, seemed initially to have too many variables, which always made her uneasy. It required some extremely complex organisation that would involve extensive travel, all completed within an ambitious timescale. However, she would take the opportunity this journey presented to consider a possible plan and decide whether the task was reasonable, achievable, and of course profitable.

As to the issue of staff, if she were to take on this commission, she would definitely need more personnel, preferably ones with contacts. She had asked Tiana, her personal assistant, to investigate and present her with a list of contractors with small businesses who might be suitable. She had no desire to become involved with larger companies or solo operators as these would bring their own complexities. Tiana had given her a list of three companies with their resumes. She had reviewed these and asked her to contact the first on the list.

As a result, she knew that somewhere on board, there were two men, who she had yet to meet who, should they prove to be capable, she might employ. Remy would not speak to the client again until she felt these or another group had, to her mind, the ability to carry out the task.

The butler having finished, asked if she wanted anything else and with a shake of her head, he quietly left the cabin. She took the star from her hair and shook it free. Walking up the stairs, she headed for the bathroom, where tall mirrors reflected her image. She thought, *At least the grey in her hair was a beautiful mix and decided that she quite liked it now.* She looked more closely into the mirror. Her face was pale; no sun touched it. Artfully applied makeup made it initially difficult for others to gauge her age, but leaning in, she used a long red vanished nail to lightly trace the lines around her clear blue eyes and scarlet lips; she sighed.

Others considered her beautiful and although this was amusing, she did not see the beauty. Instead, she noted the fine veins on her hands, that also belied her age, suggesting it was greater than the image she presented.

Undressing, her mind drifted to memories of long summer's days spent on the beach in Crete, and she smiled at memories of family trips and picnics, long since gone. Her mother, Regina, was French and her father, Ioannis, was Greek. He came from a large, close, and wealthy family and had wanted her to have a good traditional Greek name, but loving his wife, he gave way when she insisted on calling her daughter Remy after her grandmother. Her father's older brother, Panas, was the patriarch of the family and had taken on and built a large shipping firm. Her father, like his brothers, worked for him.

Each had the job of overseeing an aspect of the business and her father was focussed on developing links with an Iranian shipbuilding and offshore industrial complex, located in the Persian Gulf.

Her early life, near Kamatero, in the suburbs of Athens and summers on the Island of Crete were filled with happy, warm memories. She remembered the freedom of life in Crete, the scent of wild marjoram, valleys filled with lupins and lying reading under the olive trees. She could almost taste the ripe figs, which she climbed the tree to fetch; then sitting in the branches, she and her cousins would eat them, the juice running down her arms. She would look out at the warm turquoise seas, where together they would play in the gentle waves, afterwards going to a taverna to eat sardines straight from the grill.

Her uncle had seen her interest in ships, and having no son, and only a daughter who seemed more interested in spending her father's money, rather than joining the business, he encouraged her, especially after her father died. He watched her as she grew into a beautiful, intelligent, and focussed young woman, and so was determined that she should become the heir to the company. It was made clear to her that after school, she would go to university, first to Athens to study business management, then her uncle suggested she should go to America for her MBA and stay with her Uncle Christos.

Before she left for Columbia University, Uncle Panas announced that once she had graduated, she would be based in the US office to further develop the company's interests in America.

His daughter, Sophia, was not the least worried when she heard this and congratulated Remy; as at sixteen, she had eloped with a rich, older American actor and was living the lifestyle she loved in Hollywood.

So, it was clear, Remy's future was decided, she did not have a choice and, as she loved her uncle, she agreed.

Chapter 2

Or maybe not, she chuckled at the memory. It didn't quite go according to her uncle's plan.

As a young woman, Remy had grown into a tall, slender, radiant beauty. She had an oval face, framed by dark hair; but it was her clear blue eyes and exceptional mind that really captivated people. She intrigued but ultimately scared off most men, and if they hadn't already been frightened off, it was Uncle Christos who she was staying with who ensured that all but the hardiest were.

Remy had many suitors, as her mother called them, but few were a measure for her sharp mind and quick wit. Living at home in Athens, she knew that her mother saw every young man as a possible husband, but Uncle Panas saw them as a threat to his plans and money. He often said he had a daughter capable of being that. However, living in the States to do her MBA, Remy found freedom.

She loved life in New York and was eager to join various new groups and societies, and it was at one of these that she met Rafik and his friends, Andreas and Farzad, the three men who were destined to feature most in her life. The men were sitting outside the Green Society meeting, that she was just leaving, and were clearly arguing. As she stopped to put on her coat, she heard one talking about the interconnection between entrepreneurial thinking and innovation and, as she had just read about this, she couldn't stop herself from saying as she passed, 'Have you looked at models used in Silicon Valley to grow both start-up companies as well as innovation inside large organisations?'

'I was suggesting we looked at that but my friend here,' one of the men said laughing, indicating another, 'said it wouldn't be effective.'

So, she sat down and after twenty minutes, they had agreed that this was worth looking into further. She found that Farzad and Andreas were studying Political Science, while Rafik was on the same Business Administration MBA as her. As they got up, Farzad stopped her and asked if she would like to grab a coffee sometime; she blushed slightly and nodded. However, initially, she saw more of Rafik as they would meet up after class to discuss or argue various points, share notes, and research. She knew he liked her and for her sins, she flirted with him; but she had begun seeing Farzad and it was him she thought of at night.

One evening as they finished an assignment, Rafik took her hand and looking very serious, he said, 'I know you don't love me now but one day, my darling Remy, maybe there will be a time for us.' Then for the first time, he pulled her gently to him and kissed her with great tenderness. Then he got up and left. Remy was flustered. *Perhaps,* she thought, *she should not have led him on.* After that, although they sometimes met up, things were never the same.

Farzad, on the other hand, did not give up. He and Remy continued to meet for coffee, go for meals, the cinema, and walks. As their relationship deepened, he knew he wanted to marry this beautiful woman. Love blossomed, and on their six-month anniversary, they moved in together. Uncle Christos, who she was staying with in New York was initially furious and was only placated when he heard that Farzad had proposed. Remy was in love with this shy, quiet man with eyes as dark as midnight pools, and knew she wanted to marry him. Dealing with Uncle Christos, in the freedom of New York, was one thing, the next hurdle was her Uncle Panas.

When he heard that she was going out with an Iranian, regardless of his American upbringing, he was at first apoplectic, and then he said he was disappointed.

'Surely there were many Greek young men! In fact, I could suggest some,' he said. At this point, she told him that they had already married in a small ceremony in New York. His immediate reaction was to threaten to disown her. Deep down what he was most disappointed with was not so much her choice of a partner, who he quite liked, but the chance to give her a traditional Greek ceremony, which he had been unable to do for his own daughter.

Her mother was totally in love with Faz, as she called him. He was handsome and had the brooding looks of many men of similar family heritage; dark hair and olive skin, but it was his long-lashed eyes that seemed to mesmerise her. She had laughed and called him her "Omar Sharif" after a film star she had loved as a girl. Then hugging her daughter, she had whispered that she understood why she had fallen in love so quickly.

Having finished their masters, they moved into an apartment in New York and when Remy was pregnant, they visited the family in Greece, sending them into huge preparations for this grandchild. Uncle Panas seemed pacified by the celebration.

When they returned the following year with the baby, her uncle hugged her, shook Farzad's hand, then cooed over baby Alessia, and formally announced to all that Remy would be his heir.

Chapter 3

Before she had set out on this trip, she had spoken at length to the prospective client. While they offered limited information, they promised there would be no legal implications as the people who had the items, had chosen to return them to their rightful owner. It was clear, however, that this was an extremely sensitive issue and they wanted to remain anonymous, hence the need for a courier to act as an intermediary. Finally, he had made it clear that should she accept the commission, she might not be the only one looking for the items, and that was where possible conflict could occur.

It was necessary, therefore, that whoever she employed to carry out the task would need a broad range of skills and the ability to react to circumstances that might rapidly change. A friend had suggested some sort of covert trial to see how they coped. She agreed and the group she had chosen now had the chance to prove themselves on this trip.

The doorbell rang. She nodded to the butler who was delivering hors d'oeuvres. He opened the door and a man entered.

He walked up to the chair where Remy sat and held out an outstretched hand.

'Good afternoon,' he said and waited. She ignored the hand and he dropped it to his side. *She noticed that he moved to stand at ease, still a soldier at heart,* she thought.

Eventually, she said, 'I take it you are one of the people my personal assistant engaged for this trip?' He nodded. The cabin was silent, except for the slight hum from the engines and occasional bangs from things being stowed away. She looked down at some papers but all the time surveying the man, to see how he would react to her lack of engagement.

Finally, she looked up. He was tall, clean-shaven, and dark-haired, which she observed was beginning to grey at the temples. She noted he had extremely clear green eyes, and was well built but not so muscled that his suit looked too tight. While she considered him handsome, he was not overtly so; he would draw admiring glances from every woman but would not immediately court men's envy or threaten them, which in his job was surely important. His suit and shoes looked expensive. She thought he was around his late thirties. Interesting!

'Your name?'

'Thomas Beckett.'

'Well, Thomas, you have spoken to my PA, so you know my requirements. I take it that you were given the case that you are here to protect?' She said in an indifferent tone.

'Yes, Ma'am. My colleague has the case and will remain with it for the entire trip. I will be here to ensure your safety.'

'Yes, we both need to arrive at our destination in one piece.' She looked down amused. 'For your information, I will be working most days. I think we should meet each morning and then again for dinner. Tonight, please meet me in the Commodore Bar at 7.30 pm. Oh, and before you go, I presume you brought a dress suit?' She paused and he nodded. 'However, it will not be needed tonight.' She turned and he took it that he was dismissed.

As he left the cabin, he stopped briefly to loosen his tie. He sensed despite his initial reluctance, that this might prove to be an interesting assignment.

Thomas considered the woman he had just met. He thought she could be anywhere from fifty to sixty. Although the blush of youth had left her face, she was very beautiful. She certainly was not what he had been expecting, as he had assumed she would need protection, but having met her, he somehow doubted this. She had a real presence and he sensed that she was more than capable of looking after herself. His immediate reaction was that he had just met an extremely formidable woman, who he suspected would frighten the hell out of many people she met, which made him smile; he liked confident women. He walked away.

When they had discussed the opportunity and found out it was going to be on board the Queen Mary, his colleague, Leo, had been less than enthusiastic. He suggested that as Thomas was convalescing, he should go and enjoy the sea air. What Thomas knew Leo actually meant was that there was another job in LA that was far more interesting, and Thomas had to agree, it probably was. So, it was decided, that Leo would go to LA, while Thomas, although not too thrilled with the task, could take the opportunity to recover from the effects of his last assignment; if nothing else, these days at sea would be a benefit.

He headed for the cabin where his colleague, Jem, was guarding the case. He knocked in the agreed manner and the man opened the door. Thomas did not enter but they exchanged a few words and then the door closed, and Thomas headed for his own suite. Unlike his colleague in a Balcony Cabin, Thomas was staying in a Queens' Grill Suite, near Madam Akbari's Balmoral Suite.

As it was fast approaching 7 pm, he would shower and change, then head to the Commodore Bar at the front of the ship on Deck 9, as requested.

He arrived in good time and chatted to the barman, managing to quickly find the information he needed. He ordered two martinis, both with a twist. She arrived precisely on time, as he thought she would, just as the barman was placing the drinks on the bar. A faint smile crossed her lips as she saw the martini. Thomas pulled the stool out and offered her a hand, she took it and slipped gracefully onto the stool.

'Thank you,' she said, and as their eyes met, he was pleased to see her smile. Remy sipped the cocktail without comment. Her mind had wandered to the first time she had sat at this bar. The large model of the ship always reminded her of happier times. This, however, was not the time to dwell on the past; she must maintain her focus.

They sipped their drinks and chatted about the ship. As she became more animated, he thought that she had a sort of timeless beauty he had rarely seen before. He listened as she spoke about the arrangements in New York, but all the time, he found himself constantly reappraising this enigmatic woman. From the information he had, it was clear that she had extensive business interests, founded on a large shipping empire as well as the consignment business.

Wrongly, he had initially assumed the shipping part of the business either belonged to her husband or was a family business; however, further research had shown she had inherited the business from her uncle and had continued to run it alone. Her husband, who had worked for the American government, was dead.

She was clearly unafraid to attract attention; *her dress and jewellery were beautiful and,* he thought, *expensive.* Suddenly, as if aware of his eyes, she stood up, picked up her shawl and bag, and said, 'Shall we eat?' and turned to go. He signed for the drinks and left a twenty-dollar tip in the folder. The barman smiled and winked; *goodness knows what he thought,* laughed Thomas to himself as he turned to follow her.

Leaving the lift and walking into the Queens Grill, she slipped her hand through his arm. It seemed so natural, clearly close physical contact was not something she feared. To those watching, they made an intriguing pair. The woman in red and the man in a dark suit and red tie. Suddenly, she stopped and raised her hand to straighten his tie. Thomas had to stifle a comment as this reminded him of the times when his mother had done the same thing.

'Madam Akbari, we are so pleased to see you again,' the maître d' said, 'Please follow me, your usual table is ready, for you and your guest.' She led the way and he followed. in what felt like a royal procession. As they walked the length of the dining room, eyes turned to follow them. Although he believed she was the focus of their attention, he would have been surprised to hear that others thought he also cut a sharp, handsome figure, and that together they were an imposing couple. At the table, Thomas moved smartly forward to pull out her chair. As she sat, she briefly smiled up at him; *good manners,* she thought.

Dinner passed amiably. Initially, they talked about the weather; then she asked about what he called their insurance business. He didn't know what she already knew about the team, so provided some basic personal information and a resume of his and Leo's careers to date. He made it clear that they had developed a wide range of contacts during their military service and beyond, and that this ensured that they would be able to call in specialists when needed. She asked him about the gap between the end of their time in the military and the beginning of their business.

'I think that after time in the services, many people find it difficult to settle, and we both needed some free space before we moved forward with our plan. We work on a partnership structure, which includes Grace Holder, who now oversees the financial and organisational side. Since she joined us Leo and I can be more active which suits us all.'

As they drank their coffee, she said, 'I will not need you tomorrow as I still have a lot to consider with the commission we may discuss later. If I need you, I will call.' She opened her bag and handed him her phone. He added his number. 'I presume your colleague has the case secure.'

He nodded. 'Yes, but I will check on it again before I go to bed.'

'It is evening dress tomorrow, so 7.30 pm in the bar.'

With that, she rose and he moved to her side. He picked up her forgotten shawl and draped it over her shoulders, and she again slipped her arm through his, seen by others as a tender gesture. They left the dining room. The faintest trace of a smile crossed her lips, aware of the many covert glances they elicited.

Thomas escorted her to her cabin, wished her a good night, and then left for his own.

Speculation regarding the couple was rife. Over the days of the trip, her glamorous outfits led to envy, speculation, and animated conversations. With no facts forthcoming, gossip and rumours added to the air of mystery, much to the pair's amusement. On one occasion, Thomas overheard a couple of women wondering whether he was an escort.

Laughing, one woman said to the other, 'I wonder where she found him.'

The other replied, 'She's rich, I bet it's some high-end escort company. You know you hire them for all sorts, to chaperone them to parties and business events and things...' They both giggled. 'I bet they're at it...'

He stood up from the sofa behind theirs, walked around, beamed at them, and shook his head. To their credit, they both blushed and broke into apologies, which he ignored as he walked away.

Thomas thought the whole thing bizarre and couldn't care less what others thought or surmised about their relationship. She was always polite and professional, never giving any indication that more was expected. His thoughts were coloured by a wry grin. Would that have been an interesting option?

Remy, changing for bed, might have had similar thoughts if it were not for the diamond twisting on her finger.

Chapter 4

Each morning Thomas called on Remy at the same time. She would be taking breakfast, which he noted always consisted of fresh fruit, yoghurt and coffee. She seldom did little more than acknowledge his presence, only looking up from her newspaper briefly to comment on the day's requirements.

Time was certainly something he had in abundance. Having paid his daily call, he would call in on Jem and give him some time off, then head to the gym, then a sauna or massage. At other times, he set off running around the deck. Three times was a mile, and as the weather was often cloudy and chilly first thing, there were only a few hardy souls running, so he could complete six or nine laps, followed by a swim. He also liked to sit in the jacuzzi at the back of the ship; looking out, he thought the trail it made as it ploughed through the water was just like that of a snail. He ate lunch with his colleague, then read or caught up on whatever TV or films were on. He generally avoided contact with others.

Remy spent her time either dealing with general business issues or talking with clients. As to the new scenario, she was now developing a clearer picture of what might be needed and from what she had been told, recognised that this assignment really would require some complex organisation and timings. It appeared that the current owners of the items were extremely reluctant to reveal themselves. Transportation needed to be done by the team and high levels of security were necessary. They would collect each item at an agreed time and place, then have it transferred to a secure location in London, as this was the most convenient place for the client.

The first item would be available near London, while the others could be collected along a circular route that would take them first to Miami, next to Los Angeles, then Sydney, and then back to London. Remy had identified special cases for transportation which would provide extremely sophisticated locking and tracking systems. The keys for these would need to be kept separately.

It seemed that completing the tasks in the shortest timescale was vitally important. However, this was not fully explained initially but she had picked it up, as a concern, especially as the client's further comments had intimated a possible political interest. This was something she would need to discuss further on her arrival in New York.

Chapter 5

Thomas checked in with his colleague Jem, the man he trusted implicitly. He had promised his friend, that if an opportunity came up, he'd be in touch; he had kept his word.

Jem was over six foot six, with a body that showed hours in the gym. He had boxed for the army and still trained at every opportunity. Now in his late thirties, he still took part in some semi-professional heavyweight bouts. He also had black belts in both karate and judo, so was not someone you would want to tangle with. He had a fearsome array of tattoos, including a lion on his bald head.

Although, together the combination meant most people tended not to trouble him, he was actually quite a sensitive soul.

Alongside his imposing stature, his most surprising feature was his green eyes, courtesy of his Turkish mother, which in a light-skinned black man meant he was unforgettable. This could be both an advantage and disadvantage as it made him hard to miss. His Nigerian father wanted nothing to do with Jem's mother or his child and had gone home to Abuja. With no male role model, Jem had got caught up in the South London gang culture; that was until he met the owner of the local gym. Boxing was initially his saviour and then, so was the army.

That night like the others, Thomas walked the length of the ship and waited for her in the bar. Entering, she never ceased to amaze him. She had the look of old Hollywood glamour, he remembered from the films he'd watched with his mother.

On their last evening on the ship, they had a quiet dinner and then after drinks, a discussion about arrangements for New York, which his colleague, Leo, had confirmed with Tiana. When she stood to leave Thomas felt that he was losing something very special and that it would never be the same again. He was about to speak when she turned, she gently stroked his cheek, placed a finger on his lips, and said firmly, 'Good night, Thomas.' And with that, he knew the spell was broken.

On his way to bed, he couldn't get that moment out of his mind, then sadly shook his head.

He checked in with Jem, who moaned about the lack of exercise and the tiny shower over the bath, with a shower curtain that continually stuck to his bum. 'Never mind, Jem, home tomorrow.' Thomas left, quickly followed by a string of curses. He returned to his cabin to finish packing.

It was not yet dawn when the Queen Mary 2 sailed under the Verrazano Bridge on the Hudson River and past the Statue of Liberty on its way to dock in New York. On board, people were excitedly staring at the amazing skyline, busying themselves ready for departure, or turning over in bed to avoid the early morning charge.

Many who were still speculating about the relationship of the elusive couple would remain disappointed as the Queen Mary sailed serenely into its berth in Brooklyn. They were no closer to the answers so many sought. Lovers? Was he her toy boy? Was he gay?

Those who watched their departure were not disappointed. As Remy stepped out into the warm autumn morning sun, she had again chosen her outfit carefully. Her classic blue dress and jacket were complemented by a large-brimmed black hat, sunglasses, and accessories; very Jackie Onassis, another childhood fashion idol. Thomas made an overtly gallant gesture of offering his hand as she stepped off the ship, and then slipped it through his arm and patted it. He managed to contain his desire to laugh and felt her hand tremble. Looking at her, he realised she was also finding it hard to control her mirth.

Some might also have noticed the tall black man who paid close attention to the pair. Those with sharp eyes might also have seen the chain and not the bracelet on his wrist. Jem carefully scanned the departure hall as Remy and Thomas walked through to reach the waiting chauffeur, who held the car door open. Remy paused briefly searching for a face among the busy crowds in the departure area; with a small sad smile, she slipped into the car and was gone.

Chapter 6

As she travelled through the New York traffic, heading for her office, Remy remembered when her Uncle Panas had first bought the building and brought her to see it; it looked very different now. The original building had been designed in 1927 by a Vienna-born architect, Joseph Urban. It had then consisted of only six floors but had been designed so that it could be the base for a skyscraper to be built above it. However, this was postponed due to the Great Depression. Her uncle had been determined to complete this and employed Sir Henry Fuller, the renowned architect, to add the tower in 2000.

By 2006, Panas Petrakis's employees moved into Petrakis Tower totalling forty-six floors. The building was now owned by her company but different floors had been leased out over time to other businesses connected with shipping in some form. However, following the pandemic, the office spaces were now often empty as people worked more from home. It was often silent and she wondered whether it would ever be full again.

Getting out of the car, she walked towards the huge doorway. As a small child, she thought that giants must have lived here! But now, as she glanced up at the art deco figures, it made her think of her uncle. From here on, however, the architecture was, to her mind, cold and uninviting. The lobby was immense and busy, so she quickly headed for the escalators, which were flanked by two huge slopes of gently rolling water. This took her to the huge open atrium but she did not stop to admire the space, instead, headed quickly to a private lift, which took her to the twentieth floor, which she occupied alone.

It was both her office and her apartment in New York. Despite the views the upper floors would offer, she had refused to go any higher. Maybe 9/11 was still too ingrained in her memory.

Tiana, her personal assistant, occupied a reception area opposite the lift and rushed to meet her, taking her hat and bag. Remy greeted her warmly. Tiana had been with her now for three years and was privy to much of Remy's business and social engagements. She was of Greek descent, although as a second generation child, she had little idea of her heritage until she joined Remy's business. Her grandparents had left Cyprus in 1974 as a result of the troubles and separation of the Greek and Turkish parts of the island. Now, at thirty, and having travelled with Remy and met so many people who shared her heritage, she had really embraced it.

Last year, she had met a Greek national who was working temporarily in New York, and Remy feared she might want to go with him when he returned to Thessaloniki, his hometown. With a sigh, she thought she would deal with that if it happened.

As she entered the office, she looked out at the skyline and felt an immense longing for the expansive skies of her beloved island home. Again, she wondered why she still found herself in the city at all as she rolled the ring on her finger.

Immediately behind the screen that sectioned off the reception area, was Remy's official office, although she rarely used it; to the left, and occupying the rest of the space on this floor, was her apartment. Remy had done much to make this as warm a space as possible. She was a bit of a magpie, having collected pictures, porcelain, artefacts, and all sorts of items from across the world. She used these and warm but understated colours for furniture, to give this otherwise stark space real life. At night, the rooms were lit by pools of light from a collection of lamps. During the day when she was there, the immense windows were generally shaded, and she immediately moved to the control to lower the honey-coloured blinds halfway, giving the apartment a warmer glow. Walking over to the window, she looked out. Her office faced out towards the park, another reason for staying in this building.

Remy had much to think about as she moved to the kitchen and slipped a pod into the coffee machine. As it brewed, she again considered the man she had travelled with. Could he and his associates manage what was developing into an extremely complex, and somewhat concerning, task? The client had initially made no mention of what the items were and explained that only when, and if, she accepted the commission, would further information be provided. She had to admit this was a little unnerving but she was intrigued; always a driving force for her. Taking her coffee, she returned to her office to review the plans she had made on the ship.

Chapter 7

Despite the fact they would be going to her office soon, Thomas had watched her departure with a real feeling of sadness; the intimacy of the ship had been broken. He had only known her for just a week but he had thoroughly enjoyed her company. He felt that there had been a real connection and he recognised in her a deep sadness and loneliness that he often felt. He wondered who she had looked for so anxiously as they headed to the car; it seemed unlike her. He saw Leo and walked over to the car where he and Jem were waiting. Tomorrow they would deliver the case and then presumably wait to find out whether she was satisfied with their performance.

'How did the trip go?' Leo asked as Thomas got in the car. He gave a brief resume and then outlined the suggestion that Remy had presented.

'You sound smitten.' Leo laughed.

Thomas smiled. 'Well, there certainly is something about this woman.'

'You mean you didn't…?' Leo enquired with a mischievous grin.

'No! Will you never grow up?' They both laughed. 'Look, this could present a huge range of opportunities for us.'

Leo nodded putting his arm around his friend as they walked to the car.

The next morning, they managed to avoid much of the gridlocked New York traffic and arrived at the extraordinarily designed building where Remy had her head office. Stepping out of the car, they surveyed the art deco building with its immense blue glass skyscraper tower on top. Thomas knew she was afraid of heights and had only stayed in this building on 8th Avenue because of its heritage and the fact it was in the right part of town, among the right buildings; however, looking up, Thomas felt it wasn't really right for her.

Entering the building, they were confronted by the Ice Fall which flanked the escalators, that led to the reception area in the huge atrium. A quick call and they were taken to the lift and accompanied to the twentieth floor, by a smartly dressed security guard, where they were greeted by Tiana. She showed them through into the office. Remy had moved into the apartment and was looking out of the window.

Thomas coughed discretely. She turned.

'Hello, Thomas.' Her tone was cool.

Thomas introduced Leo and then Jem.

'Yes, business!' She declared. Thomas removed the handcuff from Jem's wrist which he rubbed and then left the room. Thomas passed the case to her. She used another key to open the case locks and then a code to release the final one and deactivate the system They were both surprised when she opened the case in front of them and even more surprised to see only an envelope inside. She sat down, indicating they should do the same.

'I am sorry for the deception, as you can clearly see you have been guarding this.' She waved at the case dismissively. 'It was important for me to be sure that the company we employed fit certain criteria. As you are no doubt aware, there are plenty of companies in the business of providing security; but other qualities are necessary. It was also important that I should feel comfortable with the person, or people, that I would be working with most closely. Well, Mr Beckett, Mr Tremaine, if you are interested in finding out more,' she rose and handed Leo a card, 'please call me. You will be well compensated, I assure you.'

She extended her hand and, despite the loose grip she had extended to so many on the ship, Thomas was pleased to find that her handshake was firm and warm. He smiled. They thanked her and as they turned to leave, she added, 'Don't leave it too long, there are always other candidates.' They were dismissed.

As they left, they found Jem chatting animatedly to Tiana. This was a surprise as he was generally very unsure of himself around women. As they headed for the lift, Thomas thought he saw Jem hand her a card. He chuckled to himself as he had only just had these printed for him. *Well, I never,* he thought.

In the lift going down, Leo couldn't contain himself and turned to Jem, he teased, 'Don't tell me you asked her out.'

Jem moved closer, towering over the six-foot-tall Leo, 'Mind your own,' he snarled and then laughed. A relieved Thomas had not wanted to try and separate them in such a contained space.

Jem said he was going back to his place and then would go to the gym, as he thought he had a lot of weight to shift. This was possibly true as he had thoroughly enjoyed the room service on the ship. Leo said they'd take a cab. 'What do you think? Will we get the job?'

'I think so if we want it,' responded Thomas.

Chapter 8

Remy picked up the phone and spoke briefly to Tiana to cancel her other appointment. She felt certain that Thomas would call her back.

With a sigh, she scrolled through the emails that plagued her life, sending them to appropriate people to deal with but responded personally to any important or serious ones. She knew she really needed to focus on the family shipping business and turned to the pile of papers, neatly sorted and arranged by Tiana on her desk. Its day-to-day running was generally overseen by an effective management team, which she had developed both in the US and in Greece. Some of the extended family were still employed but now she mostly relied on finding and nurturing talent directly out of university. This proved to be both extremely rewarding and fulfilling.

Apart from the impact of Covid, which had been a significant issue, it was only major decisions now that she had to be personally involved with. She smiled as she came across a thank you note for a commission successfully completed.

The idea of brokering and developing a courier service had initially developed from requests which came from friends or family to transport things securely and, sometimes, covertly. It was an amusing sideline and had initially taken her mind off her husband's death; but now, it seemed to be taking more of her time.

Remy considered the last week; she had enjoyed her time on the ship and Thomas' company. However, for the umpteenth time, she wondered why on earth she had agreed to even think about this new commission. When the man, who she referred to as the client, had asked for her help, she had not anticipated how involved it might be. Now it felt that perhaps this had been a rather hasty mistake. Many of the commissions and consignments she had brokered in the past had always been relatively easy—a painting, a house purchase, and even the return of a child—but this was different.

Twisting the diamond ring on her finger, Remy decided she would contact a friend to get their opinion. As they had not seen or spoken for over a month, she thought their view might be useful. She knew he was in New York, so maybe they could meet. Tapping the number, it rang. Inadvertently, she held her breath. When he answered, he sounded happy to hear from her and she relaxed. He listened carefully and then asked lots of questions. She was surprised by his interest, but finally, it was made clear that the final decision was hers.

'You know I hate politics.' This comment came as a surprise, firstly as this was an area she knew he had always been involved with and secondly, how had he made a connection barely alluded to. He wished her luck and the call ended. The line clicked; there was no warm goodbye and no offer to meet.

Remy sighed and wondered why she had bothered; she didn't really need anyone's advice; she could make up her own mind. Thinking back to the conversation, although friendly, there was no real warmth, just a feeling of distance. Having recently heard that he had lost his wife in a car accident. She remembered only too well how painful the death of a loved one was. Maybe that was the reason for the brusqueness of the call. She wondered why he hadn't called, or had he expected her to?

Suddenly, she was angry. Was she so desperate? It was not as if she needed anyone; she was extremely wealthy, having taken over the family business and developed the shipping side further, and she had her daughter, who was now returning to live with her after her divorce. But there were times when she felt physically lonely. The week she had spent with Thomas on the ship had accentuated this.

Leaving the papers, she moved to her favourite chair. Closing her eyes, her mind drifted back to the days and weeks before her husband's death. Rafik had sent his helicopter to take them across Long Island Sound to his home in Great Neck. Much to her surprise, Andreas was there also. After lunch and Rafik's surprising gift to each of them, Andreas had to return to New York for a meeting and an urgent call meant that Farzad left with him. Rafik begged her to stay, as he wanted to discuss some plans he had for decorating some of the upstairs rooms.

They laughed and chatted about his awful choices, and she made some suggestions. Having looked around, they stood in his bedroom, discussing some ideas when suddenly he pulled her to him and kissed her passionately. A distant memory forced itself to the surface. She left the room, shedding unwanted tears.

She shuddered; Love and trust she thought and shook her head, she didn't want to think anything more about that afternoon.

But thank goodness for Andreas, the other member of the Three Musketeers. She knew she had only to call and he would be there. Remy did not know how she could have gotten through the days after Farzad's death without his and Alessia's support.

Andreas had married about the same time as she and Farzad and although they were all initially close, they had lost the close contact of their youth. It was a while after his wife's death that she had heard about it, something she deeply regretted.

All these thoughts of the past and Farzad brought a lump to her throat. He had been dead for over two years and she missed him every day. Her thoughts now turned to the night he died. Rafik had joined them as they were all going to attend the graduation from medical school of an old friend's son, who they had known for many years. That afternoon, however, Rafik had taken ill with stomach pains. He had begged them to go, saying they should be there. With all the panic, it wasn't until they got to the friend's house that Farzad realised they had forgotten the present and said he would rush home and get it, as it wasn't far. He was almost home when his car was hit side-on by a truck. He did not stand a chance.

Thinking about it now, Remy recalled more of that evening for the first time, and she was sure, she had put the present on the table by the door so it wouldn't be forgotten. How could she have missed it? A tear rolled down her cheek and she brushed it away. She tried to stop herself from voicing the questions about Farzad's death that she really wanted to ask; hating herself for thinking them, fearful of what the answers might reveal. But these thoughts forced themselves into her mind again. She went into the kitchen and filled her glass again, finishing the bottle of Chablis.

Had she really been so naïve to have accepted the police report? Should she have asked more questions? With these thoughts in mind, she decided, when this job was done, she would find out the truth.

Looking out at the park, Remy remembered how totally abandoned she felt on finding Rafik had gone when she finally got home. He left a note telling her that one of his daughters was seriously ill in Iran. However, she found out later that it was a lie, the real reason was connected to his political objectives. Remy knew he had always had considerable political ambitions and had made many connections both in the US and Iran, which he claimed were to improve the two countries' relations.

Having learned the truth, it made his missing the funeral of a dear friend, just to satisfy his aspirations, all the more shocking to her. It angered her and she did not see or speak to him again for months. When he returned, he was very apologetic and wept tears of sadness. He held her tightly, stroked her hair and kissed her gently, repeating, 'There will come a time.'

She shivered, remembering another time he had said this. She had only seen him a few times since or had hurried conversations over the phone. Always, there were promises to return.

Reflecting, she knew that it was time to move on. A darkness swirled in her mind, and it was this that always held her back and haunted her. Thinking now of the three men and when they first met, she had known that each had wanted her but she had chosen Farzad. Now at night, in the darkness of her bed, she found herself thinking of those left and the one who had so recently come into her life. Could one of them fill the void? Her dreams reflected both passion and confusion.

Getting up, she knew she needed to shake off these thoughts and the negativity, that always came with them. She walked into the bedroom, removed the pin that held her hair in place and shook it loose. Removing her clothes, she welcomed the power of the shower and having dried herself, walked into the dressing room and picked out a blue silk dress. Putting on her makeup, she then brushed out her hair and remembered her mother saying that grey hair was a measure of a woman's power, not her age. She smiled as she twisted it artfully into a pleat. Picking up her glass, she walked back to the lounge, finished the last dregs of the Chablis, then settled on the settee to wait for Andreas to come, as they were going to dinner with friends.

Chapter 9

Thomas and Grace Holder had spent the afternoon at Leo's flat, discussing Remy's proposal, along with other possible jobs or opportunities that had arisen since they had returned from rescuing the daughter of a client. Thomas had already convinced Leo that unless Grace raised any valid objections, he already knew what their response should be.

'I don't have any objections to the idea, it is just the logistics I am going to have to get my head around,' she mused. 'I'll plan it out. Oh, don't forget you have a meeting with a client this morning.'

Clearly, he had forgotten! While they were considering Remy's job, there were still others that needed both consideration and deployment. He had not taken the call regarding this possible client, so had no idea what it was about and Leo, as ever, was vague. Thomas called Jem and asked him to pick them up. When he turned to speak to Leo, he was busy on the phone, arguing with his current girlfriend, Tara, or was it now Teresa; Thomas couldn't keep up. Leo looked up and Thomas indicated the door, but as he stood up, Leo kept up his side of the, "No, I didn't go round to her place" argument; Thomas had heard it all before.

While they waited on the kerbside for Jem to bring the car around, Thomas' mind wandered to his recent journey with Remy. It had been a very pleasant voyage and he had really enjoyed her company, and he had been intrigued by what he had learned about the commissions she brokered. He was sure that they could do the job she had outlined but also knew that it would probably take a great deal of time, and this could impact their other business.

The sound of a car horn brought him back and Leo finally finished his conversation; clearly, things hadn't ended well. Thomas said nothing.

As they got into the new "company" car, Jem said, 'Better than the last one, eh!'

This car was certainly an upgrade and was a direct result of their last pay cheque; although in retrospect Thomas thought, subconsciously rubbing his side, that they could have charged more. Anyway, it gave the right message to their clients, unlike his old, slightly bent, but reliable Audi. They still had some major debts and Remy's job would definitely help to address some of these. Apparently, her client must be extremely wealthy as the global sum she had discussed was well above their normal rate. However, a lot would be swallowed by travel and personnel costs.

Almost as soon as they had settled in their seats, Jem, who had not seen the inside of the case despite guarding it all week, said, 'Come on, what was in it?'

Thomas laughed. 'You know I can't answer that, or I would have to k…' Laughing, he didn't finish the sentence.

'Yeah, I know…and fat chance by the way!' They both laughed but Thomas knew he would have little chance having seen Jem in action.

Thomas explained about the envelope. 'Fuck me,' Jem exclaimed. 'We've been guarding a bloody envelope.' He laughed and put the car in drive.

The meeting they were going to was over in Brooklyn, and when he thought about it much later, he realised what a strange affair it had been. Leo explained they were going to meet a Mr Sattari. The house they were looking for was in the Prospect Park area on Union Street. Arriving, Jem drove slowly, looking for numbers and said, 'This is it,' as they stopped outside a brownstone affair, that clearly had once been a residential property; although the filthy sign showed it had more recently been a medical practice.

As they got out, it was obvious that this too had been some time ago as the building was now in a dreadful condition. Some of the houses around it had been renovated or were in the process, and the area looked as if it was becoming quite prosperous, but this place looked in need of a complete overhaul.

Leo asked Jem to stay and wait, he didn't say anything but he didn't hold out much hope for a business opportunity here. Climbing the stairs, he rang the doorbell and a small middle-aged woman answered the door almost immediately, as if she had been standing there waiting for someone to come. Waving for them to come in, she apologised for the mess and explained they had just bought the house and that renovations would begin soon. Thomas felt there was something odd about her accent, the way she spoke and moved, but couldn't put his finger on it.

She showed them into an almost empty room, with just a few chairs around a large table. They were kept waiting for fifteen minutes and just as they were discussing leaving, a tall, well-built man came in. Like the woman, he apologised for the situation.

Thomas watched him as he walked towards them. He always did this, now almost instinctively, as it had proved essential throughout his military career. His immediate reaction to this man was that he was both arrogant and ruthless. There was no warmth in the smile he gave them or his "wife". He exuded an air of malice that was almost palpable. *This was not a man to trust,* Thomas thought, *or one to cross.* Looking closely at the man, he thought that he was possibly of Arab descent, as was the woman standing beside him. He thought the late fifties or early sixties. He had a strong, handsome face but his eyes were cold. His clothes were expensive and his person well-groomed. Thomas felt he was probably quite well-off by the very expensive watch he wore, although it could be a copy, there were plenty around.

Her clothes by comparison were chain store, smart but probably not that new. He wore a gold wedding band with a large diamond inserted, which he turned inward as if consciously keeping it hidden. *So,* Thomas thought, *why would a man like this be buying a run-down office in Brooklyn?* He doubted that it was to live in.

Sensing his scrutiny, the man looked directly at Thomas, barely containing a sneer.

'You can see that the building needs a great deal of work. My wife,' he motioned to the woman dismissively, 'just loved the building and we plan to settle here.' Thomas almost laughed. A smile twisted the man's lips, making him look almost threatening. Thomas knew there was no warmth there and was getting a real sense of menace. The man sat down but his wife remained standing beside him, her hands constantly clasping and unclasping; she looked to be on the verge of tears. Thomas noted she was not wearing a wedding ring.

As was their usual practice when interviewing clients, Leo led the discussion, asked the questions, and unless necessary, Thomas would just watch and listen. That way, information was not lost, and nuanced conversations could perhaps later be given more context and clarity. The man explained that his wife's aunt was missing and that he wanted them to find her. Leo's first, and obvious question, was why them and not the police or a private detective? The man offered no real explanation, giving some vague context to his concerns. As he talked, Thomas became increasingly uncomfortable, especially when the talk turned to their current cases.

The shift was initially subtle but became more focussed on anything they might be doing in future, on the pretext that might impact their search. While this could be a purely logical line, there was something about the questions he asked that made Thomas even more suspicious.

Thomas said, 'If we take on this search, where will you be living, so we can contact you?' Leo shot him a look.

'We live upstate. We will give you our address of course.' The man looked as if he was about to put his hand in his pocket but thought better of it. 'I don't have any cards with me at the moment.' The man shrugged. 'Perhaps, I could come to your office,' he added.

Thomas suddenly stood up, catching everyone by surprise.

'No, I don't think that will be possible. I am sorry, I really don't feel that we are the right people to help you. I can give you the name of a private detective, however, who may well be able to do so.' He took out a blank card and pen and wrote a name down, leaving it on the table. Leo could see that he had written "Jack Reacher" and a phone number; a slight smile crossed his lips. They left the room and walked to the door but the man did not follow.

At the door, the "wife" thanked them and whispered quietly, 'I am sorry.' They left and Thomas felt a shudder travel through his body. He didn't know why but he feared for the woman's safety, he turned to speak but the door had closed.

'Well, that was all very strange,' remarked Thomas.

As they headed down the steps, Leo said, 'Let's just hope he's never watched the films or read the book.' He laughed.

'I doubt it, it was the first name I could think of, although god knows why.'

'Bah!' The man standing at the window exclaimed and turned, grabbing the woman by the arm and pushing her towards the door, shouting, 'Get out and tell those fools outside to follow them.' He shoved her harshly towards the door and she scuttled out.

Walking back to their car, Leo noticed the woman crossing the road to a car park down the street. Getting back in the car, Leo was mulling over the interview. 'We both know that there was something wrong with that situation. Even I didn't need your super sense to tell me that. Anyway, look I need to do something this afternoon, so Jem can you drop me off.' As they headed towards the bridge, Leo suddenly said, 'Hey, that'll do, I'll get the subway.' Jem stopped the car and without another word, Leo got out and headed for the Atlantic Av-Barclays Central Station.

Jem was surprised. 'That's not the only thing that's odd this morning, he doesn't often use the subway.'

Thomas agreed, it was highly unusual. Jem drove on back towards the Brooklyn Bridge.

But Leo did not go immediately down into the subway, he watched as the black vehicle that had been parked so incongruously down the street turned out behind the Jaguar and followed it towards the bridge. The car had the same plates as the one he had seen parked outside their office in New York.

Leo phoned for an Uber and headed back into town.

Chapter 10

Thomas arrived back at their small office on 110 West 40th Street. He thought the building, built in 1914, was architecturally stunning. There were friezes of crouching figures above the entrance and the workmanship amazed Thomas. It was one of the main reason he and Grace had chosen it; not as Jem thought the Burgers and Brew place below. It had once been known as the World's Tower Building, which Leo thought was somewhat creepy, but it came at a good rent, in a good area, so had agreed. They had a small office space on the tenth floor, where Grace was based, and another larger room that doubled as a place to meet prospective clients; but it was also where Thomas often crashed. There was also a small kitchen and shower room at the back.

The building had once been owned by a single company but now housed a variety of tenants from diverse industries, some of whom, Leo thought might be of use. Grace had become friendly with some cyber security people on the sixth floor, particularly Trent, and they had been seeing each other casually for a few months.

Back at the office, Grace had already begun to draw up some basic manpower requirements. She was amazing, and he knew how lucky they were to have her. She had been with them since the start, as she had originally gone out with Leo; however, she soon proved far too intelligent to fall for him and his games. She was certainly Leo's type; tall, blonde, and beautiful. Having done some modelling to pay for university at Harvard, she had gone on to gain an outstanding degree in corporate law. She was quickly snapped up by a top firm, but despite its outrageous salary, she had rapidly become disillusioned with the people she was expected to deal with.

One evening, listening to Leo and Thomas struggle with their plans for a business, and fascinated by their ideas, she suggested she should become a partner, provided she was allowed to develop the business side. They were amazed she would consider it and they had jumped at her offer. It was soon clear her organisational and financial skills would prove to be invaluable in setting up and running that side of their business. It was her charm and acumen that had convinced Leo's father to provide a start-up loan, at an extremely favourable rate.

Now no longer in a romantic relationship with Leo, she had taken on a sisterly role and was generally good at keeping him in line. She had even supported him through a brief alcohol relapse when a relationship failed, which she had kept quiet from Thomas. As a native New Yorker, she also knew some great hangouts and cool people in the art, film and fashion world from her modelling days. In time, this would no doubt provide them with a wealth of clientele. After Leo, she had been in a relationship with an actress, whose career was beginning to develop, but it was soon clear to both that Grace was only being used as eye candy and, although remaining friends, the relationship finished.

Still, as she said to Thomas, 'I get to go to some great film premieres!'

Thomas wanted to find out what Leo was up to but when he got to the office, he still hadn't arrived.

Frustrated and a little concerned, Thomas picked up his phone and called Leo's number; it was switched off. One thing they had agreed when setting up the business was they should ensure they kept in contact, and at the very least keep their work phones on so they could be easily tracked in an emergency. He tried Leo's private line but that was busy.

'I am sorry,' she said. 'He did phone in earlier but he was pretty vague.' Thomas opened a bottle of wine and poured them a glass.

'I suppose he's got a new girlfriend and has probably gone there. Do you know who she is?'

She shook her head.

He picked up his phone again and called. This time, Leo's mobile was on but it went to messages, so he left a brief, but rather terse, message.

Twenty minutes later, the phone rang. 'Okay, sorry! On my way.' The line went dead.

Thomas and Leo had been friends from the moment they met. They had been deployed from different units to a joint forces task force and had been involved in several covert operations. Despite the differences in their upbringing, they connected immediately. They recognised in each other strengths which had indeed carried them through many of the difficult situations they faced in the service and then the task force. Leo while clever, with a quick mind, was at times inclined to be too reckless or daring for his own good. Thomas felt his swings in mood and occasional outrageous, or brave responses to situations were probably a result of undiagnosed ADHD.

He used bravado to cover his insecurities and fear of failure. A real strength, however, was his ability to ask astute questions that often caught people out. This, together with Thomas' calm, more logical approach, common sense and understanding of people and their motivations, made them a formidable team. They quickly picked up when someone was lying or covering up the truth, then used this understanding of situations to good effect when on operational duty.

Leaving the army had been a difficult decision but one both men knew was the right one. On their last operation together in the task force, they had decided that they would work together and had talked through different opportunities. Casting around, they were contacted by and met with MI5, and were courted by some covert, not-too-legitimate groups. However, they knew that neither wanted the constraints that a government service might demand but recognised that other offers were too far outside their comfort zones.

Thomas had been thinking about some form of security work but couldn't quite frame it as he didn't want to be standing next to some celebrity nobody, even if Leo liked the idea. However, late one night, after a card and drinking session with Leo and a couple of other old squaddies, the idea for what they loosely called an insurance business had developed. As they talked it through, the idea began to take shape. It clearly would not represent the traditional image of protection. Thomas was aware from his research that there was a market for this broader remit.

The idea that emerged with Grace's help was centred around the provision of a wide range of support and security options. Clearly, these could be supplied by much larger well-known companies, but what they proposed would provide a more reactive, bespoke service. This in part, depended on the huge range of contacts they had developed from their army days and the many skills they could call on. A big problem was how to retain the interest of people they trusted in this type of ad hoc setup.

This was where Grace's experience was particularly useful. She suggested a sort of franchise arrangement where, for an agreed annual payment, members of the organisation would receive certain core benefits and opportunities. They talked it through with likely candidates, and this approach had gone down well.

However, before setting up, they needed to acquire finance. Grace suggested that Leo's father could be the perfect sleeping partner. Thomas knew that Leo's family was wealthy; in fact, Lord Gordon was a multi-millionaire. His money had come partly because of the family business in construction after the war, but it had grown exponentially because of his astute management and investment.

His father had wanted Leo to go into the business, but was aware that this would not suit his son. He recognised that prior to the army, Leo was having real problems finding his way in life. He blamed himself as he had always made life easy for his son, meaning Leo had wandered aimlessly and this lack of any real focus had led to a party lifestyle, then alcohol and drugs.

He breathed a sigh of relief when his son joined the army, albeit at a level he didn't discuss with others. Although he was pleased that his son seemed to finally have his life on track, and liked both Thomas and Grace, he had yet to be totally convinced by their plan. Fortunately, having Grace's business plan helped sell the idea, and his father recognised that the friendships he had developed since joining the army had provided a steadying influence. So, he agreed and was finally prepared to support this venture but stipulating that this was a loan, and required a clear timescale.

Lord Gordon had also been able to provide an initial opportunity as a trial. They were employed to transport some extremely important financial documents to a dissident leader in Mosul, Iraq. It was at this point that Leo became aware that his father was involved in some covert and possibly shady dealings. Talking this through, while Thomas was not totally comfortable with this, he knew that aspects of the jobs they could take on might not always be strictly legal. Following the successful completion of this task, a completely different situation had presented itself. It involved one of Lord Gordon's friends, whose daughter had got involved with some cult in Ibiza and needed help to get home.

Again, this was successfully carried out and so word of their business spread through these contacts. Within two years, they had managed to repay most of the initial loan and were almost in profit. The franchise idea also seemed to be working well as when required, people were happy to work for them whenever they could.

A world of rich clients, where money wasn't an issue, was still relatively new to Thomas, who had been brought up on an ex-council estate in Deptford, South London. His mother, a single parent, had been thrown out by her well-off but ultra-religious parents due to her pregnancy. She never told him who his father was, not that he cared. A friend gave her somewhere to stay but when the baby came, she was again forced to find somewhere to live. First, it was an emergency placement by the council in a shared house, which was small, damp, and dark.

After six months, she was moved into a tiny flat. Initially, she had no alternative but to exist on benefits and some cleaning work, while the woman next door looked after Thomas. Eventually, when she was able to put him into a nursery placement part-time, she increased her work as a cleaner in a local school.

Early one evening, chatting to the head teacher, she learned that the local council was running a scheme to pay for open university courses for those with good O and A-level qualifications. Sarah had done well at secondary school and with the support of the head, she applied. She worked hard over two years and was successfully awarded a BA in Accounting.

Despite money being tight, she managed to build a warm and loving home for her son. When Thomas started school, the head who had supported her asked her to apply for a job in the school office. Her skills in managing finance were quickly seen and appreciated. Her salary now meant that although money was still tight, it allowed her to take her son on their first holiday to Devon. He could still remember sandy sandwiches on the beach and the feel of the sand between his toes.

When Thomas went off to comprehensive school, she applied for the role of finance officer and, with excellent references, was successful. This was where she met Thomas' stepfather, an art teacher at the school. He was a bear of a man who seemed to recognise something in Thomas and always helped and encouraged him. While some teenagers hated the intrusion of another person into their family, especially when in his case, there had never been a male role model, Thomas aged thirteen, loved him almost instantly, especially as his mother was so happy. He was thrilled when the pair married.

After successfully completing his A levels, Thomas was due to go to university, but it was clear that his stepfather was unwell and within weeks was dead. When he should have been supporting her, Thomas lost his way and despite the pleas of his mother, he decided not to go to university but to travel instead. He left with little money or plan and headed off on the well-known gap year trail to the Far East. He bummed around for a while and then headed for Australia. He did a lot of bar work and became really good, so money was no longer an issue. After a couple of years, he was offered a job at a club in Los Angeles, where he met a girl and settled for a while.

Sitting in the office, thinking about the past, he thought about his mother's words, 'You can't choose what life throws at you but you can choose how you respond.' It had served him well in situations that demanded cool thinking, such as now. Should they take Madam Akbari's offer?

Thomas' thoughts were broken by Leo's arrival. His friend exasperated him at times, and Thomas was serious when he spoke to him. 'What happened this time? I'm going to put a tracker on you soon!'

'I get it, it won't happen again, and besides, it's not what you were thinking, I wasn't with a girl!' Thomas raised a quizzical eyebrow and laughed; this was a promise that Leo would find difficult to keep. Even if it wasn't a woman this time, it probably would be next.

Women fell at his feet and Thomas had to admit, he could understand why. Leo was an extremely handsome man and had the looks of a younger version of Brad Pitt. He was around six feet two, taller than Thomas and full of life, enthusiasm, and boyish blonde charm. He seemed to have all the attributes, including money, that some women could not resist, and Leo seemed intent on working his way through them.

'I have had an interesting afternoon. It seems there is another party interested in your lady friend and her client. I think there are still questions we need answering, perhaps we should invite her to dinner and discuss them.' Thomas was surprised but agreed.

Chapter 11

Thomas phoned the number on the card Remy had given him and after a couple of rings, a man with a foreign accent answered. Somewhat surprised, Thomas asked to speak to her. He wondered whether this was the elusive man associated with the ring she wore. After a long pause, she came on the line. He told her that both he and Leo were interested in discussing final arrangements and invited her to meet them for dinner. She said she was free the next evening. Thomas looked at Leo, who nodded, so he suggested he would arrange a restaurant if she was happy for him to do so.

He asked Grace to source an appropriately discrete and expensive restaurant; then, sat at his desk looking out at the busy road. He considered the information Leo had found. It appeared after getting out of their car, Leo had waited and taken the number of the one following them, noting that it had diplomatic plates for Iran. He had found an address associated with their Permanent Mission to the UN, had taken an Uber to the address, and seen the car parked nearby. Thomas wondered whether they should share this information with Remy, and if so, what this might mean for her plans.

Clearly, the strange meeting earlier, showed there was some sort of Middle Eastern connection. He wondered where this fitted in and whether this would be beyond the range of tasks they were willing to agree to. Sighing, he returned to the papers Grace had given him.

Remy put the phone down and turned to the man sitting in the chair, a glass of cognac in his hand. 'It seems they are interested.' She smiled.

'This is good, chéri, but are you sure they are experienced enough?' He swigged down the last of the brandy, put the glass down on the table, and stood up. He was a tall, well-built man of distinguished appearance. He had a moustache and well-trimmed beard, and long thick greying hair tied with a black ribbon, and as he pushed it back, as he put on his coat, a diamond ring on his hand caught the light. He appeared to be in his late fifties and had the most beautiful smile that lit up his face and crinkled the corners of his dark eyes, which shone as he pulled her up out of the chair. She took his arm as they walked towards the door.

'Yes, I believe so. Besides, more importantly, they are relatively unknown.' She kissed the man on the cheek. 'Do not worry, we are going to try not to attract too much attention, although I know that once we begin, this might be almost impossible.'

'Well, at least I have been able to confirm that there are other parties involved, so you must be really careful, chérie.'

'Thank you, the information you have given me, is extremely valuable. In a way, I almost feel that I am doing this for Farzad. You are such a good friend to me, and I know he is watching. I will do as you say and watch our friend, but I hope that you are wrong.'

'I know you do but, my darling, love can be blind and blind love can be dangerous. Perhaps instead of looking to the past, you should look forward and elsewhere.'

He turned to pick up his bag and so she missed his sad, wistful smile. 'I must go,' he murmured and gently touched her cheek, but the meaning was clear. He walked towards the door, without a backward glance.

Alone, she could not help but wonder if he was right. She sat down as a rare wave of uncertainty crossed her mind. *All those years, where had the time gone,* she thought. She remembered those early days, how they would just turn up at her flat, sit and laugh, then argue about almost everything and nothing, drinking endless cups of cheap coffee. The three of them, Farzad, Rafik and Andreas were such close friends. However, each man had wanted to date her and so a certain coldness and rivalry started to seep into their friendship. When she moved in with Farzad, there were no more happy meetings, just occasional visits, but always it felt different.

After the group left university, she married Farzad and they settled into a happy life and the birth of their daughter, Alessia. As time went on, life got busier, especially when after her uncle died and she took on the family business. Farzad was now a Foreign Service Specialist in the State Department and, although he didn't say much about what he did, she knew he dealt with the Middle East, meaning he travelled a lot. So, with time, the friendships became more distant but somehow, they had always managed to keep in touch, and she believed that if she ever needed help, one or both would come when called. That was until Farzad's death.

Following the birth of her daughter, Remy heard that Andreas had returned to Greece, had married and had two children. Through her business contacts, she heard that he had either joined or had some sort of involvement with the Greek Navy. She was surprised and always thought this was a little strange, considering his master's degree was in Political Science. They generally managed to catch up once a year when Remy and her family returned to her home in Crete, as that was where Andreas was living.

Rafik had also left the States and returned to Iran, where he married the daughter of an official in one of the more extremist political groups and had a daughter. Remy was worried when in 2009 she heard that the opposition Green Movement had launched its most serious challenge to theocracy since the revolution. Millions went onto the streets, waving banners declaring "Where is my vote?". She had called him but he had denied he was involved in anything like that and was safe. Shortly after, she heard that he had returned to America but without his wife or child.

She recalled that one afternoon, when out of the blue, Farzad got a call from Rafik's personal assistant, Mahmoud, asking whether they could meet privately as he would be in New York briefly. The man suggested that he and Remy would soon be receiving an invitation to meet Rafik for lunch. Apparently, Andreas was going to be there too as he would be there to attend a meeting at the United Nations. Farzad was interested but asked for more information, but the man was reluctant to say more than suggesting his visit might help his investigation.

Now Farzad was interested.

Mahmoud told him that a helicopter would be sent for them and that if they arrived at the heliport early, they could meet and he would explain. Considering what he had been working on, Farzad agreed.

A couple of days later, an invitation arrived, telling them a helicopter had been arranged to take them to Rafik's house in Great Neck. Remy was somewhat surprised as this was a very expensive neighbourhood across Long Island Sound. Clearly, it indicated that he was no longer the poorer member of the group, something she knew had always rankled with him.

Remy remembered thinking, how time had been kind to all of them. Rafik had built a successful mining business after his father-in-law had died; Farzad was working for the government, and Andreas was attached to the United Nations.

Farzad was keen to arrive at the airport early and while sitting in the lounge, his phone suddenly rang.

'I hope that doesn't mean you are going to miss lunch for some business meeting.' Remy remarked, clearly angry.

'No, someone just wants to give me something.' He smiled, kissed her, and headed for the door. 'Won't be long.' He heard her sigh.

The man at the desk said they would soon be clear to leave. Remy looked anxiously at the door. Farzad, beaming, returned and spoke to the man behind the desk. He gave him a case and then headed over towards her.

'What's that?'

'Work, I'll pick it up on the way back.' He took her hand and they headed out to the helipad.

It was just a short flight to the house. It was a beautiful older-style property, facing the Sound.

'Phew, this must have cost a fair bit,' laughed Farzad as the helicopter landed. Rafik came down the steps and swept Remy into his arms. Putting her down, he hugged Farzad and they walked arm in arm into the house, where Andreas was waiting.

Sitting in a modern extension, with sliding doors that opened onto the garden and down to the Sound, they ate lunch. After sitting by the pool and drinking a beautiful Chablis, they started to talk about old times. Rafik suddenly got up and said, 'In case we don't meet again, I wanted to give you something to thank you for your friendship.' He went into the house. No one spoke, as this statement seemed to denote finality. Was he ill, dying? Clearly, this thought passed through their minds.

He came out carrying three boxes. 'I want you to accept these.' He passed a box to each of them. 'I had them made for you, I hope you like the designs. The diamonds are from a special piece of jewellery I have. Sadly, it is broken and irreparable, so I could think of no better way to use it.'

Clearly, no one knew quite what to say. Eventually, Andreas asked, 'Rafik, are you okay? I mean…' His voice trailed off, clearly emotional.

'Oh, I am sorry, I see. Yes, I am not dying but I am returning to Iran and there is much trouble there. Please open them, I insist.' Opening each box, a carefully crafted ring was revealed.

'We can't accept these,' said Farzad. 'They are beautiful but...' He was stopped as Rafik raised his hand.

'Please do not offend me, I will not accept their return.'

Andreas stood up and hugged Rafik. 'Thank you, my friend. I am sorry but I must go; I am late for a meeting.' Standing up and looking at his watch, Farzad said he would join him, and Remy knowing him only too well, smiled and without speaking, waved for him to leave.

Remy's phone rang. So, her daydream was broken. It was her daughter enquiring about the meeting that evening.

'Yes, I wanted to talk to you about that,' she said.

Chapter 12

Thomas and Leo arrived at the restaurant early. The place was, as requested, elegant and fashionable, but not as some could be, busy and loud. They were shown to the bar and were about to order drinks when Remy and another woman arrived. Remy, as Thomas expected, drew admiring glances from those in the bar, as she was as ever exquisitely dressed in a sharp cream outfit, which reminded Thomas of similar outfits she had worn on the ship. Both men rose; Remy did not introduce the other woman, who remained in the shadows by the door and immediately turned to talk to the manager. Having sat down, Thomas could see that Leo was again appraising Remy, *never a good sign* Thomas thought, as he ordered drinks.

Small talk at the bar over, Remy focussed her extremely sharp blue eyes on Thomas. 'So, Thomas, you said you had found out something that troubled you.' She seemed to ignore Leo and turned to the other woman. 'Thank you, please enjoy your evening.' The woman, still in the shadow, turned to leave.

'You're not staying for dinner?' Leo questioned, walking towards the door. He briefly caught a glimpse of dark hair, glasses, and a hint of a smile.

'I don't get to play with the grown-ups,' she said quietly opening the door and before he could think of a retort, she left. The three were shown to a table towards the back of the restaurant, away from others, as Grace had requested. Remy nodded as Thomas held the chair for her.

'Just like old times,' she commented. He laughed and waited till she was seated until he sat down. Leo, by this time, was already settled. Clearly, Thomas had given thought to this meeting, she had been right about him. She had of course investigated them all, so she knew that, although he had not come from a family with money as Leo had, he had clearly been well brought up. She knew that having money wasn't always everything. She thought of her extremely spoiled niece, Sophia, who, because of her perceived outrageous lifestyle, had been disowned by her father.

Having divorced her third husband after just two years, she had recently married her fourth after a whirlwind romance, the consequences of which Remy had only recently travelled to Britain to help resolve. She had two children called Stream and Lake and had been in rehab twice. Remy hoped that in time, the love within their family would be able to rebuild the bonds and help her appreciate and understand the needs of others, and the support the family could provide, so that she would find peace.

Her mind had wandered, and she now focussed on Thomas' questions. They spent some time discussing these and she could clearly see, that like her, Leo had had enough. He was also clearly anxious to eat as he was thumbing the menu.

'Well, gentlemen.' She handed Thomas a folder. 'Please read the proposal at your leisure but to précis it, the initial contract would be for this assignment, which if successfully completed, could lead to a more lucrative arrangement.'

She reminded them that this commission was at relatively short notice, just a couple of weeks away. She reiterated that it involved ensuring some extremely valuable consignments were collected from various locations and transported to London so that the pieces could be brought together.

'Thank you for meeting me, but please let me know within twenty-four hours if you change your mind having read this, or I will not be able to make the appropriate arrangements.'

Looking towards a table of four Middle Eastern men, Thomas muttered, 'We seem to be attracting the interest of another party. Should this be a concern?'

'I don't think so. The client is Iranian, so it is possible that as there is again instability in the region, anyone from there, or having connections with it, is being watched. So, by default, those associated will also be of interest. I have Middle Eastern connections and my late husband was Iranian, but at this time, it does not appear to be a major concern. We will keep you appraised of any changes to that situation. Would that satisfy you? Obviously, once you commit to collecting and transporting this consignment, I will be able to share more information.'

Leo nodded. 'That sounds fine, okay, Thomas. Shall we order?'

As he picked up the menu for about the tenth time, a red-varnished nail appeared over his menu and pulled it gently down to the table. 'Fine it may be,' she said in a cold voice, turning her full gaze on him, 'but, Mr Tremaine, it is the timescale which could prove to be extremely difficult. When you have studied the details, get in touch. We could meet the day after tomorrow, if acceptable.

Now, enjoy your dinner.' And with that she rose, leaving both men struggling to stand before she was already halfway to the door.

'Goodness, I see what you mean,' declared Leo. 'Quite a woman! Let's eat.' He was beginning to really like this woman but wished she would smile at him, the way she did at Thomas.

They ordered and while they had an excellent dinner and talked about what they had heard and agreed that regardless, it was too good an opportunity to miss, so they would accept the commission. After dinner, they headed back to the office to finalise this with Grace.

Later that evening, Thomas opened the portfolio and he and Grace read through the paperwork together in silence. Then Thomas drew in a sharp breadth. 'Leo, come over and read this.' Leo took the papers and while reading them, scowled.

'Is she joking?' He laughed. 'To get from London to Miami, then LA and then Sydney and London in that timescale seems impossible. I can't see why it needs to be so tight. Surely, they could just wait, they have had the items for a while, so why the rush?'

'Read page three,' said Thomas.

Leo just whistled, then swore, then finally said, 'Okay then! Well, I'm off, got a date!' Thomas and Grace shared a look of exasperation.

The next morning, Leo phoned Remy and she confirmed that while the items were in these locations, for security reasons the client wanted them brought together in London for a particular date. However, she gave no reason as to why these people would not transport the property themselves, despite the many ways he asked the question, "Why?". Clearly, there was a story here but this wasn't the time to press her for it.

He asked how they would know that the items were the real ones. She explained that to authenticate the items, an expert would be accompanying them. They would be able to check whether the precious stones in the items were real. Back in London, a professor from the Victoria and Albert Museum would then confirm the authenticity of the designs and their approximate age. Leo considered everything and felt a little more reassured.

Following the call, they settled down to fine-tune their planning, so that they could see just how feasible it was. Grace and Thomas continued to work together to develop a schedule for travel that made the timescales just conceivably possible. He was amazed at the detailed planning that Grace was able to build in such a short timescale and he wondered again about how she and Leo had ended up together. Although clever in his own way, he was never her equal and it had quickly become clear that they were much better friends than lovers. Not that either had a complaint about the latter.

Leo, working with Jem, was tasked with sourcing the personnel and appropriate transport both in the UK and at the various stopping points. Remy had asserted that the finances for the operation were already available and generous; however, having discussed their plan with his father, it was clear they would again need his support. Leo had to admit that he was a little surprised at how his father seemed more than usually interested in this venture, even to the extent that he agreed to Leo commandeering the family jet, complete with crew. While he was suspicious, he decided not to say anything to Thomas, as he knew his father had some less-than-kosher deals; maybe this came close to one of them.

The use of the plane would make the trips both more possible and comfortable. He had discussed the route with the company's pilot, who recommended a refuelling stop on the LA to Sydney leg in Tahiti. Thomas met with Leo at the end of the day and having discussed it, they were confident that when they spoke to Remy, they would be able to say they had a clear plan in place and would be ready by the agreed date to fly to London.

The next morning, Thomas went to meet Remy and he explained their plan and said they were ready to accept the commission. While she agreed, she made some small modifications. She told Thomas that at each stop, the piece would be authenticated, then locked into a numbered box, which she repeated must be immediately transported by courier to a central vault in London. The key would remain with them, so the two were never together. Thomas had allowed for the couriers to London, so he heaved a sigh of relief.

'The key is able to track the whereabouts of the box,' she explained. 'Doctor Patterson will be the expert who will examine and confirm the object's authenticity and then lock the box. The doctor is currently in New York, so it would be sensible to meet them and discuss arrangements,' she said.

'I told them that you were buying dinner. They are staying at the Langham on Fifth Avenue. They will meet you at 7.30 pm.'

Following a flurry of activity towards the end of the day, everything seemed to be arranged, so he would be able to go to dinner with Dr Patterson with a clear conscience.

Chapter 13

Thomas called his favourite Italian restaurant near the hotel and booked. Then he returned to the apartment on W29th St #8N that he had once shared with Margo. Although she had left him some months ago, the place still had her everywhere he looked, from the décor to the things she had not taken with her. These included the now-dead plants that he kept meaning to throw out. The end of their relationship had been mutual. After two years together, they both knew that they were heading along different paths. She was moving to Boston to work in a hospital there and they knew this would put an impossible strain on their relationship.

He picked up a picture of them together still on the bookcase. Her strong features and warm brown eyes stared happily out as he hugged her. He sighed and knew he really would have to move out of this place soon, as it was too expensive for one person, and he seemed to be there so rarely now. Having showered, he had changed into jeans and a polo shirt. It was a short walk to the hotel, where the doctor was staying. *Doctors always seemed to be a focus in his life,* he thought, *especially after the last job, where an extremely attractive one had sewn him up.*

He had left a message for Doctor Patterson with the hotel to say he would meet them in the lobby. Arriving he stood to one side in the smallish space and as a hand touched his shoulder, he turned, somewhat startled.

'I take it you are Doctor Patterson,' he said smiling, as he suddenly realised that she was the woman who had accompanied Remy into the restaurant the day before. Although now, her hair fell loosely to her shoulders and she no longer wore glasses. In that first brief meeting, in the dim lights of the restaurant, she had somehow slipped by almost unnoticed; looking at her now, he couldn't imagine how.

'Hello, yes, I'm Alessia, friends call me Lissa.' He was immediately struck by how beautifully her face was framed by her jet-black hair; however, it was her stunning blue eyes that instantly captured his attention. She scowled a little and wrinkled her nose then, clearly aware of the impact she was having on him, her lips curled into a playful smile.

'Come, Mr Beckett, I am sure you would agree that women are far more than their looks. My mother said you were better than that!'

'Mother?' Then he realised where he had seen those blue eyes. 'You are Remy's daughter.'

'Yes, Patterson was my married name. Now are we going to continue to stand here? My mother said you were buying me dinner.'

He grinned. Yes, she certainly was her mother's daughter.

'I hope you don't mind a short walk and like Italian food.,' Thomas said.

She smiled. 'Absolutely!'

They walked to W36th/5th to a restaurant called Ai Fiori. He loved to eat there and knew that dinner would be amazing. The evening passed quickly and it was not just because the food was fantastic. It was soon clear to both that they were going to be, at the very least, good friends. Talk was easy and they shared several interests, which helped the conversation flow. Walking back to her hotel, he was sad the evening was over, but mindful of the task ahead, so he wished her good night, waiting till she entered the hotel. Across the street,-unnoticed in a black sedan, someone was also watching.

Thomas called a cab and recalling something Lissa had said, decided to pay a quick visit to the office, to check something out. As the cab moved off, so did the sedan. Thomas was preoccupied with both the job and his thoughts about Lissa, so initially he didn't notice he was being followed; however, deciding her concern could wait till tomorrow, he asked the driver to go downtown instead. The driver did a swift left and right. Hearing the squeal of tyres, Thomas was alerted and turned to see a black limo forced into a tighter turn. His years of training kicked in and he leant forward and asked the driver to do a couple of swift turns to confirm his suspicions. The driver shrugged, grinned, and then did so, rather enjoying the idea of a chase a bit too much.

'I watch James Bond!' He spoke with a thick South African accent and he beamed back at Thomas, almost hitting the kerb.

Reconsidering his destination, Thomas decided that maybe it was not a good idea to arrive at his front door, so asked the driver to stop on the main crossroad ahead. He got out and quickly paid the man, who looked sad that the chase had ended so soon. Aware the limo was now parked across the street. Thomas got out his phone and took a picture of the car number plate and then the man inside. As he did so, the car moved off. Texting Jem, he sent him the pictures and asked him to blow them up and see if he could find out anything.

A short while later, his phone beeped. Jem was in the office and had run the pictures through the police database that Leo had managed to arrange access to. The picture of the man was too unclear but the car was registered to the Permanent Mission of Iran, with diplomatic plates. Thomas instinctively knew this meant they needed to be more alert and wary.

Jem asked, 'Everything okay, Boss?' Thomas told him about the car and they laughed about the taxi driver. He was too wired now to go home and was still concerned someone was watching, so decided to go to the office and headed for the subway. Recently, he seemed to be staying there more than his apartment. When he arrived, Jem was gone. He poured himself a brandy and settled down to watch some late-night football. He could never call it soccer as the Americans did. Later, as sleep finally threatened, he made up a bed on the sofa, stripped off and settled down, knowing that in the morning, he could shower and change clothes from the wardrobe he kept there. The last thing he thought about was the car, which again sat outside.

Lissa, back in her hotel room, was confused. Her mother had already told her about Thomas but she hadn't expected him to be quite so interesting or handsome. She had thoroughly enjoyed the evening; the time had flown by and she was sorry when he had left her. She had thought fleetingly about asking him in for a drink, but then the last time she had done that, it hadn't ended there. Having only recently been divorced she wasn't yet prepared to have a one-night stand or jump into another relationship, especially when she would then have to work with him and his team.

She knew her relationship record wasn't brilliant, having only managed two longer relationships, one after uni, and then Ryan, who she had met and married. Now he was her ex-husband and thankfully they had divorced without any major issues. So, now, she was looking for some "me" time; but she sighed, her friends were mostly married, so any dating was down to online apps rather than going out with the girls. This made meeting men so much more unpredictable and, potentially, dangerous. Fortunately, she had been lucky, those she had met had sometimes been okay but mostly, they did not live up to either their picture or their profile.

She had amused her mother with some of the more hilarious or infamous lies she'd had. Now back in New York, she was waiting for her new apartment to be decorated, so was staying at the hotel rather than disturb her mother.

She got ready for bed, and as she snuggled down, the last thing she thought about was Thomas' smile.

The next morning, Thomas had gone out for a run and had seen the black limo parked across the street. It was the same car but he thought that the man in the front seat looked to be different. He stopped off at a bakery and grabbed a smoked salmon and cream cheese bagel and doughnuts, then headed back, noting the car number on the box. Grace arrived at the office early and was unsurprised to see Thomas in residence again, but grateful for the coffee he had made and the doughnuts. Following Grace, Leo arrived a little later and then Jem came in with a couple of guys to organise the equipment they might need.

When Jem finished, he asked Thomas if he wanted a lift home to pick things up. Thomas nodded. Before he left, he filled Leo in with the evening encounter and showed him the pictures.

'I'll send the pictures to my FBI contact, maybe he knows him,' he promised. Thomas headed off with Jem out to his flat to pack up a few things that he would need.

Chapter 14

Lissa arrived in the office the day before they were due to depart for London. By the time Thomas arrived from meeting with Remy, she had introduced herself to everyone, which Thomas had wanted to do. Grace laughed when she told him that Leo had turned on his typical boyish charm, which, depending of course on the woman in question, would often completely captivate them. However, by her distinctly cool reception, he quickly realised that she wasn't one of them and returned to his paperwork.

Grace put down the phone and having checked her computer, announced that the final timings and plans had been sent to their secure website and with a broad grin, wished them luck. As Thomas joined the group, he was pleased to see that everyone seemed to be getting on well and were involved in an animated discussion about an aspect of planning. Grace had used a friend in cyber security to help her set up their system, thereby ensuring it was protected. Jem, who loved computers, had laughed and initially called him just another hacker. Grace was annoyed and they had words but now having seen the system, Jem had to admit, that the guy was good.

Grace would stay behind in New York to coordinate any changes and keep them up-to-date with information as they moved from one place to another.

With everyone assembled, Jem got things going by ensuring all the luggage was taken to the cars. The cases provided by Remy were already stowed. With everything ready, they headed to the lifts and the waiting cars, for the drive to the private terminal at JFK.

As they set off, Thomas noticed the black limo pull in a couple of cars back.

'It's okay, boss, I've seen it,' Jem said and relayed the message to the other car. The journey was uneventful and luckily there were no hold-ups on the interstate. As they cruised along, Jem shrugged as he realised that the tail seemed to have disappeared. Leo's phone beeped and checking it, he saw he had a message from his FBI contact to say that this car was also registered to the

Iranian mission to the UN as Iran no longer had an embassy. The man however, remained a mystery. Leo's request had raised his friend's interest and he questioned what was going on. Leo was good at being evasive but on this occasion, he didn't need to try too hard as he had yet to have any clear idea himself.

Arriving at JFK airport, initially involved passing through the outside security gate; once through, they were directed to the private terminal. It was here that they would complete the necessary immigration checks and then wait till they could head to the plane. Thomas was pleased that so far, arrangements for the trip to London seemed to be falling into place. It was about forty minutes later that a steward greeted them and told them that the plane was ready. The terminal was not very busy and their luggage and stores had been checked and taken out to the plane. Lastly, they had to clear personal customs, so they would be able to board.

Nobody was carrying any weapons, aware that in the UK this could cause a problem on entry. They would, however, be sourced on arrival as a precaution. Thomas thought that with the time difference, it would be early afternoon when they arrived at Biggin Hill Airport. This would give them time at the hotel to finalise any last-minute issues or personnel arrangements so that they were sure everything was in place. They followed the steward through the air side doors and walked across the tarmac to Lord Gordon's brand new GULFSTREAM G650 jet. Leo hadn't seen it yet and whistled, adding, 'Nice one, Dad!' only too aware of his father's threats if he "dented" it.

Jem did not like flying very much and was grateful the flight across the Atlantic was smooth. They arrived on time at the small airport to the south of London. On approach, Thomas couldn't help but think about the hundreds of men who, during WW2, had flown out of this airport, never to return. The arrival formalities were much the same in reverse to those in New York. Grace had clearly ensured absolutely every form and bit of paper was in place. Once this was completed, they headed out to the front of the building, where Jem and the other driver went to pick up the cars that had been arranged.

As the others stood in the late afternoon sunshine, waiting for him to bring it around to the front of the terminal, Thomas couldn't help but scan the area, but nothing seemed out of place. When their car driven by Jem arrived, he helped the others load the hand luggage into the boot and then got in.

Jem had already set the satnav to the hotel postcode and turning out of the airport, headed out left towards Westerham, then turned towards Turner's Hill and the hotel. This had been selected as it was near to where their first meeting would take place. Meanwhile, two of Jem's men had picked up a van and were loading the cases and some equipment into it. They had donned yellow high-vis jacket covers, so that to onlookers, this group would appear to be ordinary baggage handlers, meaning anyone watching would not connect them to the other car. When they left, they took a different route to the others.

Jem drove easily through the country lanes, despite the sun flickering through the trees and being on the wrong side of the road. The forest was wet following the morning rain, so large puddles caused considerable spray and waves as he sped through them. Thomas, sitting in the front seat, looked at Jem's face and realised he was having great fun making sure he hit as many of these as possible. Unfortunately, this could also mean some sharp bumps as the water hid some deep potholes. It took less than an hour to arrive at a curving bend in the road and a sign which pointed to the Ravenwood Hotel.

As the sun disappeared again behind some dark clouds, they went through the gateway to the sixteenth-century hotel. Jem stopped as a smartly dressed doorman walked towards them. He gave Lissa's name and the man removed a private sign for them to park. Once everyone had headed into the hotel, Jem got back into the car and disappeared up the drive. He was staying elsewhere with the others.

The doorman led them inside through the heavy doors which gave way to an inner lobby. The hallway was beautifully oak panelled and to one side, there was a small reception desk, where a smiling woman stood up and greeted them. They completed the necessary paperwork and she said their rooms were ready. She picked up three keys and showed them upstairs.

His room was delightful and looked out onto a beautiful formal garden. It had stopped raining and the sun glistened on the ivy that crept up the side of his window. He was of two minds, either to head for a shower or get some air. He decided it would be good to stretch his legs.

He headed down the stairs, through the bar and out onto the porch that was filled with flowers and Wellington boots. He had been right; the air was beautiful. Following the rain and in the early evening light, the gardens seemed magical. Despite the dampness, he decided he would climb the steps and as a light breeze stirred the grasses, the shifting of some stones ahead made him realise that he was not alone. Coming the other way was Lissa.

'It's so beautiful here,' she gestured up the path. 'I have been right up to the top and to the right is a huge vegetable garden.' They fell into step as they left the terrace and chatted about different plants as they wandered around the garden, stopping at a small hidden pool.

'I didn't take you for a gardener.' She grinned.

'And I didn't take you for a mineralogist!' he said.

'Touché! Do you fancy a coffee?' He agreed and they headed back inside. Initially, they did not talk about the next day but when their coffee arrived, eventually and inevitably, it happened.

'What do you know about what we will be collecting?' She asked.

'Nothing specific, just that the pieces are extremely valuable. Presumably whatever they are, they must contain precious stones, as you are here. I also understand that it was broken up many years ago. Oh, and we need to be there tomorrow.'

Lissa began to explain that the pieces they were collecting were originally part of an ancient treasure. She said there was evidence that over the years, the various pieces had been bought, traded, fought over and stolen many times, often in particularly brutal circumstances. As she talked, she became more and more animated. 'The regalia, that's what my mother called it, is made up of a dagger, sheath, belt, sash and clasp, along with several other items. Following the last robbery, the thieves found no one wanted to buy the items, because of their history. Oh, and goodness, it starts to get really gory again, as they were found dead with their throats cut.'

Thomas nearly laughed as he could see how much she was enjoying retelling the tale. She continued by suggesting that whoever killed them, split up the regalia items.

'Do you mean the people we are dealing with are murderers?' He asked with mock horror and a barely hidden chuckle.

'Oh no,' she said still oblivious to his amusement. 'The people who have the pieces now inherited them and appear to have no knowledge of how they were obtained. I am sure there is some connection between them but I don't know how or why. What I do know is that the whole item has some sort of significance to the client and their family, but again, I am unsure what this is, and I am sure, we will not be the only ones trying to recover these pieces.'

Thomas was now totally captivated both by her enthusiasm and by what he thought sounded like it might be an exciting task. 'I expect that together, they would be worth many millions today,' he said.

'I doubt they could sell the whole thing completely; they would probably break it up for the stones. But my mother found some references to rumours that the items as well as the stones, appear to have a more profound cultural significance to the people of Iran. Apparently, Persian history places them as an important part of the royal ceremonial dress of the Shah. We do not know what the client wants with the regalia or those who have been following us. But it is clearly possible that they represent at least one other client.'

The conversation continued until they had drunk their coffee and then they returned to their rooms. That evening, they met Leo in the bar. They had an excellent meal, then settled quietly in a corner of the bar to talk about the arrangements for the next day.

With Lissa's story still swirling around in his mind, Thomas found it difficult to sleep; the bed was comfortable but he couldn't get her or it out of his mind, especially her comments about the items they would be collecting. Eventually, he drifted off but his sleep was fretful, unusual for him.

Chapter 15

Breakfast the next morning, while looking out at the garden, was wonderful, but they couldn't afford to linger.

Lissa told them she had received some further information from her mother about the item they would be receiving today and showed them the picture on her phone. Leo whistled. She said this, like all the other items, was coming from private sources and believed that the woman they were meeting today had no knowledge of its history. Apparently, when her husband, who was of Iranian descent, died, instructions had been left in his will for it to be returned to his homeland. There were also clear instructions as to who to contact, which was exactly what she had done. The team would meet her at her house, where Lissa would verify whether the stones in the item were real; if so, they would lock it in the box and send it directly to London.

The woman from reception came over and told them that their car had arrived. Thomas went to finalise the account and then met the others outside. Jem had turned the car ready to go, so they stowed their luggage in the boot and left. Leo asked whether there had been any issues. Jem shook his head. 'All quiet,' he replied.

The house they were going to was not far and they soon arrived at another impressive driveway, with a sold sign hanging precariously by the gate. They drove in and pulled up outside a large, somewhat neglected house. As they got out of the car, the front door opened and an elderly woman appeared.

'Good morning, Doctor Paterson?' She asked.

'Yes. Thank you for agreeing to do this.' The woman nodded and they shook hands. 'Please come in.' She showed them into what had once clearly been a beautifully proportioned hallway but it, like the rest of the house, was empty and felt uncared for.

'Thank you for coming.' Recognising the look on their faces, she hesitated. 'I don't live here anymore. My husband died a while back but it has taken time to resolve his finances. The house will have new owners tomorrow and I hope they will be happier here than I ever was.' A sad look passed across her face.

She started to walk towards another door and they followed her into what had presumably been the drawing room. There was a small table and in the middle was a leather-bound box. 'My husband's will specified that he wanted this to be returned to its rightful owner. It has brought this family nothing but grief, so I shall not be sad to see it go.'

'Do you know what is inside?' Leo asked.

'No,' she replied, 'and I don't want to know. It is evil. I will wait for you in the hall.' With that, she turned and left the room.

Once she had gone, Lissa moved forward and opened the box. On the blue velvet interior lay a gold, heavily jewelled dagger, its pommel mounted with what appeared to be a huge ruby. Leo whistled. Lissa opened her bag and put on a pair of white gloves, picked up a small eyepiece and then the dagger. She let out an audible sigh.

'Its colour,' Lissa exclaimed, looking at Thomas and pointing to the ruby. 'It's the colour of blood, which is why someone might think it was evil.'

Turning the dagger over, Lissa examined it closely and then placed it back in its box. Out of her bag, she took a portable gemstone estimator to check the quality of the stones. Holding it first against the ruby, then the other stones, she confirmed it and the others in the dagger were real. Putting the dagger carefully back in its box, she closed the lid. Jem laid the travel case on the table and Lissa placed the box inside, secured it, and closed the case. She turned the key, and as she did so, it was clear that its tracking device had been activated, as a blue light seemed to briefly flash over the surface and then disappear. She put the key on its chain around her neck.

They returned to the hall, where Lissa shook hands with the woman, who walked with them to the door. 'Thank you,' said Lissa. 'This is from the client to who you are returning it, I believe this will explain matters and will help you.' She handed her an envelope. They left the house and the woman locked the door.

'I fear it may have come too late. Be careful, the house was broken into recently and I think it was because someone else wanted this.' She indicated the case, then turned and got into her car. Thomas didn't question her comment but it made him uneasy and again, he fleetingly wondered just what had they got themselves involved with.

The silence in the car indicated a change in mood. Each held their own thoughts but perhaps they were all struck by the same sense of foreboding. With the box nestled between Thomas and Leo on the back seat, Lissa sat up front. Thomas was unable to shake the uneasy feeling from the night before that although no one was seen, they were not alone. But he noticed nothing on the drive back. At the airport, however, he felt one of the desk staff at the car rental place seemed to engage with Jem rather intently.

'Was there a problem?' He asked Jem.

'Nah, she suggested we might have scratched the car but I'd taken photos, so no contest. She was just a bit too nosy. Anyway, I'd scrubbed the navigation data in the car system and told her we were heading home to New York.'

Dennis and Rab waiting in the carpark, had arrived to pick up the case and deliver it to the safe house. The pair were good friends of Jem's from his boxing days. Rab was around forty and had been in the police but was now "retired". Dennis, also ex-police, had taken a slightly different path in personal security; or at least that was what he called it. Before this job, he had been a bouncer at a top nightclub. He used to quip that, unlike Rab, he had two ex-wives to support. Jem had vouched for them and Grace's clearance checks had raised no red flags. Thomas secured the case to Rab's wrist, then watched as they got into their car and set off. Jem had arranged for an escort car to cover them, just in case.

'Belt and braces,' laughed Jem, as they set off with the first box destined for a very secure location in South London.

The team watched the cars leave and then entered the terminal. They went through customs and security once more and while they waited in the lounge to board the plane, Leo checked the new crew manifest. He was pleased to see that the pilot and crew were the same. He put in a call to his father to thank him and to say all was okay. His father said he had nothing to report but that he should take care, nonetheless. Leo was somewhat surprised as he detected a slight tremor in his father's voice. They boarded the plane for the second part of their journey. Leo checked his phone, it was 4 pm. He thought they were making good time.

Thomas' phone rang and after a brief conversation, he turned to the others. 'Dennis just got word that there was a car accident near where we met the woman this morning. A lorry hit a car side-on, there were no survivors.' A thought crossed Thomas' mind but he dismissed it as coincidence.

Lissa looked at Thomas and it was clear that this had unnerved her. She was clearly thinking about what they all were but was there something else that she was not saying?

Finally, she responded, 'Why? She didn't have the dagger anymore.'

'There is a lot more to this dagger than we know. Clearly, it's an expensive piece and maybe part of a ceremonial outfit, but killing someone who was associated with it? Well, I think it's time to find out as much as we can about these objects,' Thomas scowled.

'Looks to me as if someone is "circling the wagons", keen to dispose of any connections or loose ends maybe,' added Leo.

'What do you think that means for us?' Lissa asked.

'It means we need to be more watchful and get the job done asap,' Thomas replied as the plane taxied to the runway. Silence descended as each contemplated the news and prepared in their own way for the flight. At the back, Jem gripped the arms of his seat and with eyes closed, repeated a well-used Muslim Dua, or prayer, for their safety.

Lissa was clearly worried and only when the plane climbed away from the airport, did she seem to relax a little. As she looked out of the window at the clouds below, she was only too aware that this wasn't the first time that she had heard of someone being killed in this way. She tried to shake off the feeling, hoping against hope that she was making connections that were not there.

She considered whether she should talk to her mother about this but then, bringing up old wounds may not be a good idea.

Chapter 16

The plane was quiet, except for the hum of the engines. It would take around nine hours to fly to Miami. Considering the time they left, they would arrive early evening because of flying west. Jem, having got over the take-off, went immediately to the back of the plane and put on his headphones. He wanted to watch a boxing match, and to everyone's amazement, he did so without letting out a sound, although he demonstrated much of the action. As everyone settled, Lissa told Thomas and Leo that she had received a text from her mother, telling them she would be joining them in Miami. Lissa had told her mother that the dagger appeared genuine, but to be truly authenticated, they could not do this until they could finally fit it into the jewelled scabbard in London.

She also told her that they thought the woman they had received it from was dead but didn't say how. This was greeted initially by silence, then "Take care, my darling", and the line went dead.

Thomas saw a look of concern on Lissa's face. He moved to sit next to her. 'Was there a problem? I hope she trusts us,' he quipped.

'My mother doesn't really trust anyone, not even me!' She smiled.

'I have a question though bearing in mind what has happened.'

'Okay, but don't expect an answer!' She said still smiling.

'The ring on your mother's finger, she is inclined to twist it repeatedly whenever she is thinking, or I imagine worried about something. I noticed she did that the last time we saw her. Has it got anything to do with this trip?'

'No, I don't think so,' but she immediately looked away, leading Thomas to conclude otherwise. However, he decided it was best to leave her to her thoughts and went over to sit with Leo.

'Not having any luck? I could give you a lesson if you want,' laughed Leo.

'Leave it. Let's just check through the schedule now Remy is joining us.'

Not giving up, he said, 'You're going to have to work a little harder on this one, I think. You do know she thinks that you're after her mother, don't you?' This time, Leo's grin was warm.

Thomas looked aghast, then looked away, leaving Leo surprised to find he had hit a nerve. He knew Thomas well and could tell when he was interested in a woman and knew not to cross that line, but he was up for a bit of fun. So, with that, he got up and moved to the seat opposite Lissa. It was soon clear that they were chatting amiably and Thomas swore to himself.

From their days with the joint task force, they had established a good friend in the FBI and Thomas decided that as long as he was careful he might also turn out to be useful. He got out their schedule and checked the name of the hotel in Miami, then picked up the phone.

'Hi, Wes, how are things?' He had met Wes when he was on a covert op in Afghanistan while still with the task force. The man had all but saved his life, when, after a brutal fight, which he had to admit he was losing, Wes had come to his aid and killed the attacker. Since then, Wes had joined the FBI, and on more than one occasion proved to be a useful contact, as they had for him.

'Hi, stranger! Look, I haven't much time, I am on a team op. If you need more help, you'll need to share.'

'Okay, so we'll be in Miami tomorrow morning, staying at the Fontainebleau, South Beach, any chance you can meet us, we can chat then.'

'Yeah, should be okay, will call you later.' The line went dead.

Leo called over, 'Is he free?'

'Think so.'

The rest of the flight was calm, so they made excellent time and they all managed to get a little sleep. They landed at Miami International Airport a little ahead of schedule. The plane taxied to the private terminal, where entry requirements would be completed. Despite having travelled to the States often and still having military and NATO connections that allowed residency, the paperwork and searches were tedious. Lissa had dual nationality, so passed through easily. However, as they were ushered through to customs and passed endless queues for immigration, Leo held his breath and was again thankful for Grace and her careful planning.

Customs were also straightforward, as again any resources they might need would be sourced locally, so as not to alert the authorities to anything other than returning after a business trip. They walked through the green exit and Jem headed for the car service desk. Leo ensured their luggage was collected and they walked out onto the main pick-up area, where they waited in the increasingly warm Miami sun for Jem to bring the car around. Walking to the car, Thomas turned to see that Lissa had stopped and appeared to be in conversation with a man, who was partially hidden by a pillar.

She leant forward to kiss him, so clearly knew him. Thomas could just see his profile; he was older, he thought late fifties, with a shock of long grey hair. Then he moved back and only his hand was visible as it gripped Lissa's. On his finger was a thick gold band, with a large diamond inset, and then it and the man were gone. Thomas decided now might not be the time to raise the question but he was curious to have an answer, as this was the third ring of similar size and design he had seen recently. Circumstances as they were, there should be no secrets. As he was about to ask, the car arrived and there was no time.

It was a straight run on the interstates, so the journey to the hotel turned out to be easy as the traffic was light. The hotel was enormous and had been chosen well by Grace, as it would help them remain anonymous. The entrance was all marble, glass and huge chandeliers, not Thomas' style at all. Checking in, their rooms were ready early, so they headed up and agreed to meet later for lunch.

In his room, Thomas headed to the window and looked out at the ocean. He was always amazed at the different shades of blue against the almost white sand. He could see that the hotel was separated from the beach by a stretch of grass that then led down to rows of umbrellas, pools, and sunbeds. He watched as the waves rolled in and people jumped and swam in the clear, calm waters. As he turned away, he thought that this all seemed so unreal. They were entering a period of uncertainty and he sighed, wishing he and Lissa could enjoy this scene together. He turned, stripped off his clothes, and went into the bathroom to shower.

As the hot water hit his body, it relieved some of the bruising that still added a faintly yellow tinge to parts of his body. Drying himself, he examined his newest scar, a wound from the knife of one of the cult leaders from whom they had rescued the daughter of one of Lord Gordon's friends. It was healing well. At thirty-eight, he maintained his body through regular exercise and diet. He was not into fad training, pills, or anything like that. He was well-muscled but somehow managed to remain lean. He had only one tattoo, worn by all the men in the task force, a beautifully stylised wolf's head on his chest, above his heart.

It had also cleverly covered a shrapnel wound, the result of his time in Afghanistan. He shaved and then dressed.

Downstairs in the bar, Leo was sitting with Lissa and, much to his surprise, Remy. He smiled. 'Good to see you again, Madam Akbari.' Remy nodded.

'I thought since you were early, I would catch up with you and discuss your progress to date and whether you had encountered any unexpected issues or problems. However, I have heard from Alessia that things have gone smoothly so far.' Thomas looked at her and Leo, who were both smiling and nodding, he thought, a little too vigorously.

'Most pleasing. Well then, I will leave you to enjoy what is left of the day and will see you tomorrow.' She got up and both men rose and watched her as she left the bar.

'No one told her about what the police in the UK are calling "a terrible accident" then?' Thomas queried.

'No. Jem called in a couple of favours and it appears the police are keeping the woman's name quiet, however, they have already established that the driver of the lorry had been shot and died well before the accident, so for the press, they are just saying it was an accident.'

'That poor woman. Whatever is going on here, she had nothing to do with it.' Lissa was clearly upset.

There was silence. They were all keenly aware that since then, the trip had taken on a new light. Someone chasing them was willing to kill.

Jem got up, saying he was hungry, and despite the somewhat sombre atmosphere, they laughed and headed to the Oceanside Bistro. Having lunch together seemed to relieve some of the tension and they agreed to meet the next day for breakfast. Thomas and Lissa walked to the lift.

'What are you going to do for the rest of the day?' He asked casually.

'Sleep! The next flights will be gruelling, then I'll decide,' she said. 'Where's Leo?' She stopped looking around.

Thomas indicated the door. 'He'll be back by breakfast. Do you want to meet up for dinner?'

She hesitated, then said, 'Why not, about eight in the bar?' He nodded and they got into the lift.

'What about you, what will you do?'

'I'm going for a swim and then I'll see.' He smiled as she got out of the lift. 'See you at dinner.'

Having gathered his things, Thomas headed straight for the sea, enjoying the surprisingly cool water. He relaxed on a sunbed, then decided to head back to the hotel. Later, he wandered along Ocean Drive. He remembered his days working the bars here; although the scene was very different now, much more touristy and a lot less seedy. He stopped for a drink at the Betsy and was unsurprised that there was nobody there he knew. Bar staff were like the ocean, constantly moving.

As he was finishing his Mai Tai, he got a call from Wes, who apologised and said that he wouldn't be available after all but might catch up with them in LA. Thomas was sorry to have missed him; although, knowing Wes, once he knew they were in the States, he had made it his business to find out as much as possible about what they were up to. It seemed he already knew they were going to Los Angeles, so no doubt had been checking up on his "old friends" movements.

Thomas headed back to the hotel, unable to shake the feeling that he was being watched, although he saw no one. Back in his room, he stripped off to cool down and stretched out on the bed, his mind still trying to put pieces of information together. He had lots of scraps but nothing yet seemed to make sense. Eventually, he gave up and drifted off to sleep.

He woke with a start, realising he had only ten minutes to get dressed and meet Lissa in the bar. A hasty shower meant he was just able to get there before her.

She arrived and he was momentarily taken aback as she looked just like a younger version of her mother. Her dress followed her curves and almost took Thomas' breath away. He ordered martinis and she sat on the bar stool next to him. They chatted about their day, which for her had been mostly sleeping.

'But I did go out and got you this,' she said handing him a small box. Inside was a fridge magnet with "I love Miami" on it.

'Just what I always wanted! Anyway, how do you know I have a fridge? Margo might have taken it with her.' Then he realised, he had never spoken about her.

'Oh, I am sorry,' she said, clearly embarrassed.

'Come on, let's have dinner and I will tell you all about my disastrous love life,' he laughed.

'We can swap stories,' but her laugh lacked warmth.

He took her arm. 'Sounds like fun,' he lied but smiled.

They had dinner at a restaurant on Ocean Drive recommended by the concierge. After dinner, they shared stories and a good deal of laughter, then walked back to the hotel, and ordered Black Russians, settling into a corner by the window in the hotel's bar.

Thomas decided now was the time to broach the question he was concerned about. 'Who was the man you spoke to at the airport? I ask only because we are clearly being followed.'

'He is a friend of my mother's. When my father died, he was there for us and has always supported us.'

'I see,' said Thomas. 'I thought there must be a strong connection, the diamond on his hand is similar to the one your mother wears.'

'There are four, one belonged to my father, which mother has, hers and the one Andreas wears.' She stopped as it was clear that Thomas was about to ask the question, that would lead to one she did not want to face.

'So, who has the fourth?'

'Someone who should have been there to support us at that time but wasn't. I will never forgive him.' This was a conversation that she clearly was not going to elaborate on.

With that, she got up. 'Thank you for a relaxing evening, just what I needed. I will see you tomorrow. Goodnight, Thomas,' she said and without giving him a chance to say anything further, she turned and left. He ordered a brandy and considered what they had discussed and the events of the day.

Based on this, he felt the need to check in on the whereabouts of the first box on his way to bed. Jem said that the men had safely deposited the first box at the safe house, so all was okay so far.

Chapter 17

Meeting for breakfast, the next morning, Leo looked a little worse for wear. Thomas suspected that one of the city's casinos was probably light a few thousand dollars.

He was partly right as Leo had spent part of his time at a casino, and then his winnings in a club. He had initially gone to Rockstars and met up with someone called Mirana. Based on the area and her appearance, she was unsurprisingly of Cuban descent, as many dark-eyed, dark-haired women in the area were. They had ended the evening with a meal at a small Cuban restaurant, where the food was great and the music and dancing even better. They wandered back to his hotel and as he pulled her towards him, she whispered that this was a one-night-only affair, which suited him. The sex was great. She had kissed him as she left the next morning, which roused him, but he just turned over. It was Thomas' thoughtful knock at the door that warned him to get up and shower.

After years of wasting his life, like many young men with money, he had wandered from one party to another. Drink, drugs, and sex were part of the scene, and he was hooked on them all. Following a failed marriage, two stints in rehab and a final warning from his father. It was the threat of being cut off, not just from the money but his family, that finally seemed to get through to him. With their support, this led to his sudden decision to join a friend who was going to enlist in the army. No one was more surprised than he when not only did he do well but gained a promotion as a non-commissioned officer.

It was this that started the process of "finding Leo". The friendships he made, especially those with Thomas and Jem, helped him develop and grow further. It was meeting Grace that finally made him take responsibility for his life.

Today, however, the hangover threatened to blow his head off as he dragged himself out of bed. He still had the odd minor lapse, particularly with alcohol, but nothing he couldn't control any more. He showered, which helped, and then shaved and dressed. He no longer took any drugs, so the headache would have to wane in its own time. *So stupid,* he thought, as he remembered the AA meetings he had attended. When this job was over, it would be good to catch up with his sponsor. Picking up his wallet, he was glad to see no money had disappeared and the cheque for his $20k winnings was still there. He headed for the door.

Downstairs, the others were coming out of breakfast. Leo helped himself to some complimentary coffee but had no time for anything else. Remy arrived, so they moved to the private meeting room arranged by Grace. Thomas handed Leo a serviette with several pastries in it; he nodded, thankfully, as he was now feeling hungry. A short while later, a call announced that a visitor had arrived and Thomas asked for them to be shown to the room.

A knock and Leo opened the door. Outside, stood an extremely small, older woman dressed in black. Her dark eyes darted from face to face. Jem was holding her arm and it was clear that she was incredibly nervous; although being held by Jem, no matter how gently, could have that effect. She looked reluctant to step forward, so Jem almost lifted her off her feet and into the room. The woman carried a large bag over her shoulder and clasped it tightly to her chest. She spoke softly in Russian.

'Pozhaluysta, my dolzhny byt' bystrymi, oni budut skuchat' po mne, yesli ya budu otsutstvovat' slishkom dolgo (Please, we must be quick, they will miss me if I am gone too long.)' To everyone's surprise, Remy immediately translated and then asked the woman to speak in English.

She nodded, clearly terrified of whoever they were.

'Don't worry, we will be as quick as we can,' Lissa said, as she held out her hands for the bag. At first, it almost seemed the woman would not give it up. Then, with her eyes darting from one to another, she held it in front of Remy, not Lissa.

In halting breathless English, she whispered, 'Take care, they kill him when they know he had it. He gives it to me, tells me to come. I owed him my life, so I do. But now "he" knows, now they come for me.'

'Who will?' Remy probed.

The woman shook her head. *'Ya ne mogu,* no tell, let me go. You have,' she said as she thrust the bag into Remy's hands.

'Go with this man,' Lissa indicated to Jem. 'He will make sure you are safe.' The woman looked unconvinced but headed for the door with Jem, then stopped and turned.

'You do not know what he will do. My family gone.' She started to cry. Jem hustled her out of the room.

Remy stood apart, stoney faced, the others just looked at each other. Finally, she moved forward, opened the bag and took out a box. Almost reluctantly, Lissa joined her and they both put on gloves and then Lissa moved forward and opened it. She carefully took out an amazing intricately jewelled scabbard, which she laid on the table. The room was completely silent, it was as if everyone was holding their breath. They examined the scabbard carefully. As before, Lissa checked each of the main jewels and then nodded.

Both Leo and Thomas stepped forward and were amazed at the intricate design on the scabbard. From what he remembered of the knife, Thomas thought it appeared it would be a good, if not perfect match, to the dagger. Having no experience with fine gems, he could only marvel at the size of the monetary value of such an item. He knew from what the Russian woman had intimated, that if for no other reason, someone would be very angry to have lost this.

Finally the spell was broken, as Lissa gushed, 'I can't wait to see all the pieces together,' as she put the scabbard back in the box, indicating to Thomas to bring the case over. She ensured the box was safely installed in the case, then she used the second key, to lock the case in the same way as before, which activated the blue light, indicating that the tracker was triggered. The case would be given to Remy, while Lissa took the second key and passed it to Thomas, so the keys were also separated. Leo put the case on the floor by the chair, while Thomas picked up his phone and within minutes, a sharp knock on the door drew everyone's attention.

'Probably your escort, Madame Akbari,' announced Thomas, who got up and opened the door. A tall man dressed in black, with a fearful scar on his cheek, entered. Spider was well known to Thomas and he remembered how he had got the scar in a bar fight in New York. They shook hands. Another man Thomas didn't know stepped into the room.

'Why the change?' Leo asked concerned.

'This is Pete,' Spider indicated the man, who nodded somewhat nervously. Thomas didn't like last-minute changes.

'Apparently, Cooper's flat out with Covid and he sent him; they were in the same unit.' Thomas was still wary but knew and trusted both Cooper and Spider. They would only be responsible for taking Remy to the airport for her private flight to London, and the case and keys would be in different places, which somewhat reassured him.

Remy seemed to catch his mood. 'Remember,' her voice was deathly serious, 'whoever is watching, will know that we now have two pieces, so time is even more of an essence. We are all in danger, so take care and trust no one.' She glanced at Spider and Pete.

'You must go as soon as possible. Do we know when the plane will be ready?' Leo asked.

'I had a call from Grace to tell me that the plane is already at the airport.'

Jem returned to the room and told them the woman had been taken somewhere safe.

Remy kissed her daughter and smiled briefly at Thomas, she ignored both Leo and Jem. Thomas picked up the case and chained it to Spider's wrist. They escorted her out.

'She doesn't like you as much as Thomas.' Jem laughed as he nudged Leo, almost pushing him off his feet. Leo just grinned.

'She'll come around,' he said with a smug grin. 'They always do!' Everyone laughed and the tension eased slightly.

Reaching down, Thomas took a case from behind the chair. 'Do you think Remy noticed she has a dummy case?' Leo said. 'Let's hope she isn't too annoyed when you tell her.'

'It's not a surprise, she already knows. It was her idea. When I spoke to her after Grace called me last night about the change to personnel, she said she had a feeling she would be a target. I wanted to change things but she thought that changes would alert whoever was following. Besides, she was sure that no one would hurt her. Of course I tried to argue but she was adamant. That's when she showed me the copy of the case.'

'What!' Lissa shouted, clearly angry. 'You shouldn't have listened to her, she couldn't be so sure she would be alright.'

'Bloody dangerous! What did she mean do you think?' Leo was interrupted by Lissa standing up and walking away.

'I don't know, and she wouldn't say.' Thomas was clearly exasperated. 'Look it's clear that we need to get ready as quickly as possible. She is giving us this time to shake off whoever is so eager to get this.' Leo and Jem took the case containing the scabbard down to the car, where Jem's men were waiting to take the second case to London.

When Jem came back, he asked if there was any news on Cooper. Thomas shook his head. He had asked Grace to investigate, but despite there being no news, he was still suspicious until he heard more. So, he said nothing, just shook his head, 'I'll let you know when I find out.'

Leo returned to the room, grabbed his bag, and took the lift to the lobby to pay their bill. As he waited outside for the others, he was aware of at least one person watching him. He went back towards the lift and caught Thomas as he was coming out. Smiling, he called him over and said, 'Dark-haired woman by the door, a man with phone by the blue car. Can you get pictures?' He handed his phone to Jem, who had just arrived, and looked a little confused but soon saw Leo's head indicating the car.

'Hey, come on photo op,' he said, Lissa raised an eyebrow but also immediately got his gist. They gathered and Jem took a picture to include the man and after moving around, to include the woman. Jem gave him back his phone. 'I'll send the pictures off to Wes,' Leo said smiling.

Chapter 18

Remy was expecting to see a car and driver waiting downstairs but was surprised and pleased to also see Andreas leaning against it; although she thought this might complicate matters. He waved and walked towards her beaming, wrapping her in his arms. Despite her concerns, she immediately relaxed, feeling his strength comfort her.

'What are you doing here?' She wondered how he could possibly have known.

'I have decided that I am coming with you,' he said, and there was a note of finality in his voice.

'You can't.' She stopped, searching his face, but something in his eyes made her reconsider and she just nodded. Few people could get her to do something she did not want to do, but Andreas was one.

'I can catch up with a few things in London and then perhaps once we have ensured this,' he indicated the case, 'is safe, we can spend some time together.' To this statement, Remy raised an eyebrow and Andreas laughed. Although Remy did not know it, he knew a lot more than he was saying, and she need not have worried. Lissa had decided to tell Thomas about Andreas and through a quick call to Tiana, Remy's PA, he had contacted him. Following a long conversation, Thomas was surprised to find out exactly who he was and what he did. It was agreed that he would meet Remy in Miami, so had flown down from New York overnight.

Remy had known Andreas Metaxas since her time at uni when she had sat and argued with him, Farzad and Rafik. She knew his family was wealthy, so was a little surprised when she later heard he had joined the Greek Navy after he had married. Whenever they met, he said little about his job, so she had no real idea of what he actually did. He was in fact a highly decorated senior officer and part of the Hellenic Navy General Staff.

After his wife died, he left the Navy and spent much time in New York, but on one of her visits to Crete, Remy heard that he had also set up an antiquities and art business on the island with his son. At their next meeting, she chided him for not telling her and laughed when he told her that to match the image, he had grown his hair and lived a somewhat bohemian lifestyle. It also appeared that he was developing a growing reputation as an artist. Although he loved this side of his life, it was also a clever cover story, as for many years he was, in fact, still in the Navy but as part of a covert operation task force based on Crete. He used the business as a cover.

Now, as he neared sixty, he was less involved in this and more concerned with the business; although they sometimes still crossed when required. He was an extremely fit man and had excellent skills in both the use of firearms and self-defence.

Andreas smiled as he took Remy's arm. 'Come, my dear, we should go.' They got into the car with Pete driving and Spider in the front seat.

Leaving the hotel, Remy felt things were going well but she reminded herself that they still had a long way to go. *The initial part of this journey,* she thought, *would be straightforward.* Remy's phone cut through her thoughts, it was Lissa. She grinned at Andreas and mouthed, 'She's checking up on me.' She reassured her daughter that they were almost at the airport.

Chapter 19

The journey to the airport would not take long but between two longer sections of the interstate, the traffic slowed to a crawl. Pete's phone beeped. He picked it up, and turning around, he said, 'There's been an accident up ahead but it's clearing. We should be on our way soon.'

Their car came to a sudden stop; however, the car behind did not stop in time and ran into the back of theirs. Pete said that he would go and check out the damage as the traffic didn't seem to be moving. As he got out, two men walked towards him. Recalling the events later, Remy said that it felt like time had unexpectedly sped up as so many things seemed to happen all at once. One moment, Pete was out of the car, then there was a popping sound and he seemed to have a gun and fired at Spider. The front door opened and someone was cutting the chain on Spider's wrist.

Then, suddenly, there were several shots, one narrowly missing Andreas, who, like Remy, was now crouched down. There was a moment of silence and then another round of shots and then apart from the engine, it became quiet. They sat up; Remy and Andreas were aware that Pete was holding a gun and pointing it at them.

'Get out,' he said as the car doors opened and both she and Andreas were pulled from the car and pushed towards a dark transit van, a couple of cars ahead. They were shoved inside and the doors slammed. Rough hands grabbed her and told her to sit down, then Remy was aware that the van immediately moved off, swerving violently as they pulled out of the line of traffic onto the side lane. There were no windows, so she could not see how they managed to get through the almost stationary traffic. They were quickly tied with zip-ties and these were anchored to the side of the van, with one man cradling a gun, sitting up at the end.

No one spoke. Remy could tell that they were now picking up speed, so thought they must be off the interstate. She did not know who had taken them, although she had a good idea. She thought that as long as Alessia and Thomas were sensible, they would be safe. She was calm and, not afraid for herself but was more concerned for Andreas.

Andreas however, had been in many difficult and dangerous situations before, and was not therefore inclined to panic. He also knew that if these men had wanted them dead, like Spider, they would be! Clearly, they wanted Remy, not him, so he played it low-key. Having only had a brief view of their faces, he was aware that they appeared to be Eastern European in origin. They wore no masks, therefore were probably low-level local thugs, and whoever had organised the kidnap, would likely kill them when their task was done.

Andreas was aware of Remy's commission, as was the task force he worked for. He had heard the men in front speaking a few words of Russian, which he understood, and wondered how they were linked to the regalia she had been asked to gather.

After about thirty minutes, the car came to a halt. The man driving spoke in English to someone about a gate and then finally, the door opened. The sunlight was bright as it reflected off the large jet they were parked next to. They were pushed towards it and up the stairs. Inside, they were directed to two seats. The plane door closed and the engines started. A voice behind them said, 'Welcome!' Without turning, they both knew who it was.

Chapter 20

Leaving about an hour after Remy, Thomas and the others on their way to the airport encountered only light traffic on the freeway; but to Jem, it was clear that a dark SUV was paying rather too close attention as he switched lanes. He decided to test his theory by taking a sharp turn onto the I95 heading south. It was a big junction and he could swerve around traffic, making it easier to spot any tail.

'Hey, Jem, what's up?' Thomas asked as the car rocked violently.

'Your friends are still with us, Leo!' He growled, not sounding best pleased. Leo turned and saw the car he meant then nodded.

'Okay, I'll contact Wes, and see if there's been any chatter.' He picked up his phone as Jem swung back onto the I27.

'It's all clear now,' Jem said. 'They seem to have gone,' and a smile crossed his face.

The number Leo called clicked and an answerphone kicked in, 'Hi, Wes, on our way out of here but we seem to have picked up a tail, anything you can tell? Thanks.'

They reached the security gates to the private hangers on the airfield with no further sign of anyone following, a fact that Thomas found somewhat unnerving. Having passed through security, they drove to the private lounge, where immigration and customs were completed. After a short wait, they were able to walk out to the plane. The luggage had already been stowed and the steward, from the same crew as before, said that they had clearance for their flight. As he settled into his seat, Thomas' phone rang. 'Hi, thanks for getting back. Anything?'

Wes said, 'Nothing on the pictures you sent but there is some noise, not about you, about another guest in your party. Are you sure everything is okay?' Thomas was a little surprised by Wes' tone but guessed he was with others and didn't want to alert anyone. 'Thanks, Wes, will check in with you again later,' he said and rang off.

'Leo, who's with Remy?'

'Spider and Pete, why?'

Speaking quietly to Leo, he said, 'Odd message from Wes, the focus isn't on us but on one of our guests.'

He turned to Lissa. 'Think we should check up on your mother, she should be well on her way to the airport now.' She nodded.

Leo finished his call when Lissa smiled and mouthed that all was well. Thomas let out a sigh and buckled his seat belt. Maybe it was just one of the various groups in town who kept a careful watch on the comings and goings.

Thomas looked across at Leo, who had again sat himself opposite Lissa and looked back at him with a grin. She clearly didn't mind his company and he found himself a little annoyed that Leo had got there first. He knew he was attracted to her. She was beautiful but it was more than that. She looked at him across the aisle and he thought he caught something in her eyes. She lowered her chin and looked at him again, but this time her look, as she turned her head, seemed more intimate. He reminded himself that this was business. The team had agreed at the start of their partnership not to engage in any romantic liaisons with clients; not that Leo ever seemed to take this fact into consideration.

The flight to LA was turbulent, as they encountered quite a significant storm as they left Miami. Although the jet rode the turbulence well, it was clear that much-needed sleep was not going to be easy for some. Looking at Jem, it was obvious he was praying. Turning to the window, Thomas could see that the lightning was intense. He was a reasonably good flyer but storms like this were inclined to make him wish they were on the ground. The pilot came on and apologised that the flight time would be around six hours or maybe a little more due to the poor weather. They had left just after one, so arrival could be after three in the afternoon. This was not a problem as their next meeting wasn't until the evening.

As they passed through into calmer air, Thomas decided he would get on the internet and email contacts, trying to find out whether there was any more information about who might be following them. Out of interest, he also did some digging into ceremonial daggers. Looking at pictures, he tried various combinations of words till he was able to pull up some pictures that resembled the one he had seen. He concluded that the dagger was most likely Persian in origin. One article caught his attention and, although the picture showed a dagger much larger than the one he had seen, it was clearly similar in design, particularly the flower pattern around the ruby on the pommel.

There was also a snake design on the dagger similar to the one on the scabbard. The larger dagger was apparently part of the Persian Royal Crown Jewels, some of which were in the Victoria and Albert Museum in London, while others were spread across museums and private collections across the world, or reported lost, or stolen. *Not surprising,* he thought, as so many valuable pieces of jewellery changed hands in this way.

The royal treasure, as it was once known, had been added to, sometimes pieces were stolen, and others broken up for the stones or lost. In recent times, they were stolen by a man who worked for the British East India Company, who claimed he had been given them. However, before he could sell them, he was apparently caught and killed. Nothing further was known, regarding his killers, or what happened to the jewels. However, some, including the regalia, found their way into the Persian Crown Jewels and wearing them became part of the Shah's symbol of power. It appeared that there had always been stories and legends about pieces in the collection, but especially about a central stone that locked the pieces together.

This was the main stone in the clasp, which was apparently a huge ruby. This alone, depending on its origin, size, and quality, could be worth over a million dollars. The legend seemed to suggest it had often lived up to its association with blood. This stone was supposed to be very old and predate the regalia. It was rumoured, for example, to have belonged to Cleopatra. The story suggested it was red with her blood and had mystical powers. Another story said it was used to buy the release of a royal prisoner following the Crusades. Some suggested that this was King Richard, who was captured and held, and was only released following the payment of an enormous ransom.

Reading on, he found that it seemed to have ended up back in the Middle East as part of a hoard stolen by the Persians in the Ottoman-Persian wars around 1500. It was next heard of in Russia, again as a result of war, but its fate was unknown until it appeared as the centre stone of the regalia and given to Fath' Ali Shah in the early 1800s. It was apparent that it had forever been fought over and Thomas worried that it appeared never to have brought about anything good.

Next, he found a piece about a previous owner of many of these antiquities particularly interesting. It spoke of a man called Fath' Ali Shah who had died in suspicious circumstances in 1834. During his early reign, he apparently had some dealings with the British East India Company, and stories about his connections with Georgia, and then Imperial Russia during the Russo-Persian War.

One story however, brought a wry smile to his face. It claimed Ali Shah was said to have had two hundred and fifty sons. He had built a special slide of marble in the harem. He would lie on his back naked, at the bottom, as one by one harem beauties would slide into his arms, before being playfully dunked in a pool; Thomas laughed, but his own thoughts were more X-rated. He found his mind wandering, as he imagined what Lissa might look like naked. He turned to see her sleeping peacefully and sighed.

He returned to his research. When the Iranian revolution deposed the Pahlavi dynasty in 1979, it was feared that in the chaos, the Iranian crown jewels had been stolen or sold by the revolutionaries. Although it was suggested only smaller items were stolen, in fact, key items of the regalia had already been smuggled across Iran's borders. On the next page there was a picture of the Shah and around his waist was an intricate belt and from it the sheath that the Russian woman had given them. The revolutionary government of Rafemi Rafsanjani later reopened an exhibition of the Iranian crown jewels but without the regalia, and no mention was ever made of the missing items.

Considering this information, Thomas concluded that the regalia, although now Iranian, could be of older construction and the jewels could be from even earlier origins. So, who would want these items now and why? Apart from its possible monetary value, what reason would there be for anyone to kill an old woman in England? With that thought in mind, the pilot announced that they were on their final approach to Los Angeles. This roused the sleepers, who gathered belongings, as the flight attendant collected the final glasses. They strapped in ready for landing.

Thomas wondered what sort of reception they should watch out for.

Chapter 21

'My dear Remy, I am so sorry we must meet again like this. Oh, and I must congratulate you on your clever little ruse. I take it that the case swap was your idea, Andreas. Untie them,' gestured Rafik. One of the men who had brought them to the plane took out a knife and cut the ties.

'Well, I didn't expect to see you.' Rafik said as he sat down opposite Andreas with a smirk that made Remy cringe. 'Have you nothing to say, Andreas? You who have been hunting me for so long, I thought you would be pleased to see me.' His smile became even tighter and more unpleasant.

Remy looked from one to the other, seemingly unable to understand what was going on. She wasn't afraid as she knew both these men, but then she thought in a moment of panic, *Do I really?* A dreadful memory flashed into her mind, reminding her of a past event. Rafik could be dangerous and this made her shiver.

'Of course, I am happy to see you, Rafik. Goodness, hunting you? Why on earth would I want to do that? I am sure Remy would love to know. Anyway, I take it we are not going to London.'

'No, I am sorry, and we will miss your friends and the delightful Lissa in Los Angeles. But don't worry, I have a surprise waiting for them. So, all we need to do is just bide our time and let them do the work.' His words conveyed no warmth. He turned to Remy. 'My darling Remy, I am so pleased to see you.'

Remy recoiled, 'We have missed so much time together.'

'Rafik, what's going on?'

'Not my darling? Or is that now reserved for Andreas? No matter. What is going on, my love, is as Andreas has already surmised, a change of destination. We are on our way to Sydney.' A woman moved forward holding a hypo gun. Remy's eyes widened as she tried to move away but Rafik moved forward onto his knees in front of her and grabbed her arms firmly. He moved closer and she felt his hot perfumed breath on her face. He whispered, 'It is a long flight, my darling, this will help you sleep. Remember, I said, "There will come a time", he paused, soon my love,' and kissed her, then laughed.

She glared at him as the drug was quickly administered. Andreas did not fight it and as the effects began to take hold, with his voice hoarse, he whispered, 'This is not over, Rafik!'

As she fought sleep, Andreas said, 'Don't struggle, you…' She never heard the rest as she drifted off but those words floated in her subconscious like a tether.

Checking in, the woman who had administered the sedative to Remy began to be concerned as she seemed to be reacting badly to it. From time to time, she moved violently and seemed to murmur words or strangled cries. However, the woman knew enough to stay away from Rafik, so said nothing.

Remy's dreams were filled with strange images and forgotten memories. She floated and drifted through them until she saw Farzad. She called out to him but he didn't seem to hear. So, she ran towards him and as she got closer, he burst into flames. She tried to scream but a hand covered her mouth, and she was suddenly, violently grabbed. Turning, she heard a familiar laughing voice, saying, 'Together, we must be together' Then the faceless man was grabbing at her. She fought and screamed but the more she tried to push him off, the more he laughed. Finally, she pulled free and ran. With enormous mental strength, she forced the scene to darken and closed the box that had rested so long in the deepest parts of her memory.

It was many hours later when Remy woke. She felt awful, her mouth was dry and her eyes stung. A woman brought her a bottle of water and a face cloth and then helped her to the bathroom and said she should take her time. There was a shower, so despite her situation, she stripped off and felt the hot water revive her. Drying herself, she found a change of clothes on the back of the door and slipped into the sweatshirt and pants. Picking up her clothes, she opened the door. The woman put her clothes in a bag and then indicated a seat but Remy went over to where Andreas was still asleep.

'Why hasn't he woken?' She asked.

The woman felt his pulse. 'Soon,' she replied. 'I will bring you some food.'

Remy struggled to put her thoughts together. She realised that a memory which had been buried had surfaced and, at some point, she would have to deal with it but not now. It seemed almost impossible to understand what was happening as she struggled to organise the pieces. What the hell was going on? She had known these two men most of her life and now she felt she didn't know either of them. Why was she being held by Rafik and what did he mean about Andreas hunting him? Things had clearly become a whole lot more complicated than she had ever imagined they would when she had agreed to take on this task.

A tray was placed on the table in front of her but she wasn't hungry. She nibbled some fruit and drank the tea. After a little time, Andreas stirred. She got up and went over to him.

'Andreas, it's all right, take your time,' she said, stroking his brow.

He opened his eyes and smiled at her. 'Are you okay?' He asked, and she nodded. The woman gave her a bottle of water, which she undid for him.

'There is a shower in the bathroom and some fresh clothes,' the woman indicated the door.

Andreas got up, a little unsteady, and some twenty minutes later, re-emerged from the bathroom dressed like Remy in a sweatshirt and pants.

'Where is Rafik?' He asked.

'I haven't seen him but I think he is beyond the curtain,' she indicated behind him.

The woman brought food but unlike Remy, he ate everything, aware that he would need the calorie intake for whatever happened next.

'Andreas, what did he mean about you "hunting" him?'

'I think you already know or have guessed that the regalia you have been asked to collect and deliver is being sought by others. What you may not be aware of is its importance to people in Iran. Clearly, there are different sides hunting for the pieces and they represent different views. There are those who support change and those who oppose these and enjoy the life they have. But there are also people trying to steal it for themselves. Rafik is one. I work with an organisation which wishes to ensure that the people have the right to determine the future of their country, not just those who want its wealth and power for themselves.'

The curtain behind Andreas opened and Rafik came through, flanked by another.

'Ah, I see you are both awake. If I heard your speech correctly, you think you are right that helping one group will ensure some sort of peace. But one thing you forget is that with change, lives will be lost. I would be doing the country a favour by keeping the status quo.'

'Come off it, Rafik, you know countless lives are being lost already through torture and murder by those claiming to be religious. Is killing of those who want freedom right?'

'Don't be so naïve!' His laughter was mirthless, 'You forget the crimes and greed of those noble families that would seek to regain power, the fortunes they withheld from the poor. Having the regalia will bring a people...'

He didn't finish as Remy interrupted angrily.

'Save the rhetoric, I know who it will benefit. There is no way that you have become a man of the people! And as for religion, you are no man of God.'

Rafik laughed. 'Too true on all counts, my love. Enough for now, we can debate this further later. Sit comfortably, we are nearly at our refuelling stop in Tahiti. Sorry, no time for sightseeing.' With that, he left the cabin.

Remy said, 'I still can't believe it. It would seem there is much I do not know about either of you.' Her eyes clouded and she turned away from him. Andreas reached out for her but she got up and went back to her seat. Looking out of the window at the blanket of clouds below, it was as if they were the veil that had covered her eyes. What was hidden below? What else had she not seen or had been kept hidden from her? Just as she didn't know what lay beneath the clouds, was it sea or land? What were the true motives of these two men?

Her mind was in turmoil, on the one hand, there was Rafik, the man who claimed to love her. She shuddered at the memory, now fresh in her mind. And hadn't he left her during those most awful days following the death of Farzad? Was he really going to try and steal the regalia under some pretence of returning them to the people? Of course not, he was going to make himself even richer. She knew he craved power, so would he use it to either curry favour or satisfy his political ambitions? Or would he just find a place somewhere and live out his dreams?

Then what of Andreas? Had he really lied about who he really was, or had she just been too blind to see that this man was more than she gave him credit for? Or was he using her too, just to get to Rafik? He had supported her and even encouraged her to take on this commission; by doing so, he had put her in danger. Was she just a means to an end?

When the woman with the hypo gun appeared again, this time Remy did not struggle. A final thought came to her, as her eyes once again started to close, had one of these men been responsible for the death of Farzad?

When she woke again, the plane was just coming to land again. She felt sick, aware that the drugs they had used were leaving her system, so she felt disorientated. Andreas sat opposite her; he smiled reassuringly and handed her a bottle of water.

As the plane taxied to a stop, Rafik and two men came over to them. 'Well, my darling, it seems we must part again.' He reached forward and caressed her cheek. As she pulled away, he laughed. 'You may have robbed me of one case, however, it appears you have presented us with an even better opportunity, and the chance to collect several pieces, while disposing of some annoying *alhamqaa waghayr almuminin* (Idiots and non-believers). These men will take care of you, and I will see you later.'

Andreas could not stifle a smile, which made Rafik stop. His response was swift as he hit out at Andreas, who immediately ducked and then stood up, so he was face to face with Rafik, who took a step back and indicated to his men, to grab Andreas. They pushed him back into the seat. Laughing, Andreas said, 'Really? Are you sure?' He had realised that Rafik did not know that the other pieces were already in London.

Rafik turned with a huff and walked down the plane followed by a man, who caught Andreas' eye. As he passed, he stopped, pretending to threaten him but to cover him slipping a knife into his pocket. He called two men forward and told them to take them but to zip-tie their hands, then he too left the plane.

Chapter 22

While Rafik was on his way to Australia, Thomas and the others were arriving in Los Angeles.

Thomas hated Los Angeles. It was too vast a city, too flat, too grey, and the freeways were always clogged. Although the valley no longer contained the smog of the 60s and 70s, there were still days when the San Bernadino mountains could barely be seen. He had to admit, however, that he loved the fact you could go up into the mountains that surrounded the city in the morning in winter, ski, and then head back for a swim in the Pacific in the afternoon. He particularly liked the areas around Idyllwild in the San Jacinto mountains, but he still much preferred San Francisco as it felt more like a European city.

As they drove through the endless traffic, he remembered his early life here. After his stepfather Bill had died, he decided not to go to university but instead, head off on a gap year which he extended into his early twenties. At first, he travelled in the Far East and then Australia, working in bars and nightclubs. Eventually, he crewed a yacht across the South Pacific to LA, where he met an English girl, who was on a teacher exchange program. So, he stayed, working in various bars. When their relationship ended, he travelled around the US, again working in bars, front of house, or waiting in restaurants.

He regularly spoke to his mum and when she told him she was ill, he immediately went back to the UK, and although extremely unwell, she still had the strength to give him a few home truths. She was right, it was time to sort his life out. He had drifted for too long. He stayed with her till the end.

After her death, the money she had left helped straighten out his finances. He decided not to sell the house but to use it as a base and get his life in order. He met up with an old school friend, who was in the army and with no ties or clear direction, listening to the stories of the life he led, he felt drawn to the structure this could offer him, especially as this was a route to obtaining a degree. He had achieved a good set of exam results from his grammar school, so he applied to the army, and it was suggested he apply for the Officer Selection Board.

Through the interview process, he was selected to train at Sandhurst. Although this did not commit him to joining the British Army, he felt it would give him the good grounding he needed. He never looked back. The comradeship he sought was there. He was good at all aspects of the role and graduated as a second lieutenant. He completed a full master's degree through further electives and a dissertation. Within eighteen months, he became a full lieutenant and attained his final rank of captain within five years.

He met Leo, who had travelled to the army via a different route, as they were both seconded to a task force, carrying out highly specialised reconnoitring and rescue missions. Jem had been their sergeant and two of the men who they really trusted, Cooper and Parsons, were on their squad. The group made up of twelve men had come through some tough situations and they had learned to rely on one another implicitly.

His mind had wandered, so he was surprised when the captain put on the seatbelt signal. Having landed, he stretched and grabbed his bag and helped Lissa with hers. Their routine was less onerous this time as they were on an internal flight but because of his, Leo's and Jem's status, they had to present passports. With no problems, they were soon waiting in the hot late afternoon sun on the tarmac as Jem loaded the last of their kit into the SUV. They would be staying at the Hotel Bel-Air and if there were no accidents or hold-ups on the interstate, it should take about an hour and a half. Leaving the airport, Jem said, 'We've picked up a tail again.'

He kept watch on the car following them, but as they turned onto Sunset Boulevard, he was surprised when it didn't turn off after them.

'Hey, that's odd,' he said, as much to himself as the others.

'What's up?' Leo asked.

'The car following us since the airport has gone. Mmm, don't like it!'

They all turned to check.

'It might be time to check in with Wes again.' Thomas picked up his mobile.

The call was picked up. 'I tried to reach you earlier,' Wes began, 'I'm sorry I have to tell you that Remy and the man she was with have been taken.'

Shocked, Thomas asked, 'What happened?' Although they had discussed this possibility with Andreas and Remy, he was still worried. But he said nothing as he knew Lissa would never have agreed to something so dangerous.

'The car they were in was stopped by an accident on the interstate. Early CCTV images suggested two, maybe three, men approached the car but no firm IDs. They killed one of your guys, and when my men intervened, they were shot at. I lost a good man, which is going to take a lot of explaining to my boss. A spray of bullets kept others away, although an off-duty cop tried to intervene. He was shot but survived and maybe our best chance for info. Witnesses said one of the men in the car pulled the other two out and pushed them at gunpoint into a van. I didn't find out about it immediately, sorry. I'll let you know when I hear more.'

'Do you know which of my guys died?'

'Early ID seems to suggest a Stephen Pinder.'

'That's Spider.' Thomas recalled the nervous "Pete" and was angry. He began to wonder again what had happened to put Cooper out of action. He was one of the original group of guys from Thomas' army days and he trusted him. Now he was concerned for his whereabouts.

He would put in a call to Grace and ask her if she knew where he was and to make arrangements for Spider's body to be collected and his family informed. She would be more than capable of sorting the fine details of insurance and compensation. He also asked her to contact one of their police contacts to see if there was any news about Cooper.

Wes said, 'We found the van that took them, inside were two bodies, the ones seen on CCTV taking your guys. I've also found out that a private plane, with two extra passengers added to the manifest, left shortly after on route to Sydney. The flight plan is registered to a man called Yazdi, he has an Iranian and US passport. Do you know him?' He paused. 'Thomas, what have you gotten yourselves into?'

'I wish I knew,' Thomas said angrily. He thanked Wes and cut the call, unwilling to put into words what he was thinking. As he turned, he saw the shock on Lissa's face. 'Lissa, I am so sorry. Try not to worry. I know I don't know your mother well but I am sure she will be all right.'

Leo asked, 'Lissa, do you know anything about this man Yazdi? There is a growing body count, so there has to be more than Remy has told us.'

'I did think that Rafik Yazdi could be the client, but now I'm not so sure. I know that he held a special place in my mother's life and they were close before my father died, but all my mother told me about the client you already know. He won't hurt her, will he?'

'I don't think so, I think there is much more to their relationship than we know,' replied Leo. They arrived at the hotel and while they checked in, Jem realised that Lissa was finding things hard to cope with.

He was right, Lissa felt completely out of her depth, and unable to breathe. She grabbed her bag and headed out of the main door of the hotel. Thomas got up but Jem was quicker and shook his head. 'She doesn't need you or sympathy right now, we need her on her A game.' And went after her.

Chapter 23

Thomas' phone rang. 'Wes, what's the news?'

'Sorry, we missed them. I have to tell you that there are now real concerns and rumblings here. Any time there is even a whiff of a Middle Eastern connection, the wires crackle. Their flight plan has them heading to Australia. Are you sure there isn't anything you want to tell me?'

'It's all to do with some expensive jewels, that's all I really know at the moment. Thanks for your help.'

'That might be good enough for now but you know I will be digging! Watch yourselves. We will follow the trail and get back to you when we have more news.' The line went dead.

Leo said, 'Wes clearly knows more than he's saying. Now we all have secrets. Anyway, whoever has Remy and Andreas, obviously knows our next stop and is trying to get there first. With Remy, they must figure they have a chance to gain a piece, which would stop the whole thing being put together.'

Thomas picked up the phone and asked Grace to arrange local contacts to meet them when the plane landed in Tahiti to be on the safe side.

'Any news about Cooper yet?'

'Yes, finally found him. He's in a bad way but he'll live. He's in hospital and I'm on it.' Despite his fearsome reputation, Grace had a soft spot for Cooper, so she would see he was all right.

They arrived at the hotel. Thomas recalled having worked the bar there when he had first arrived in Hollywood. He had excellent references and they were thrilled to employ him as bar manager. He just remembered it was a beautiful establishment and he had enjoyed working there.

Lissa and Jem came into reception and although she was clearly still upset, she seemed calmer. Thomas smiled at Jem, who clicked back at him. They checked in.

As they walked to the lift, Leo turned to Thomas, 'should we tell Lissa about the case? Even if the kidnappers find out it is a fake, Remy and Andreas should still be safe, if Andreas was right about who had taken them.'

Thomas thought about it for a minute, then said, 'No, let's just keep it between us. Besides, I think she already knows more about Andreas' background than her mother. She seems very positive about him, that's probably because she is confident he can handle any situation.'

They headed for their rooms, having arranged a time to meet, ready for the arrival of the courier.

Thomas quickly showered and as he shaved, he tried to focus on his main concerns and the best actions to take to ensure they were in control of how this would play out.

He was dressing when there was a knock at the door and a muffled voice said, 'Room Service.' He was instantly alert and almost laughed at what he suspected was an old ploy.

'Just a minute,' he called out. Moving quietly to the door, he looked briefly through the spy hole and saw exactly what he was expecting; a clearly inappropriately dressed "hotel waiter" carrying a tray with a bottle of champagne in front of him, so that it covered his face. Thomas picked up the gun Jem had insisted he took in Miami and slipped it into the waistband of his trousers.

'Coming,' he called as he picked up his belt from the bed. He made sure he slid the restraining bolt back, clunking it hard against the door, loud enough to ensure it was heard outside, then leaning around, he pulled down the door handle and stepped back against the wall. As Thomas expected, the door flew open, almost unbalancing the man who entered. Thomas heard the hiss of a silencer shot. He stepped forward behind the man and kicked his knee from under him, so he fell forward, which knocked the gun from his hand. As he struggled to his feet and turned, Thomas used a fist, hitting the man full in the face, then followed this with a chop across his throat, making him fall to his knees, gasping for breath.

Thomas caught him and dragged him, coughing and limp, further into the room, he closed the door with his foot. Pushing the man face down to the floor, he used the belt to bind the man's hands and then sat him up, against the bed. The man's eyes were streaming and his nose bleeding heavily. Apart from the silenced gun, he didn't seem to have much of a clue about how to fight an opponent. Thomas checked his pockets but they were empty. The only thing of note about him was a small intricately tattooed designed cross symbol between his thumb and first finger.

He picked up the phone and took a picture of it, then called Leo. 'I've had a visitor, not the one we were expecting.'

'I'll be there.' The line cut but Thomas heard the familiar sound of a line tap. He scowled. Was that Wes or someone else?

Leo arrived with a familiar knock. Opening the door, Jem stood in the doorway, then as he often did, he stooped to enter, making him seem even larger. His presence had an immediate effect on the man propped up by the bed. His eyes clearly showed the fear many before him had shown at the sheer size of the man.

'This man is going to have a chat with you,' said Leo. 'I suggest you comply.' The man started to speak rapidly in Russian.

'Don't worry, my friend speaks Russian,' said Leo with a smirk, as Jem moved closer, levered the man to his feet, and propelled him out of the door.

Thomas' phone rang. Lissa said the person they were expecting had arrived. Leo said, 'See what he has to say Jem, and then contact Wes for a cleaner service, it looks like the room could do with one.'

They went to Lissa's room where a tall blonde woman was sitting cross legged on the settee.

Leo beamed as he saw her.

'Hello, can I offer you anything?' He said immediately. She gave him a withering look and leant back. He went and sat down opposite. She had placed the case next to her and it leant against the curve of her hip.

'You have the case,' he said unnecessarily.

'Clever boy,' she said. Then in a Sharon Stone moment, Leo remembered only too well from *Basic Instinct*, she slowly uncrossed her legs and stood up. Moving forward, she bent down and put the case down between Leo's knees, snuggling it up to his crotch. Looking up through her lashes, her blonde hair falling onto his knees, the front of her dress opened, showing an extremely good "boob job", he thought but not his taste. It was clear that he was having real problems containing himself. She smiled.

In a drawling southern twang, she purred, 'Eyes back in,' then she wriggled the case closer and looked down at his crotch, 'oh, and down boy,' she said to Leo. Then, coming closer, she ran a diamond-crusted nail under his chin, and whispered in his ear, 'I think you were expecting this.' She slowly pulled the chain from around her neck up through her breasts and, taking it from over her head, dropped it into his lap. Then she stood up and turned to leave.

Leo stood up, clutching the case to himself, and moved in front of her, his eyes twinkling. 'Is that it?'

'Yes, I was just paid to deliver the case, the man said that no response was needed and nothing else was expected.'

'Let me show you out at least,' Leo tried.

'Thanks, but no thanks, honey.' She ran the diamond-covered nail under his chin. 'You can't afford me.' And with that, she turned and left as the others stared at the case, then dissolved into fits of laughter.

Leo looked around. 'What?' His expression was one of injured pride.

'Oh, come on, Leo, you were practically salivating!' Lissa chortled.

Thomas was serious. 'Lissa, you should open it.' The atmosphere changed as he carried it over to the table. Taking the key from Leo, she moved forward and turned the locks then slid them open. Inside, wrapped in silk, was the most exquisite, intricately woven belt. It was made of a number of small interlocking rectangles of silver and gold in three rows. Each had a floral motif in the centre, set with diamonds, rubies, and emeralds. The large clasp was an arrangement of the same rectangles but set vertically.

Leo whistled. 'The dagger was beautiful but wow, the workmanship on the belt here is superb!' The others nodded.

Lissa put on her white gloves and Thomas noticed her hands trembled slightly as she looked at it. She pointed out the two clips at the side that would secure the sheath and identified how the central jewelled decoration, the last part of the regalia, would fit onto the clasp. As she brought the belt together, the clasp clicked, and they were all surprised when the back sprang open.

Inside was a small, folded black and white photo of a little boy. As it was not stuck in, it fell out into Lissa's hand as she moved the clasp. Turning it over, there was a name written in a very small flowing hand—Darius, son of Shahtiar Shafiq—who was assassinated by the Islamic Republic, Paris, in January 1984.

'Well, if there was ever any doubt, this clearly indicates that we were right about there being an Iranian connection, but it is still unclear what is going on here,' mused Lissa. 'This isn't a name I have heard of. I do know from my uncle that what remains of the Persian royal family is widely spread. Maybe this relates to one of them. Not long ago, at a family gathering, they were talking about the situation in Iran and he said that he thought that there were some of the Shah's extended family there who were more involved and had political ambitions. I'll speak to him and do some more research and see what I can find out.'

'Could it be these people who are after the regalia? Or are they our clients I wonder? Or does this point us to the Shafiq family? And if it does, are they in it for the money, or something else?' Thomas wondered, still so many questions. He cursed.

Lissa just shrugged as Jem came into the room and dropped a large hotel laundry bag on the floor. As it unrolled, the man Thomas had captured fell out.

'Thought it'd be a bit too obvious carrying this piece of shit in the lift with all the nice people. Surprise, surprise, it seems he speaks English,' said Jem. Kicking the man, he said, 'Tell them.'

The man groaned but looked up. 'They have your friends and intend on taking them to Sydney; they know that is where you are going. You must let me go or it will not go well for your friends.' His voice trailed off. As this was news to Lissa, her audible gasp made Thomas turn. He could see she was close to tears and he instantly regretted not telling her earlier.

'Why should we believe you?' Her voice quivered.

'They have people watching and if I don't kill…' He didn't get to finish as Jem kicked him.

'Don't worry, Lissa, he isn't worth their time. They sent him in to scare us and hold us up. If they had wanted to kill us, they would have sent a professional. Stay with him, Jem, but no touching.' He laughed as he could see the amusement in the big man's eyes. 'While I phone a friend in the local cops, they can handle it.' Thomas nodded to Jem as he picked up his phone.

Leo was puzzled. 'Well, we know his employers have Remy and Andreas. Do you think the people who are bringing the pieces together are the ex-royal family, or am I missing something?'

'I don't know for sure,' Thomas replied, 'but I get the feeling there may be three groups, let's say they represent: money, power, and altruism. Maybe one of them is playing a very devious game and has ramped up the stakes.'

Chapter 24

The rest of the day, they spent time discussing how things had changed. It was clear that they were going to have to adapt their planning in order to deal with the circumstances they now faced. They were deep in discussion about the best way to proceed when there was a knock at the door. A tall man with glasses entered and showed his badge. The police officer greeted them warmly.

'Is there anyone you two don't know,' laughed Lissa.

'A few! Hi, nice to see you again, Frank, did you manage to find his friends?' Leo asked.

'Just heard from my guys that they have them. I'll take this one off your hands. Hi, Jem, see he had a bit of a fall.'

'Not on me, mate, that's the gaffer,' he said pointing to Thomas and hauled the man to his feet and walked him to the door.

Looking at Leo, the man said, 'Short visit, is it, Leo?'

Leo nodded.

'Just as well,' he snarled, then mock-saluted and winked at Lissa as he left the room.

'I won't ask what that's about,' said Thomas, knowing full well that the last time Leo was in LA, he had left quite quickly and at short notice. From what he understood, he had become involved with some rather shady characters; although to his credit, it was more a result of the female company he was keeping at the time that caused the problem. Frank had been the investigating officer and had warned him that if he didn't "leave", he might not be able to. Fortunately, Leo took the warning seriously and returned to London.

'Okay, so when we get to Sydney, we will need to find Remy and Andreas as well as the next courier, so to make things practical, I suggest we should split up. This might also make it more difficult for those following us to know what we are going to do, so keep them guessing. Sorry, Leo, but there is someone in the police who we both know in Sydney, who should, if she's willing, be able to help us. It's okay,' he replied amused as he saw Leo's face, 'I'll speak to them.'

Leo groaned, 'You mean Julia, don't you? Fuck me! You know what she'll say and even if she agrees, I will never hear the end of it.'

'Who's that?' Lissa asked.

'My ex-wife!' Leo snarled.

'I never knew that you were married,' laughed Jem, 'and to a policewoman.' He almost fell off his seat, he was laughing so much. 'Boy, you kept that quiet, fancy that!' He was beside himself now and Leo moved to punch him but thought better of it.

'So, we all make mistakes, she was a fucking huge one!' He snarled. However, over time that was no longer what he actually thought anymore, as he now recognised how she had tried to help him, but sometimes he still found it difficult to separate her from the difficulties he had faced managing his addiction.

'Okay, everyone agreed?' Thomas asked and they all, even Leo nodded.

As people stood up, Thomas put his arm around Leo's shoulders and then moved to pick up the case. He said no more as he knew how much Leo regretted this part of his life; Julia was only a small part of that but he wasn't about to share that story with the others. After they had left the army, Leo had decided to live a little, to put it mildly. Thomas had tried to stop him but he knew he would lose his friend if he pushed too hard. Therefore, when Leo said he wanted to go to Australia to catch up with some uni friends, Thomas agreed to go with him.

They had only been there a few days when Leo was arrested by Julia, then a detective sergeant, along with a group of old friends from uni. Although someone else at a party was dealing, when the police arrived, his friend had planted his stash on Leo. It was only thanks to a witness, Daddy's money, and friends in high places that seemingly got him off. It turned out that Julia had found the witness, who confirmed that it wasn't Leo dealing. He had met her later to thank her and, one thing had led to another, as it so often did with Leo.

Six months down the line, it was meeting up with Thomas again that helped Leo finally kick his habit for good. Thomas despised drugs and having spent some time working with ex-soldiers to quit them, he was able to support and help Leo. They lived in Leo's flat in Mayfair and Thomas saw him through withdrawal and got him signed up with a rehab group, AA and a sponsor. That was three years ago and he was still clean. Somehow, none of this or his previous run-ins with the police were ever recorded and no charges were ever made, so the army and US border control were never alerted.

Standing looking at the case, Leo nudged him back to the job at hand and locked it, ensuring that the tracker's blue light flashed. It had been arranged that Rab and Dennis would take the third box to London. Leo took the third key, as the first was with Lissa and the second with Thomas. With the case secured to Rab's arm, he, Jem, and Dennis left the room and headed for the hotel lobby, where they waited for the valet to bring back their car. Jem tipped the guy and, the two men got into the car.

'Take care,' Jem said and they nodded. They had an escort car, which would support them if needed, and then they would fly commercial to London. There would be no problems with security, thanks to the case's amazing construction, indicating to all sensors that it contained only papers inside.

When Jem returned, he said, 'Okay, folks, let's get going.' They all stood up, gathered their belongings, and headed downstairs.

On the journey back to the airport, they were all on high alert. However, Thomas guessed that whoever had been following them would not trouble them now. At the airport, although formalities for Australia were far more stringent but, again there were no problems thanks to Grace's careful planning, they were soon seated on the plane ready for take-off. This was a new crew but they had already been cleared by Grace and information forwarded. It showed this crew had also been with the company for many years and were experienced long-distance flyers; it was important as this would be a long flight.

They would stop over in Tahiti for refuelling in the early hours and hoped for a swift turnaround, so they would be in Sydney the following day around eight a.m.; a flight and stop time of some twenty hours plus.

Having agreed that they would split up in Sydney, they decided Jem and Leo would go and meet the last courier, while Thomas and Lissa would work with a local team to search for Remy and Andreas. As the plane taxied and took off, Thomas wondered what the next hurdle might be. Leo's phone rang. *That didn't take long,* thought Thomas.

Leo got up and walked to another seat to take the call. Thomas knew this was in case there was news regarding Remy and Andreas that he didn't want Lissa to hear. When he came back, his face clearly showed there was a problem. He sat down opposite Lissa.

Chapter 25

'Lissa, that was Wes. He said there are reports from British sources that the body of one of the professors at the V and A Museum in London had been found. Apparently, he was a renowned gemmologist and considering your job, he wanted to know if you knew a Professor Whiter?'

She shook her head, 'I wonder if it was the man I saw in my mother's office before I knew all about this trip.'

'Wes didn't say a great deal more and I just wondered whether this man could have been the client?'

'I very much doubt it. Although she said he was an eminent scientist, I certainly don't think he'd have the money for something like this. But he might have been working for the client. I believe he could have been the logical choice to authenticate the items. With his assertion that the stones were real, they would have been accepted immediately and become, if anything, even more valuable.'

'Mm, so why kill him?' Thomas mused. 'That probably rules out anyone in it for the money and altruism, leaving power. What power might they believe that gives them?'

'Could it be that if they could discredit the gems, pronounce them as fakes? Maybe they couldn't convince him to do that and because he knew their plan, they killed him?'

'Possibly, no doubt we will find out in time,' he replied.

Lissa's phone beeped. 'Message from my uncle. It appears that the people who have my mother have been in contact with him. You can imagine he was both surprised and concerned. They said that they were extremely keen to acquire the items we have, and if that did not occur in Sydney, there would be consequences for everyone. Apparently, when we arrive in Sydney, someone will phone with instructions.' Lissa groaned. 'It's not as if we own these things, for all I care they can have them.'

'I know this must be terrible for you but there is something else going on here. This isn't just about someone wanting to gather some jewels to add to their collection or to sell. Come on, Lissa, who might the client be?' Leo's voice was slightly raised and Thomas shot him a warning look.

'Look, just let me think about it.' She was clearly distressed and got up and walked to another seat.

Sitting staring out into the darkness, sparked only by the flashing of the wing light, she tried to think back to a day about six months ago when she had gone to her mother's office to talk about something else, not connected with the commission. She remembered that she had been running really late and as she arrived, she saw a man briefly as he left. She remembered he was tall but his hat was covering his face as he leant in to kiss her mother. She paused her thoughts and concentrated on the man, his shape, size, and hands and then she had it; the ring. She was pretty certain it was Rafik. She had met him a few times a long time ago but she particularly remembered him the day of her father's death.

He had been ill and unable to go to the party, so she had gone to pick her mother up. When they got home, he had gone. After that, she hadn't seen him for a while. She knew from what her mother had said recently that he was enormously wealthy and she had known him for a long time and that he had once been a close friend. Maybe that was why the kiss seemed longer and more familiar than expected, although her mother had seemed tense. Having arrived hot and exhausted from the New York traffic, her mother had chided her for her lateness, but never actually said anything more about the meeting, whether the man had been there for it or who he was; so she could not say for sure that he was the client.

Okay, so what did she know about him? Well, he was Iranian and her mother had once intimated that he was a descendant of one of the greatest Persian dynasties, the Safavids. She had told how one day, he had arrived with the diamond rings and had given similar ones to her mother, father, and Andreas; so it seemed more and more likely that he was rich enough to be the client.

'I think the client might be, a man called Rafik Yazdi.' Leo and Thomas moved closer to listen as Jem's snores were quite loud.

She explained that it was the ring that made her think it could be him. 'There had been four rings; one he had, one was given to her father, one her mother wore, as did Andreas. The four of them were friends when they were young. Apparently, Rafik had suddenly become very rich but mother never knew how.

He had given each a diamond and said that they were a token of their friendship. On the band of each ring is inscribed *Doret begardam*, which literally means "let me circle around you", in English I suppose, "I would do anything for you". After my father died, I know she was very angry with Rafik, and they were never really close again and she always seems so conflicted whenever she speaks about him, and I know she was wary but wouldn't say why. I supposed it was because he spent a lot of time in Iran where he has strong political ties. Although she never said this was the reason, so I don't know for sure.'

'So, what do you think the connection to the regalia could be?'

She paused before speaking, thinking carefully about her words, she said, 'My guess would be that this must be linked to some sort of political ambition. Either he or someone he is supporting wants to use the regalia in some way. After all, it was part of the crown jewels. There is currently huge turmoil in Iran.'

'Your father was Iranian, wasn't he? Could there be some link, maybe your uncle?' Leo queried.

'He was but my uncle and family have not lived there since he and my father were small children. Our family came to the US and my uncle never went back.'

Thomas took a chance, 'Can I ask you about your father's accident?' He asked tentatively. She nodded. 'I remember you said there was no investigation,'

She shook her head, 'No, the other driver died in the accident, so it was just deemed an accidental death. Why?'

'Did the police give you the report or any of his belongings?'

'Only his watch and ring, both of which my mother has,' and reaching into her bag, 'and this.' She pulled out a small silver lighter, with "Love ♥ NY". 'I keep it with me always as a reminder of him.'

'And those were the only things?'

'Yes, why?'

'I'm not sure. I think I need to speak to someone before I say anything else. You should try and get some sleep now as the next few days will be hard.'

Lissa nodded, 'I wish you'd tell me what you're thinking, I'm not sure I'll sleep now.'

Thomas got up, and handed her a pillow and blanket from the locker above and she extended her chair into a sleeper bed.

'As soon as I am sure, I promise I'll let you know.' He turned and went over to join Leo.

He lowered his voice and said, 'I think there is more we need to find out about Rafik and Lissa's father's "accident". I'm going to contact Wes and see if he has any info. In the meantime, I will also contact Gerry in the NY police and find out if a report was made about the accident. Can you contact Julia and get her to put the word out to her contacts and then alert the team Grace set up for us in Sydney, so we can get an early lead on any possibly related action by an Iranian group?'

'Couldn't we swap, you phone...'

'No, Leo.' Thomas was emphatic.

Following several phone conversations, Leo got up and poured two brandies.

Thomas smiled as Leo didn't seem to have had the "difficult reception" he thought he might.

'She spoke to you then?' He laughed.

'Yes, we had quite a decent conversation. Thanks for pushing me, I know I should have done so before now. And, yes, before you ask, I did apologise for the way I treated her.' Thomas just nodded.

The plane was quiet, except for the drum of the engines and Jem's snoring.

Leo's brow furrowed, which concerned Thomas as so little ever seemed to trouble him. 'The further we go with this, the more I get the feeling that we are involved in something a lot more than just ensuring an expensive dagger reaches its destination. This is beginning to feel political to me and maybe not something we should be involved with.'

'I know what you mean, I certainly have had similar thoughts but sadly, it seems we are, like it or not. Whether it is this Rafik guy or another group, or whoever, they have two hostages who we can't just leave.'

'Yes, but are we making things worse for them as maybe we're in danger of getting in way over our heads. I think we should involve the UK Intelligence Services. What was that guy's name we met before we set up the company? Was it Michael...something? Can't remember. Dad will know, he set up the meeting. I'll give him a call.'

'I agree but downplay the Iranian bit, stick with just the jewels for the time being.'

'Sorry, mate, he already knows most of it. I had to tell him. How do you think I got the plane? Remy's money was good but not that good! He said that unless I agreed to keep him informed, he wouldn't help.'

'Okay, let's see what he says. I'm going to get some sleep.' He got up and moved to another sleeper chair, grabbed a blanket and pillow, and settled down.

Leo phoned home. He explained to his father exactly what they knew, what Lissa had told Thomas, and what had happened in LA. He made it clear that while they were dealing with the situation, they felt that it was time to ensure that should things spiral out of their control, they would welcome some backup. His father confirmed he needed to contact Michael Raffy, sooner rather than later.

'Thanks, Dad. I don't want to give him names just yet, as these people might not be involved at all, but could you find out anything about these three men connected to Remy, called Rafik Yazdi, Andreas Metaxas and a Darius Shafiq.'

He heard his father laugh, 'Who's doing the work here, son? Perhaps I should join you?' The question hung in the air.

'No, but thank you, Dad, we've got it covered for the moment.' If he could have seen his father's face, he would have been seriously shocked as he would have seen a look somewhat akin to pride. *Finally,* his father thought, *he seems to be taking things seriously.* But at the same time, sadly, he knew that it was a shame this would probably never transfer to the company or his business.

'Take care, son, from what you have told me, you're in dangerous waters. Oh, and I don't just mean Julia.' He hung up. Leo chuckled, as he got a blanket and pillow, and settled down to sleep. As his mind drifted through the events so far, he couldn't help but feel his father was right, they were in very dangerous territory. He tried to process all the information and thought, *Maybe we have got this all wrong, maybe it is just about the money for this man.* He phoned the number his father had given him and then slept fitfully.

Chapter 26

Their stop in Tahiti was as expected only brief to refuel. The extra security organised by Grace met them on the tarmac and stood guard around the plane. Once fuel and food had been loaded and the plane checked, they were soon back on the runway and taking off again. Thomas slept intermittently.

Descending into Sydney, the smell of coffee woke him. Jem, it seemed, had slept soundly all the way from LA. Leo and Thomas looked at each other and smiled as they both looked somewhat the worse for wear. Lissa appeared from the toilet and also looked clear-eyed and chic. Leo's phone rang. It was clear from his face and tone that he was talking to his father.

When he finished the call, he turned. 'Well, there is a lot more than meets the eye with this Rafik Yazdi. He shows up on more than one international watch list. There are questions about the level of his involvement in the Iranian secret service, which were raised after several of his trips and stays in the States. Eventually, he seems to have carried a diplomatic passport but his visits became fewer, as relations between the two countries weakened. There are unconfirmed reports that he may have been involved in the deaths of several anti-government dissidents in the US but also in Iran. The list goes on!'

Leo looked at Thomas and the question hung in the air between them: Was Lissa's father's death an accident? Neither spoke.

Then Lissa said, 'I am sure that my mother doesn't know anything about this.'

Thomas nodded. 'When we find your mother, we'll talk to her, so don't worry about it now. Jem get Yazdi's picture out to all the team; instruct them to follow if seen but stay clear, don't get caught, this man is clearly dangerous.'

Leo confirmed what they already knew from the picture that Darius was the son of Shahtiar Shafiq, assassinated by the Islamic Republic, in Paris in 1984, but there seemed to be little about his later life. He appeared to live most of his early life in Paris and then he moved to the UK to go to University in Oxford. After that, it all becomes a little vague.

He had wondered about telling everyone about Andreas Metaxas but was saved from further comment as the pilot announced that they were circling in on their final approach to Sydney airport. He pointed out that if they looked out on the port side, they would get an amazing view of the city, Opera House and Bridge.

Getting off the plane and taking in a lungful of somewhat fresher air perked everyone up. They headed across the tarmac to undertake the formal parts of landing in Australia. They were prepared for there to be stringent and extensive customs searches, paper checks and questions. However, these were completed with good humour on everyone's part and presented no issues. Thomas had wondered whether Leo's brushes with the Aussie police regarding his drug use would be an issue but as they passed immigration with no issues, it seemed that his father's contacts and connections to the Foreign Office had made sure that any record of past problems had disappeared.

He had never quite figured out what exactly these "connections" were but he promised himself that one day, he would dig a little deeper as he was intrigued.

Having completed formalities, they headed out for the cars and soon picked out their team, as the group of men sweltering on the tarmac. While the others got into the cars, out of the strong Sydney sunshine, Thomas shook hands and spoke with all the men, and then spoke to one and asked him to arrange for two groups to meet later that day, one to go with Leo, while the others would go to a pre-arranged meeting point and wait for instructions. It had been decided that he and Lissa would meet Julia at the police station, while Jem and Leo would head to the hotel to meet the courier.

Splitting up, he and Lissa headed for the first car and set off to the police station. Jem and Leo would travel with the men they had met at the airport, ensure they had any necessary equipment and then head for the hotel to wait for the meeting. As Thomas was getting in the car, his phone rang. Lissa was concerned as she watched him, he became more and more animated; it was clear he was angry. Getting in the car, she asked, 'What's happened?'

'It was Leo. He said he had just had a call from the kidnappers, they'd given us a deadline. We need to get a lead quickly.' Turning to the driver, he said, 'How quickly can you get us to the main police station?' The driver caught his eyes in the mirror and nodded.

'No problem, Sir,' he said.

The driver of Thomas' car was clearly an experienced city driver and snaked his way easily through the Sydney morning traffic into the city, showing great skill.

Impressed, Thomas asked his name. 'Tyrone O'Brian, Sir.' The tone was clipped.

Over time, Thomas had developed his innate ability to quickly discern and understand people's characters and motivations, which had stood him in good stead in the army. He had used these skills already at the airport, having noted how the group were gathered and how they interacted. He had considered their body language and watched their expressions, and it was clear that this man stood out. He saw the way he had stood outside the car, the way he had held the door for Lissa, and the use of the word "sir", he knew from experience were indicators that this man, with the Birmingham accent, had clearly been a soldier and probably an experienced and extremely effective one.

'Which service?' Thomas enquired.

'Commando, green beret, Sir.'

'You're a long way from home, marine.'

'I go where the work is, Sir,' Tyrone said holding Thomas' eyes in the mirror.

As the car came to a halt at the police station, Thomas said, 'Call me if you fancy something more interesting than just driving,' and handed him a card. 'When we leave, we'll be with the police. Follow discreetly, you'll be the spotter, keep watch.' Tyrone nodded.

Lissa and Thomas got out and headed in. As they did, Lissa said, 'He seemed nice.'

Thomas nodded. 'He is certainly someone we could use, especially with those driving skills. He could fit in well with the team, should we make it out of this mess, of course!' His laugh was mirthless.

They introduced themselves at reception and were asked to take a seat but didn't have to wait long before Julia arrived. Thomas didn't quite know how he would be greeted but was not expecting the warm hug he received, which came as a nice surprise. He introduced Lissa and they followed Julia through to her office. As soon as the door closed, a string of questions exploded from her. 'I am happy to see you again, how are you? How did you end up working with my beloved ex-husband? He sounded fine when we spoke, even apologised, but how is he really? Leo told me a bit about what you are doing here, how can I help?'

Thomas decided on the somewhat short version. 'Good and still clear. But you know there are parts of Leo that are never going to change!' They all laughed.

'I am sorry, that was too much, wasn't it?' They all nodded. 'So, would you like some coffee?' Again nods.

As he watched her, he could see why Leo had fallen for her. She was exactly like all his other women, totally stunning. Typically, Leo favoured models who were tall, blonde and beautiful, and she certainly qualified. But she was also very different; like Grace, she was intelligent, highly organised, and motivated, therefore, not swayed by his usual approach. She was already an excellent copper when Thomas first met her and he again wondered how she had managed so successfully in the still somewhat misogynistic world of policing. Unlike her days in uniform, where her looks and figure were disguised by her clothes, he wondered about the impact that this smartly dressed woman had on both her colleagues and the criminals she apprehended.

She was now a detective inspector, so clearly extremely capable. This was something that they definitely needed.

'Thanks for seeing us. I don't have any new info, other than what Leo told you, but we have now been given a deadline. Have you managed to find out any information about where our friends might be being held?' Thomas asked.

'There have been a couple of leads but nothing definite yet. You gave me so little to go on. What's this all about anyway?'

'Leo and I are working for the lady who has been taken, this is her daughter. We were hired to find and return some items of jewellery to their owner. We believe that the people who have taken her also want the jewels and that is why she and her friend have been taken. We have already collected three of the pieces and the person who we think has the final piece is apparently here in Sydney. So, these men are holding the hostages as a bargaining chip; we give them the items, and we get her and her friend back. But both you and I know that it doesn't always work out like that.' He looked directly at Julia, not daring to look at Lissa.

'As Leo intimated, there might be an Iranian connection. I have a couple of contacts with the refugee and asylum seekers communities if you think these might be useful, we can try these out.' Thomas nodded. 'Let me make a couple of calls,' she said as she walked out of the office.

'Do you really think they might not keep their end of the deal?' Thomas was loathe to answer.

Fortunately, he didn't have to as Julia quickly returned. 'Good news,' she smiled. 'I'd asked one of the guys to check out his contacts and it looks like we have a lead. It seems there is a group of migrants who he thought might be useful. Hopefully, they might have some ideas.' She smiled at Lissa. Thomas stood and turned towards the door. 'I have had a word with my boss and before you go running off, he would like to meet you. 'Spect he'll give you the "don't do anything" talk!' She looked amused.

With that, they left the office and they headed up the stairs. Chief Inspector Carmichael was probably younger than either of them had expected. He was a tall, thin man with a mostly bald head and a poor combover. His somewhat awkward appearance was not helped by a beak-like nose. He walked over to them with his hand outstretched as they entered the room. 'I am pleased to meet you,' he said, shaking hands, 'but obviously concerned about the situation that Julia has outlined to me. I can see that we have a potential hostage situation and have agreed in the first instance for her to try and help you. She knows the conditions and I am sorry, but at this stage, we can't offer any additional people until we have clearer information.'

'We understand, it is a difficult situation,' Thomas replied with a smile, to which Carmichael nodded. 'We are just grateful to be able to call on Julia's skills. Hopefully, we will be able to resolve this swiftly and get out of your hair.' Julia coughed and Thomas looked at Lissa, who had turned away.

Carmichael's laugh was strained from the many times this unintended comment had been made. As a still youngish man, he was acutely very aware of his baldness.

'Oh,' spluttered Thomas.

'Don't worry,' interrupted the inspector. 'Not the first time. Seriously, however, please don't think that you can do whatever you want, be careful and remember if you break the law…' He left the threat open.

'Understood,' said Thomas. With that, they stood and returned to Julia's office.

'I thought I would explode! Good job he has a sense of humour,' laughed Lissa.

'Let's move on…we are on the clock, where do we need to go?' Thomas asked.

'Okay, so I presume you have some guys, somewhere.' Thomas nodded. 'I'll give you the reference points where they need to head to meet us. The people we are going to see are asylum seekers, so we need to be cautious for their sake, as well as ours. Apparently they have built a strong network between groups, so hopefully one of them will have some idea where your mother might be being held. They will only appear when they believe it is safe to do so, so we may have to wait. Okay, let's go.'

Chapter 27

Thomas phoned his group's driver and gave them the reference for the place to meet. Leaving the building, they headed for Julia's car. It was a solid SUV, which probably held a variety of useful equipment, that he hoped they wouldn't need. As they set off, he made a call to Grace, gave her Tyrone's name and asked her to check him out, although he felt sure that the results would be positive. With a quick look back, he saw the man's car fall in behind.

They passed through the city, out into the suburbs, where they began to see more industrial areas. Some of these were quite run-down and this appeared to be where Julia was heading. Several buildings looked as if they had been deserted for some time, as vegetation was beginning to grow through the concrete; while others as if they had only just become empty. Where there were small stores, they saw some people but they weren't like the smiling faces of people in the "Visit Australia" adverts. There seemed to be an air of sadness and despondency.

'There are a lot of disused buildings here, especially after the pandemic. They are now being squatted by refugees, illegals, drugees, and asylum seekers, you name it, they'll be here. But that means we need to be careful; some groups, especially the Eastern Europeans, are not welcoming. They run several illegal operations but are difficult to catch. They are not keen on being seen and depending on the group, they can be aggressive. I don't know a great deal about the group we are going to, so watch your backs.'

Julia stopped the car at the gates of one of the factory developments. She motioned for them to stay and then got out and walked over to the car with Thomas' men in. The leader of the group got out and having spoken to Julia, he gestured for his men to do so. Thomas looked around but could not see Tyrone but knew that he would have taken up a support position.

It was clear she was giving instructions to the men and they nodded and started to head away from the car to other locations as directed, disappearing behind the fence. They would remain out of sight unless needed. Julia had made it absolutely clear that they were there for protection not for attack. She walked back to the car with the team leader, who Thomas recognised as Parsons.

'What's the layout of these buildings?' Thomas asked. She explained that this was a disused factory. The machinery had been taken out, so the floors were mostly open, which was why they had been squatted.

'When we make contact, I suggest one of the men comes with us to protect the main door, while the others stay out of sight. When we see any sign of movement, that'll be the time to move.' The team leader nodded, gave Julia a radio, and checked in with the other men who were now in position, having skirted around the fence. He then headed for the main gate. With everyone in place, it appeared it was going to be a waiting game. As they settled down, Julia passed out some chocolate bars, particularly welcome as they hadn't had any lunch. After about an hour, Julia's radio buzzed. One of the men reported having seen some movement in the far corner of the building.

'Okay, here we go. Remember, these people are going to be easily spooked,' she cautioned. 'You and Lissa come with me; I have told your men to stay on watch but not move unless there is an obvious threat. These people don't cause any problems as a rule but it pays to be cautious.' Thomas checked in with Parsons who was watching the door, who told him that it had been opened slightly.

They got out of the car and walked through the gates of the site. The padlock hung limply on the chain. They were cautious, as they knew crossing the open space to the building's door could be dangerous as they had no idea if there was anyone else besides the people Julia had described inside. However, they saw no movement and they reached the door without a problem or any sound from the building. The door was clearly open and Julia pushed it cautiously, calling out. Silence, then the sound of footsteps.

The man who came to the door was clearly very wary and stayed in the shadows. Julia gave the name of her contact and he just nodded, and pushed the door fully open, then turned and walked away. They entered the building. Inside, they climbed the first few steps, then reached the first room, where they were surprised to see what appeared to be a collection of mismatched tents and dwellings, some made of blankets, tarpaulins and others just cardboard. Clearly, this open space had given them the opportunity to set up a kind of camp. What was eerie, was that there were no people or sounds of any kind but Thomas had the distinct feeling they were being watched by many eyes. They followed the man up more stairs to another room and again, there were tents and makeshift dwellings.

'It's a village,' said Julia. 'Some of them are legal, others aren't, but if they don't bother us, so generally we leave them alone. Although you can't see them, there are many families here with children, but they will stay hidden when "outsiders" come.'

Lissa, clearly uncertain, asked, 'This must be a difficult life. How do they cope?'

'You'll see.'

They walked to the end of the room, where the old offices were located. Thomas noted that this was the only place that appeared to have light. The door was open and there were three men and a woman in the room.

'*Ahlan wa Sahlan*,' said the man in the centre, who moved forward.

'*Shukran*, for seeing us,' said Julia. Thomas thought that, although this looked to be a poor collection of temporary buildings, they seemed to have an extremely sophisticated array of surveillance systems, that had clearly shown their arrival. They also had cameras that had picked up the team. He noted, however, there was no sign of Tyrone.

'My colleague said that you might be willing to help me.'

'Yes, but first, I need to know from your friends why they are here and what they seek?' A man moved forward and stood in front of Lissa. His appearance was intimidating as he was well over six feet, with long black hair and a beard. He was clearly well built, despite his loose robes. He surveyed her intently. Thomas could see her breathing had increased but she stood her ground. *Well done*, he thought. He guessed the man was in his thirties and his appearance clearly suggested Arab in origin. He held out his hands, palms upwards, and without questioning, she placed her hands on his.

'You are of the blood and I will answer your questions.'

'Yes, my father came from Iran. I am looking for the men who took my mother and her friend,' she said, 'we would be grateful for any information that might help us find them.'

'Why have they taken her?'

'She has something they want.'

He spoke in a voice that resonated around the room, 'I know why you are here. The things you seek are for the Persian peoples, your ancestors, not Iranians or Arabs.' Lisa turned to Thomas, clearly amazed.

'I am Bizhan. I speak for these people,' he indicated the tents outside. Then he looked at Lissa. 'Your goal is important to us, to our people, and this is why we will help you.' He spoke in Arabic to one of the men in front of the computers. They pressed a button and the screen split showing two images. One was a boarded-up motel, another showed that there were two men guarding the gate. Then he spoke to the woman, who left the room. She came back with a carved wooden box, which she opened. Inside was a beautiful, bejewelled clasp plate that matched the pattern on the belt, lay on a blue velvet cushion.

'Is that?' Lissa stammered.

'Yes,' said the man. 'We were preparing to meet you elsewhere but circumstances would have made that unwise.'

Bizhan told them that his family, the Abbas, had been in possession of this since the death of the Shah. It was their family's duty to protect it, just as others had been selected to guard other pieces until the time when all would be brought together and Persia would live again.

He believed that when complete, this would be the flame that would light their cause, and his voice almost sang the words, 'The return of our land from the religious fanatics and traitors.' He pointed to the clasp, 'you can see that the central stone, a ruby, has been removed; this was done by my grandfather but remains within the family.' He paused. 'To ensure its safety, he did not tell us who had it, so I do not know who that is. I believe that after the fall of the Shah, it was smuggled to the UK. You must find it so that once again it can be reunited with the whole regalia. When it is, we believe that the one who will lead us will come forth.'

'Thank you, I don't know what to say.' Lissa's voice was unsteady. She held the item lightly, as if afraid it might break. 'I promise we will take great care of it.' She laid it back on the velvet, and the box was closed, put into a velvet bag, and presented to her. She took it, almost bowing. Thomas' radio beeped, picking it up, Tyrone warned he had seen a man climbing a building across the street, who he thought was carrying a long gun.

'I think we have a problem,' Thomas said and turned to the man at the computer, who immediately started to scan the outside camera on the door side of the building towards the place Tyrone had described. The camera caught the faintest flash of light. Bizhan spoke rapidly to the other man and woman, who immediately left the room.

Thomas got on the radio. 'Tyrone, do nothing, stay safe, just observe then follow when you can.' He told Parsons about the gunman and told him to get his men back, staying out of sight and to meet behind the factory, he didn't want to risk a fire fight. Bizhan said they should follow him and they headed across the way they had come, which was now suddenly alive with people, gathering things together and dismantling tents and buildings. He quickly led them across the floor towards a side door, near where they had entered. He said that they would be protected by the fence.

'What will you do?' Lissa asked.

'Like always, we will move on. Take care and *liakun allah maeak* (God bless you). Quickly, we must go.'

As they hurried through, Thomas was surprised by how many people had emerged from their shelters to watch the outsiders walk back through the building. Those who could, had moved to touch the box that Lissa carried, Whispering *min agle baladi libaladina*, "for the sake of our country". Lissa was clearly moved by the experience and nodded to each as they touched it. She felt so sorry that their arrival had caused this panic but moved as quickly as she could through the people.

Leo's phone rang. 'What's up, Thomas? The courier didn't turn up.'

'I know, as we are with the guy who was going to deliver it. We are on our way back. Where are you?'

'Over at Manly, following a lead.'

'Get back to the hotel as quickly as possible. Julia and her team will meet you there. They have the location where they are holding Remy and Andreas. Be careful, it appears we may now have someone with a long gun following us.'

Leo groaned, not because of the possible sniper, but because he had heard Thomas snigger and he knew he could not avoid meeting Julia face to face any longer. 'By the way, Grace phoned, said to tell you that the name and ID you gave came back amazingly positive; she sent you some documents. What's that about?'

'Will explain when I see you.' He hung up, opened the email from Grace and whistled. He had been right; Tyrone would certainly be useful by all accounts.

Leo picked up his gun from the table and called Jem. They met back at the hotel and headed down to the carpark under the hotel. Jem opened the van parked there and took a large bag from it, which he put into the back of the hired SUV next to it. Jem drove out to the main road, where he parked up, to wait for Julia and the others.

Meanwhile, having made it out of the factory, Thomas and Lissa met the others. Apart from Parsons, the rest of the team was sent off to meet Leo at the motel as backup, while he would accompany them as they headed back to the city with the clasp. They stowed the box in the boot and headed back to their hotel in town.

It was a quiet journey back, clearly the way that the people had treated the passage of the box had affected them both. Arriving back at the hotel carpark, they were met by two men who accompanied them to Lissa's room. She opened the last of the cases and they placed the clasp inside and locked it, securing the tracking device. Thomas, for the time being, took the fourth key as well as the second one.

Thomas' phone rang. Tyrone explained that he had followed the sniper to the outskirts of the city. He was now at a disused motel, in a forested area, which made tracking him more difficult. He had let Leo know that the man was somewhere on site but as the team were already in place, Leo did not want to search and spook whoever was holding Remy and Andreas, as they might lose the element of surprise.

Thomas told Tyrone to head back to Sydney as he had a job for him.

Lissa had ordered some coffee, and they were just finishing it, when there was a knock at the door. He was instantly alert and picking up his gun, he checked before opening the door, and motioned for Tyrone to come in.

'Must have been an empty road,' Thomas said smiling. Tyrone laughed. 'All okay?' Thomas asked.

Tyrone nodded. Following Grace's call, Thomas had decided that since they were a man down, as a result of Spider's death, he would ask Tyrone to stand in with Parsons. 'Good. Listen, Tyrone, I am going to offer you an opportunity, a chance if you like, and a trip to London. Added to this is a promise that if all goes well, there will be others. This was supposed to be someone else's job but if you want it, it's yours.' He paused, thinking of Spider. 'We don't have time for formal interviews, so I'm going on my gut,' he said, smiling, he held up his phone. 'Nothing is secret these days. You have two hours before the flight goes to decide.'

Tyrone stood up straight and said, 'I don't need the time, Sir, thank you.' They shook hands.

Thomas explained, 'You will have company all the way, Parsons will explain the job. All you need do is take this with you,' he said holding out the case.

Parsons offered his hand to Tyrone, as the man said, 'No problem.' After a quick discussion, it was agreed that the case would be attached to Tyrone's wrist.

'Thank you, Sir,' said Tyrone, again shaking Thomas' hand. 'I won't let you down.'

'I know you won't!' He smiled as he turned and the two left, passing Lissa coming out of the bedroom.

'Wasn't that rather reckless? Can you really trust someone you've only just met?' She asked. The smell of expensive toiletries filled the air.

Thomas laughed. 'I trusted you!' He ducked as she hit out at him. 'Besides, looking at the info Grace sent, we will be lucky to keep him. The man left the service as a warrant officer with a host of commendations.'

'So, that's good but,' she said plonking herself down on the settee beside him, 'where the hell is the stone?'

For the moment, he found it difficult to put his thoughts together. The smell of her freshly washed hair, perfumed from the shower, and her closeness were almost too intoxicating. She started to brush out her hair. He got up suddenly and poured them both coffee.

'We could start by trying to trace the family tree of Darius Shafiq,' she said. 'Maybe someone at the *Khabar* (news), the paper banned in Iran, will be able to help us. We must be careful not to make them aware of what we are doing though.'

'I wouldn't be at all surprised if they already knew. I don't think there is anything else we can do until Leo lets us know whether they have been able to find and release your mother and Andreas.' Thomas shrugged.

'I don't want to think of that right now, if I do, I'll not be able to stop worrying. They will be all right, won't they?'

'I think whoever is doing this is more interested in the regalia,' he lied, but he just sensed that there was something more personal going on here.

'Hey, I am starving.' He was finding it difficult to keep his thoughts in check.

'Let's have room service, I can't face a crowd right now,' she said.

They ordered steaks, salad, and a good red wine from the menu. It arrived quite promptly and they sat chatting about Lissa's childhood visits to Crete as they ate. Taking the rest of the wine to the sofa, they talked about all sorts of things as they finished it. Despite it not yet being 5 pm, Thomas yawned as he realised that he hadn't had much sleep in the last twenty-four hours and what with the red wine, they were beginning to have an effect, so he could feel his eyes wanting to close.

'You do look tired.' Lissa ran her hand across his brow. 'Come on, you can sleep here, then I can make sure you'll know if anything happens,' she said, waving towards the bedroom. 'As you said, there's nothing to do until we hear from Leo. I'll wake you when he calls.'

She held her hand out and tried to pull him up but ended up being pulled into his lap. He caught her in his arms and despite all his qualms, said, 'I can think of something that might keep me awake.' Then with a smile, he leant in and kissed her. At first, she seemed a little surprised and her body tensed, but as he deepened the kiss, seeking out her tongue, he felt her relax.

'So, you're not too tired.' She laughed and he stood up with her in his arms and beaming down at her, shook his head.

Her voice was husky, as she looked up into his eyes and stroked his face. 'I wanted this from the moment we met at the hotel in New York, and…' His kiss stifled her words. He carried her into the bedroom and closed the door with his foot. He put her down at the edge of the bed and let her go, he did not want something to happen that they would regret.

'I felt the same in New York,' he said, as she started to unzip her top. He took the zipper from her and eased it down. She had nothing underneath. He eased the top off her shoulders and as she took it off, her beautifully curved and full breasts took his breath away.

'Wait, are you sure?' He said and clearly she was, as she was slipping her trousers over her hips, then moved to unbutton his shirt. He removed it and then his trousers.

'Yes, I am sure,' she said, slipping her fingers into the front of his briefs, caressing his already erect penis.

He kissed her breast and teased her nipple with his tongue till it hardened in his mouth; his hands caressed her firm bottom, hooking his fingers in her panties, which she wriggled out of. The words, 'I want you,' were barely out of her mouth before they were wrapped in each other's arms. He picked her up and she wound her legs around him. He entered her as they moved to the bed; the urgency of their lovemaking left them both panting.

Lying together, through gentle touches and kisses, they started to explore each other's bodies. She found the scars and wounds, kissing each one gently.

She traced the wolf's head with her nail, making him shudder and he kissed her neck, then her breast. 'You are so beautiful.' His voice was soft and full of emotion. He slipped one hand down her stomach, his fingers seeking entry, ensuring that she was fully aroused. He caressed her inner thigh and she opened fully to him. This time, his movements were slower, deeper, ensuring she would really enjoy their lovemaking, which by her cries, she clearly did.

They came to the climax together, then lay wrapped in each other's arms, hot and tired, till sleep took them.

When they awoke, it was dark. Thomas looked at the clock. 'Much as I want to stay here, I think we had better shower. Leo could call at any time.'

They showered together, kissing, and teasing each other's bodies until he picked her up and with her back touching the cool tiles; they came together again, the steaming water adding to their pleasure. Rubbing each other dry was very arousing! As they were about to…Thomas' phone rang.

Chapter 28

Leo had not had a chance to speak to Julia before they were in the cars and on their way. As he watched her organise the team she had managed to put together without the chief knowing, he admired the way she worked. There was no suggestion of coldness and as he watched her, he remembered how brilliant she had been at her job when they had been together. He was pleased that her career was going well, and from the way the chief spoke to, and about her, he felt sure that there was more to come.

It was late afternoon when Leo and Jem followed Julia out of the carpark. Arriving at the location, they parked up in a wooded area, close to the boarded up motel. She told Leo to wait and walked to the other SUV. When she returned, it was clear she meant business, as she was dressed in the same way, as the three heavily armoured men who got out of the jeep.

Julia said, 'This is the place. Thomas said there were a couple of men outside but who knows? I take it you and your people will be able to protect yourselves?' She laughed, as clearly, she knew they would be armed. They were all aware of what Tyrone had reported seeing at the factory and Julia immediately got a couple of men to do a sweep of the woods nearest to the motel. She was concerned about the sniper and told her men to spread out but they were under strict instructions not to engage, just report back.

Leo and Jem were told to remain undercover, and Julia made it clear that Leo's group should stay outside the perimeter and only engage if it was clear someone was escaping or taking a hostage away. He nodded. Getting out of the SUV, his team collected their weapons.

Using a heat scope, she worked out where the group was located inside the building and one of Leo's guys sent a mini drone to survey the outside. Using the information they had gathered, the group split up as they moved into the forest. Turning to direct her men, he noted their focus and the positive way they instantly reacted. He was captivated and only Jem nudging him drew his eyes away. Jem smiled. 'Come on.'

Leo's men moved through the trees to take point around the building, able to see all exits and watch the guys patrolling. If they came into view, they would be taken out. As it was getting towards dusk, the lack of bright sunlight and longer shadows helped Julia and her men move around the edge of the carpark unseen, quickly and silently taking out the two guards outside. They reported no sign of a sniper. They closed in on the entrance nearest to the heat signatures. The plan was to send two men to enter by the door from the corridor, accessed from the back, while Julia and another entered through the door from the carpark.

Through her earpiece, she heard the guys in the corridor confirm they were in place. Mentally she counted, *3,2,1*, and the back door was kicked open and a flash-bang thrown into the room. Then all hell broke loose; the front door burst open and two men stumbled out to be met by Julia's gun pointed at their chests. She screamed instructions and the men immediately dropped to their knees.

Leo and Jem made their way to the group to find Julia's men had already arrested the kidnappers, who appeared by the tattoos on their hands to come from a local Russian gang. She explained that inside they had found Andreas, who had managed to free himself somehow. He had told her that the moment he heard a noise at the back of the motel, he'd grabbed Remy and pushed her into the bathroom. The bang startled the men in the room and in the confusion, he was able to disarm one of the disorientated men, the others had fled outside. The other man had simply crumpled to the floor coughing. When the police entered, they found Remy somewhat bemused, and Andreas, with his foot on the last man, and pointing a gun at him.

'Well, it appears you didn't need rescuing,' Julia laughed. 'You'll have to tell me more later!' Then she turned and briefly spoke to Remy, who, although dishevelled, had clearly regained her poise.

Remy beamed at Andreas, said nothing and then just laughed and kissed him.

Leo was amazed at the scene but knew he needed to quickly search the men to see if they had any information that might help them. He dragged the two men onto their feet; they were clearly groggy but able to stand.

He grabbed one of the men's hands and said, 'Thomas showed me that the guy who tried to kill him had a cross symbol tattooed between his thumb and finger, seems they are from the same group.' Julia looked concerned.

'That's a worry. They don't usually get involved with this type of job. It's usually drugs. Looks like they may be branching out.'

One of Julia's team brought a third man round from the back. All the captors were searched but nothing was found.

'Okay, which of you geniuses is the leader?' The men, heads down didn't move. 'Well, look at it this way, the one who is, is in for a shit load of trouble, while the rest, well!' She didn't finish the sentence.

One said in a heavy Russian accent, 'No one will speak.'

'So, it's you then,' Julia smiled. 'Put the rest in the vans.'

Except for the man who spoke, the kidnappers were marched away to the two police vans that had arrived in the carpark. She called a policeman over to take him to the station separately. As the man was moved towards the car, they heard a single shot and the man crumpled to the ground. All except for the policeman who had been holding him ducked for cover; he remained upright, frozen in shock.

'Get down!' Julia screamed but there was no second shot, as the policeman belatedly dropped to the ground.

Julia was the first to react. 'Where the fuck did that shot come from? We checked the perimeter.'

One of the policemen who had searched the area started to explain but Leo interrupted, helping the man out. 'By the sound, it was a long-range shot. The sniper will be somewhere in the woods to the south and could be a long way off. As there was only one shot, it's clear that he aimed only to shut the leader up. I think we should get going but maybe it would be a good idea to bring a vehicle across to protect the door and another to cover the police car.' The policemen nodded to Leo as he spoke into his mike. Everyone stayed low but there were no other shots.

The sniper's nest in the wood was already empty.

Leo said, 'We'll make our way around the back and see if we can find any evidence of the shooter. But likely a professional, so I wouldn't hold out much hope.' Julia nodded and said that they should meet back at the station.

The two groups split, with Leo and his men skirting around the building back into the woods, while Julia, Remy and Andreas climbed into her SUV and headed back to the city.

Leo indicated to his men to spread out. They searched the bushes but unsurprisingly found no evidence of the shooter, so they headed back to their vehicle. They did not see the man following them on his rifle scope. His instructions were to take out any loose ends and at this time, this did not include any of the team or the police. He was well camouflaged above them and had moved positions. Later, the autopsy carried out on the dead leader revealed the bullet's trajectory showed it had entered his body on a descending angle, tearing through the man's chest and out his back at a lower angle.

This, and other potentially useful information, were noted in the forensic report but were never actually discussed with the team, as there was a large pile-up on the motorway, and the report was mysteriously lost.

Back at the station, both Remy and Andreas were seen by a police doctor and were then interviewed by Julia, with the chief behind the two-way mirror. Unfortunately, apart from identifying the men who had taken them and who had treated them reasonably well, there was little they could offer the police. The men were part of a Russian drugs gang and it seemed they were used to moving people in and out of the country with no questions asked; neither Remy nor Andreas dissuaded the police of the notion that this was who and how they had arrived in Australia. They had agreed to their story and once they had given very vague statements, Remy asked if they were able to leave.

Julia had her doubts about the Russian connection but said, 'You are free to go but please take care and do not leave the city, no doubt we will speak again after we have tried to resolve your immigration status.'

Thomas and Lissa, who had arrived earlier, were now able to greet the captives. Clearly, she had been worried about her mother and hugged her tightly, then did the same to Andreas.

Thomas grinned at Andreas and as they shook hands, said, 'Good to meet you.' Then he said they should all go back to the hotel. As they left the station, he held Remy's elbow, reminiscent of the times he had walked her to dinner on the ship. This time, he steered her to the waiting car.

'When we get back, we will all be really interested in the real story,' he suggested.

'Why, Thomas, don't you believe me?' She raised a beautifully styled eyebrow and he laughed.

'Just glad to see you are both okay.'

Andreas, Leo and Lissa followed; each had a smile as they watched the pair ahead.

'Do I have competition?' Andreas asked and they all laughed.

Chapter 29

As the car headed for the city, Thomas knew that the danger to everyone had increased substantially. Initially, they were just being followed, not unexpected given the nature of their commission. But when Remy and Andreas had been taken, this had raised the stakes. But now, it seemed they had someone far more dangerous on their tail. Whatever reason or group they represented, obviously considered they were a threat. Were they the same people who were responsible for all the killings that had occurred? Was the "someone" so desperate to stop them from gaining the regalia that they would employ an assassin?

What would happen when they located the person with the stone, would they cease to be of use? So many questions raced through his head. Whether they were in danger or not, it was obvious from the man's death at the motel that they did not want anyone revealing their identity.

Arriving back at the hotel, it was clear everyone was a little on edge. Thomas felt that in the centre of town, they were probably safer, but he was still hyper-alert as they got out of the car. Once in the carpark under the hotel, they walked to the lift with Julia at the rear, surveying cars as they walked past; but there was no problem and they reached the suite that had been reserved for Remy without incident. Thomas went in and closed all the blinds. They all sat down, there was silence. This was suddenly broken by Andreas, who stood up.

'I am sorry, Remy, everyone, I have not been open with you. I need to explain. I am currently the Greek Naval Liaison Officer working with a NATO task force. We are presently focusing on the unrest in Iran. A few years ago, rumours regarding the regalia you have been collecting started to spread. There were suggestions that those who opposed people's democratic right to choose their leaders were so worried about it that they would do anything to find it. We have also known for some time that there was an Iranian spy working in America, whose job was to find and destroy it. We have been following him and his friends for a while now. I think it…' he never finished the sentence, as his phone rang, and he immediately picked it up, he listened and then with a curt, 'Yes,' he closed it, his face a mixture of emotions.

'I am sorry, but I must leave you. I need to get back to the team.' He looked at Remy. 'I know you will be safe with your team, chérie. I will catch up with you later.' With that, he kissed a stunned Remy, then Lissa, shook hands with Julia and the men, and then without another word left, leaving behind startled faces.

'Well, I didn't see that coming,' replied a bemused Leo.

'Could this day get any stranger? Come on, mother, we all know that it wasn't a Russian gang that was behind your capture. What's the truth and what do you know? No more stories or lies.'

'I'm sorry, my darling, for the moment I don't think I can.' She paused, clearly conflicted. 'I can say no more than it wasn't anything to do with the client.' As there were protests from the group, she got up. 'I am sorry, but you must trust me. Now, I need a shower,' and with that, she turned to go into the bedroom.

'We do trust you,' Thomas said. 'and I think we could all do with a shower,' he smiled broadly at Lissa, 'and a meal. We'll leave Jem with you,' insisted Thomas, then to everyone, 'In the meantime, get some rest and food. We can meet tomorrow and plan what to do next.' There were some sighs, then nods. Jem left to have a shower and then quickly returned munching a steak sandwich.

'That was quick,' said Leo as he walked to the door.

'You gotta know the right people, I ordered it on the way in,' he laughed as the others left. With Remy in the bedroom, Jem settled on the settee.

Across the road, high on an empty building under renovation, a man dressed in black screwed in a rifle scope and swore as he realised he was too late as someone was closing the blinds. He sat down and opened a bottle of water, annoyed that he had been caught up in the early evening city traffic. He cursed his luck as he knew he had missed a perfect opportunity. He lit a cigarette. Maybe tomorrow, he'd have a chance to remove the men. He was being paid a lot of money to dispose of them. As he settled, he thought he may now need to deal with the policewoman also.

His thoughts were distracted by a noise. He stubbed out his cigarette and crouched down lower as a security guard swept a brief light across another part of the roof. When it was gone, he pulled his bag closer. A breeze, caught a can and rolled it across the roof, sweeping it, the dust and debris into a corner, then all was still.

Remy looked at Jem and smiled. 'Thank you, you need not stay, I will be quite all right.'

Jem's face was stern. 'Thomas said stay, so I ain't moving, luv, and I'm sleeping on this settee.' Remy laughed. Jem wasn't sure why but it was his term "luv" that amused her; no one ever addressed her that way. She gave a slight shrug and went into the main bedroom in the suite and closed the door. She walked to the bathroom and was appalled at the image she saw in the mirror. She was grimy, her hair, usually so carefully arranged, had broken free of its clips. She stripped off her clothes. She wanted to scream, she hated the feeling of being out of control. However, she knew if she did, Jem would be there, so decided instead to shake the tension out of her body under a hot shower. As the water streamed over her body, she wondered what she really knew of the client. She was sure that this had nothing to do with him. As she lathered her hair, her thoughts turned to Andreas; just who was this man who she had known for years? She shivered as she dried herself. How could she have been so wrong about everything? Now they were all in danger and that was her fault.

She began to plan.

Tiana had arranged for Remy's luggage to be sent from Miami and it was now in the closets and drawers in the room. The shower had done its best but she was still uncharacteristically shaken. As she dried her hair, she considered what she should tell the others about Rafik and what she had learned. She tied her hair in a ponytail and dressed in pyjamas and a dressing gown, she went into the bedroom, checking the handbag for the new phone and cards Tiana had organised. She phoned her, first to thank her and then listened to the intel that had arrived. Some of this she had guessed but it was still difficult to form a complete picture; perhaps with the help of the others, it would all become clear.

She phoned Andreas but their conversation was stilted, and he told her he would meet her in London. She was disappointed. So much had happened and as a result, had changed her perspective on their relationship but she wanted to be with him when they talked, not over the phone. Next, she went into the lounge with a blanket and pillow from the closet.

She realised that it was now early evening and it was almost twenty-four hours since the men had given her and Andreas water and sandwiches, which she had hardly touched.

Addressing Jem, she said, 'I am hungry, are you?' He looked mortified at the thought he might have to share a meal with her; he didn't do fine dining. However, much to his delight, he heard her order him a T. Bone steak, two lots of French fries and beer. For herself, she ordered a Salad Niçoise, French fries, and a bottle of Chablis. She sat on the couch and caught up with her emails. He relaxed into a chair with a satisfied sigh.

When dinner arrived, they ate together in companionable silence. Jem was clearly hungry but left the beer. After the meal, Remy stood, and Jem, mid-bite, immediately did the same. Picking up the glass and bottle, she went into the bedroom calling "good night" as she went.

Jem smiled and replied, 'Sleep tight and don't let the bed bugs bite.' Remy laughed as she closed the bedroom door.

Jem finished his meal and pushed the couch over to the door. He grabbed the blanket and pillow and settled down with his iPad to watch the football with West Ham beating Manchester City. He did not sleep and neither did the man on the rooftop.

Leo caught up with Julia just as she was about to leave. She intended to go back to the station and complete some paperwork but Leo caught her arm and said, 'Hey, where you going? It would be good to have some quiet time to talk.' *He looks a little like a puppy dog*, Julia thought, *but I'm not falling for that!* As she turned to look at him, she could see something in his eyes that she had only seen in the early days of their relationship and it made her heart jump, just as it did then. *Oh God*, she thought, *here we go again.* He asked if she had eaten and she shook her head. He took her hand and they headed towards the main restaurant. They ordered and then there seemed to be an uneasy silence. *Maybe this was a mistake*, thought Julia.

Finally, Julia spoke, 'How have you been Leo, really?' This was clearly a loaded question as she knew only too well the problems he had when they were together.

He knew he should be honest, he owed her that. 'Good. All that's in the past. Look, I know you won't believe me, seeing as how things ended with us, but you did make a huge difference to me. I had a relapse I know, but after you left me and I went back to the UK, well, I sobered up.' He laughed. 'Dad saw to that,' remembering how much he owed his father. 'Then I met Thomas again. He had experience helping ex-army guys totally get off drugs and he helped me sort things out and put them into perspective.'

'I am so glad. It wasn't the right time for us. I know my job made it hard for me to be sympathetic but I just didn't know how to help you. It seems you're doing so well now though. Well done.' Having somewhat cleared the air, they finished their meal, chatting about their lives since they last met.

'You haven't married again?' Leo asked.

'No. You?'

It was clear to both that the chemistry between them was still strong and the air seemed electric.

Her words were whispered and she found herself saying, 'Shall we take this conversation upstairs?' He nodded.

He paid and then took her hand. Julia caught her breath; she knew that as much as he wanted her, she felt the same way. In the lift, he pulled her to him and kissed her; it was almost like he was asking her a gentle question. She smiled and gently touched his cheek; this was unlike the Leo of old and she kissed him back.

Reaching his room, he opened the door and she walked in past him. He suddenly felt uncharacteristically unsure. Was this wise? Hadn't they been here before? He stood perplexed. Julia had her doubts too but felt her body burning and walked towards the bedroom. Leo considered the implications so did not immediately follow. When he did, Julia was already naked, standing in the middle of the room. Leo stood in the doorway, his breath was taken away, as was his uncertainty. He had kept his feelings contained up till now but his erection on seeing her amazing body again was immediate.

As he undressed, she moved to the bed and he was soon running his fingers down her body as she arched her back and opened to him. Their bodies seemed to remember the positions and touches each enjoyed. Later, Leo went into the bathroom and she heard the shower running and laughed; she went in. He turned under the hot water, clearly ready for her as she joined him under the rainwater shower.

They weren't the only ones enjoying each other. Lissa drew in an ecstatic breath, as Thomas, lying behind her, slid his hand over her hip, pulling her onto him. He reached round to her stomach, then down till it reached her mound and played there to excite her further. She groaned as the orgasm started to pulsate through her body, and they came together.

Clearly exhausted, they all slept. Thomas woke as the dawn broke. He got out of bed and walked to the window to open the curtains.

Chapter 30

He was about to walk across to the bathroom when he felt rather than heard the huge window shake; it was followed by a loud bang and a neat hole appeared in it. He felt nothing initially but then touching his arm, he felt the blood. He dived down as a second shot passed his head and he heard Lissa scream. He turned; she was on the floor, face down beside the bed. Instinctively, he wanted to go to her but he knew he would be a target. He called but she didn't respond. He crawled to the window and pulled at the blind managing to drop it down the window, so he could get up and go over to where she lay still on the floor.

Turning her over, he could see no sign of a wound but a red mark on her forehead, thankfully there was no blood. Looking at the headboard, he could see where the bullets had ended, they had been lucky. As he held her, she sighed, and opened her eyes.

'Thank God,' he said and gently touched her forehead. 'I thought you'd been hit, but I think you might have caught your foot and hit your head on the bedside table and knocked yourself out.'

Her hand went to her head and she mouthed a silent ouch! 'You're bleeding,' she gasped, her eyes now wide and scared, as she tried to focus on what had just happened.

Shakily she got to her feet and went to the bathroom. Thomas stood up and grabbed his phone, dialled 000 and asked for the police. Lissa came back and using a damp towel inspected his arm; he had been fortunate also, as a bullet had only grazed his arm.

'Stay here, I have to warn the others, just don't go near the window. I doubt there will be another attempt, they will be long gone by now. I'll be quick.' He grabbed his shirt, wrapped it around the flesh wound on his arm and pulled on a dressing gown as he left the room.

Thomas knocked first on Leo's door and was greeted by a sleepy, abusive response but the door opened. Seeing blood, Leo was immediately awake and as

Thomas explained what had happened, he clearly understood the need for action. He called to Julia to keep the blind closed and grabbing a gown, followed Thomas to Remy's room on the other side of the building. Jem, freshly showered and clutching a bacon sandwich, answered the knock immediately and reassured them that all the blinds were closed. Hearing the voices, Remy appeared fully dressed from her room.

Listening, she calmly suggested that they should all get dressed and meet in her room as soon as possible.

'I agree,' said Leo.

They separated and within a short time, a fully dressed Julia knocked at Thomas' door and handed him a first aid box. 'How bad is it?' She asked.

'Nothing much, just a flesh wound, I was lucky!' He said wryly. Lissa took the kit and busied herself finding things to steri-strip Thomas' wound.

'I used my badge and spoke to the hotel. They will send someone to ensure the window is safe and a replacement ordered. A forensics crew will be here shortly, best you shift your stuff to Remy's room for the time being while we decide what to do next.' With that, she left. He had noted the use of the word "we" and smiled.

Having cleaned and dressed Thomas' wound, she helped to gather their things to move to Remy's room. Jem answered the door and saw the bump on Lissa's head.

'Shit, your mother will have a fucking fit' Which, when Remy saw it proved to be right. It was the first time Thomas had seen Remy anything but completely in control.

Across the road, Thomas was right. The man had rapidly gathered his belongings. He cursed, as he knew that he had wasted an opportunity. Looking around to ensure he had left nothing to identify him, in his haste to leave, however, he missed one of the stubs of the many cigarettes he had smoked last night. He left the roof and headed down to his car, which was parked on the access road at the back. He climbed back through the neat hole he had cut in the fence, so avoiding security at the entrance. As he loaded the gun into the boot, he could hear sirens approaching and knew he needed to be quick.

He got in and started the car; driving to the corner, and turned onto a side street, which then joined the main road. As he did so, a police car and PTG van turned in at the other end, just missing him.

The man focussed on driving normally, so as not to attract attention, and headed towards the airport. He ditched the car on a road near the Wolli Creek metro stop and got the metro to the Novotel, where he was staying. He had chosen this as it was near the airport and busy, which meant he could disappear in the crowd. He knew he would be contacted with information as to where the targets would be next; in the meantime, he needed a shower and food. Reaching his room, he stripped off and showered, then dressed in a business suit, he left to get some food.

In Remy's room after some frenzied and angry communication with the hotel management, things were finally settled and everyone had gathered together. She suggested that they should eat and despite Lissa's objections, almost immediately a knock at the door announced room service. Everyone was on high alert but Jem, with his foot ready and hand on his gun, opened the door. Plates of fruit, eggs, bacon, toast, and coffee were ferried into the room. The smells of bacon and eggs quashed any doubts and silenced them all as they focussed ravenously on the food. This included Jem, even though he had clearly already eaten.

Once they had finished, Remy said, 'Well, hopefully, you are all now more relaxed. I think it is time for you to know the reason why I think we are being chased.'

She said she knew they had already guessed it had something to do with Iran and the troubles there. She said she thought it was time to tell them what she had found out, been told, and had already known. She explained how Iran's Islamists had been waging a campaign against the country's indigenous culture for at least sixty years. They had worked relentlessly to erase all vestiges of it, or tried to incorporate it into a state-sponsored, political and ideological form of Islam, that was totally alien to Iran's traditional Shia Islam.

She explained that "The Assembly of Experts" were the powerful elite. Like the Vatican's College of Cardinals, and were seen as "virtuous and learned". They determined who could run for a seat in the assembly and they elected the Supreme Leader from within but it seemed after that, they either did not or could not challenge any of the Supreme Leader's decisions.

Saudi Arabia, Qatar, and others were concerned that Iran planned to convert Sunnis to Shi'ism. It seemed that many Arabs believed that Iranians were not real Muslims as they had never fully converted to Islam. They suggest Shi'ism was nothing more than their old religion with a thin guise of Islam. Some believed that the Iranians aimed to subvert and undermine true and pure Islam.

It was whispered that if Iranians were non-Muslims, then Islam's edict that Muslims should not fight other Muslims did not apply, which would have considerable political ramifications. For example, it could help the Saudis enlist other Muslims in their fight against Iran.

Remy paused, then said, 'However, it is still unclear to me exactly who is orchestrating the attacks and which side they represent, or even if some other force is engaged.'

She went on, to explain that each faction might want the regalia to push for their cause. This could lead to catastrophic events, such as a revolution, to bring about change. However, others may seek the regalia to destroy it to stop this happening. Information she had received did not indicate which faction had which belief or tell her their intent, or even which, if any party, or person she knew, was involved. She had not yet included the extended family of the previous, exiled Shah. There were some suggestions that it could be a move by them to re-establish the royal family.

She suggested that if someone had the royal regalia, then perhaps they could act as a figurehead for their cause, or perhaps someone else's ambitions. The last possibility to consider was that this was simply an attempt to steal the jewels, as had happened in the past. Did someone want them purely to break them up?

Thomas said, 'Yes, it is as we surmised: money, power or altruism; it doesn't matter which of these three, we are dealing with, or even if it is all of them. Whoever they are, they are playing a very devious and dangerous game.'

Remy looked weary. 'Yes, you are right. Suffice it to say, none of this was made clear to me when I agreed to the client's request. I also need to tell you that I am concerned, as I have repeatedly tried to contact them, and have not yet managed to do so. Since it is now clearly an extremely dangerous situation,' she stroked Lissa's cheek, 'it is also possible they are not safe either. Before you ask, I have been in touch with and gained the support of various agencies, thanks to Andreas. I have spoken to the intelligence agencies in New York and London, and they will investigate the client's whereabouts and safety.'

'For the moment, because of political ramifications, they do not intend to become openly involved. They are content to watch, so as not to escalate the situation. To outsiders, we are still just working for a client to complete a job.

Thanks to the change of cases in Los Angeles, we now have three pieces safely locked away.'

Finally, she drew a breath. 'What I have been told is that a contract was issued by someone in Iran to kill both Thomas and Leo, arrange for the capture of both Alessia and me, and secure the regalia. We have so far thwarted their attempts but I doubt that we have seen the last of these attempts to stop us.'

Everyone was silent, as they contemplated all that Remy had just said. Then Lissa broke the silence. 'Wait, I think I might have found something that might be useful,' she exclaimed and went to her backpack. From a folder, she produced the tiny black and white photo of a small boy, dated September 1971, which she had found in the clasp. Turning it over, she showed Remy the name, Darius, son of Shahtiar Shafiq. The man who they knew had been assassinated by agents of the Islamic Republic.

Remy drew in a sharp breath. She thought this would make Darius about the same age as Andreas. Could this boy be the man she knew as her client? He would certainly be about the right age, but why was he using a different name? She tried to match features but she couldn't be sure.

Although he knew they should pass the picture onto the intelligence services, Thomas was exasperated and said, 'Remy, I believe we must go on the offensive, and to do this we need Andreas to be more upfront with information. If he had been, maybe we would have been more prepared.' Thomas was clearly angry. Partly due to the lack of clarity but also because he felt that the situation was being taken out of their hands and he was worried about this; after all, they were the ones literally in the firing line. Remy nodded.

'Tell him about the photo but only give it to him if they are willing to be more open with us.' Exasperated, he had clearly decided to take control. A small smile crossed Remy's face. Standing up, he suggested that he, Lissa and Jem should work to find the clasp stone, while Leo and his team located and neutralised the gunman.

Julia nodded. 'But I should go with Leo, as it would be better if this person was not killed, unless unavoidably, of course. With me there, it would be easier to argue an "unintended" kill.' She glanced at Leo, who smiled broadly.

Remy said, 'I think it would be better for everyone that I go back to London. I can ensure that all is ready there. Please stay safe,' she said as she hugged Lissa, as people started to move away.

Thomas smiled for the first time, 'Immigration has agreed to your departure and two of our team based out here will escort you to the airport and ensure you get to the Qantas flight safely. Parsons and Tyrone will meet you in London, they have delivered the fourth box.' Thomas' tone was adamant. Remy just nodded.

'Again, I do not think there is any need to worry,' she said enigmatically. and stroked Thomas' cheek, 'if I am right, I will be exactly where he will want me. It isn't me he is trying to kill.' Thomas was beginning to put pieces in place but said nothing. There was clearly a lot more than she had told them, including who was trying to kill them both. 'Take care of my daughter,' she said and gently kissed his cheek. Was there a look of sadness in her eyes, he wondered?

Thomas whispered in her ear, 'You know who it is, don't you?'

She said nothing but he was sure that she gave the briefest of nods, then walked to the door where the men were waiting.

Chapter 31

Once Remy had left, everyone felt a sudden need to do something. Leo beamed at Julia. 'Just like old times,' he said.

'I hope not,' she replied laughing. 'I seem to remember things differently. Let's see if we can find out where the sniper took his pot shot at Thomas from; bet he was pissed he missed. He'll have gone to ground now but may have left some clues to his identity. I alerted HQ and once we find the site, and any evidence, the forensic guys will put it at the top of their list.' Her phone rang. It appeared that the hotel was still arguing over which insurance company was liable for the bloody great hole in their window. Julia suggested they contact Chief Carmichael to sort it out. She hoped that she would be out of his way when he got the call.

Julia, heading for the door, called, 'See you later, Thomas. Remember, you are a guest in Australia, so take care, keep it legal.' She grabbed Leo's hand and pulled him up.

'Take care, everyone.' Thomas thought Leo looked more relaxed than he had seen him for a while but also remarkably focussed. Julia was obviously good for him. *Long may it last,* he thought.

Outside their hotel, they stood and looked at the buildings that faced Thomas' room. From the evidence she had put together in his room, Julia had already calculated roughly where she felt the most likely location for the shooter would be. Crossing the road, she showed her badge to the site security at the gate of the building being restored. The man called his boss, who arrived; once he understood, he handed them hard hats and pointed to the stairs.

'I think we should try either the top floor or the roof,' she said over her shoulder to Leo, who was climbing the stairs behind her. Reaching the top floor, they split up to cover the rooms on the side of the building facing their hotel. Returning, they both shook their heads and went back to the stairs. The door to the roof was unlocked. As they opened the door, they stopped, noting the clear indications in the dust-covered roof of footsteps and a disturbed area where someone had recently lain against the small wall facing the hotel.

'This'll be it,' she said, and they started a careful search of the area. Leo moved along the wall and called out. 'Someone has been careless,' he said, holding out his hand. He was holding a cigarette butt in the centre of a tissue.

'Well done. Let's hope it has some DNA on it. There's nothing else here. Let's get back to the station and get this to the lab.' With that, they left the building. Leo was watchful as they left the site and crossed the road. They walked down to the garage, got into Julia's car, and headed for the exit. As they turned out onto the main road, Leo saw a grey hatchback, which appeared to follow them.

'Change lanes,' he said, and Julia immediately did so without question, squeezing through a small space. 'Can you make a sharp turn up ahead where the traffic slows? I want to try and get a look at this guy.' As she did, Leo got a glimpse of a man he thought he had seen before.

'I think that is the guy who was in the carpark when we got back yesterday. He was parked opposite us and was unloading something. Nothing strange then but Thomas hadn't been shot. The man just nodded and turned away; I didn't think any more of it.'

'Think what was he unloading, what did it look like?'

'I think it was a suitcase, I didn't pay much attention.'

'I had better get our bomb squad to look, just to be on the safe side. Remember Remy said that she thought that maybe more than one group might be involved in trying to stop us.' Julia made the call to central control and immediate orders were issued to investigate. As they drove into the station, news was coming in that a suspicious device had been found under one of the team's cars. Taped to the underside was a phone that was linked to an already primed detonator, but the wiring wasn't connected, so maybe the bomber had been disturbed.

Later speaking to the tech officer, he said, 'If it had been activated, the bomb squad determined that any explosion would have blown the boot open at the very least, but it had the potential to ignite the petrol tank. By the way, we found this lodged in the device.' He held up an evidence bag and inside was a small silver lighter with "Love ♥ NY" inscribed on it.

Leo's face showed nothing, but like Thomas, he was beginning to put pieces together.

'It could be we have two groups here, one prepared to set a device; another, trying to shoot us. Happy days!!' Leo said with a wry smile.'

'So, who set it? Was it the man who tried to take out Thomas, or was it someone else? There are still way too many variables for my liking,' Julia mused.

They took the cigarette butt to a team member, who headed for the forensics lab, saying they would ensure testing was expedited. In the meantime, despite Remy's concerns, Leo put in a call to Wes at the FBI.

Wes had already made the Iranian connection and had a good idea of what was going on. In fact, he had just been in contact with the task force that Andreas was working with. Leo presumed that all the security services were now linked, and thought about phoning to update his father, but would lay bets that the old man would already know. Anyway, he wanted to hold back telling him that he was working with Julia; he didn't want to give the old man a heart attack.

Wes remembered, 'By the way, Thomas asked me about the death of Farzad Akbari. Well, nothing on the report seemed to suggest any real concerns, although it appeared the fire burned extremely hot. As a result of the rapid action of the fire crew, some small things were saved or there would have been nothing left. He mentioned a lighter. Well, that got me thinking and I did some research. Did it have anything inscribed on it?'

'Yes, Thomas said that it had "Love ♥ NY".'

'Well, I'm pretty certain that Akbari's death was no accident. This is the calling card of a serial bomber and arsonist; we have been trying to catch him for years. I'll do some more digging and get back to you.'

Leo drew in a sharp breath. He was right, there were two different people trying to kill them. He phoned Thomas but said nothing to Julia when she returned with some sandwiches and coffee. 'I have updated my boss, and unsurprisingly, he said something about how he would be glad when you all left. I have some leave and I asked him if I could use this to go with you to London.' Leo pulled a face, half grimace and half laughing. She hit him. 'You can't leave me out now.' She smiled and he pulled her to him and kissed her.

Leo munched his sandwich; secretly he had hoped she would want to come with him.

'I'll go and see if there's any news from forensics.' When she returned, she had the results from the cigarette butt. It had been run through Interpol's DNA database. This showed that the shooter was an Iranian man called Imram Karimi, known by his pseudonym, "The Arrow". The report added that he was a known assassin, who had been linked to a number of high level kills, but never caught.

There were no suggestions that he was a bomb maker. This confirmed Leo's conclusion that this was the man Wes had mentioned.

'Fuck, now we've got two murderous bastards chasing us and both are clearly very dangerous.' Reading the notes, it was clear there were no useful pictures. The only one was marked "presumed" sniper and that was blurred and side face.

'I don't think it was the man in the garage,' said Leo as Julia came back. 'The description says they believed the sniper was a tall, youngish man, the one in the garage was neither.'

'Well, we have a name for one, the sniper, now all we have to do is catch both him and the bombmaker,' grinned Julia, looking at the picture. Without warning, Leo stood up, held a finger to his lips, and put his phone on the desk, indicating she should do the same. She took it out of her pocket and placed it next to his. Then he grabbed Julia's hand and with one look at his face, she just followed him out of the building.

'What's up? Do you think we're being bugged? I don't believe anyone in my...' Leo interrupted her.

'I don't know, it's just a feeling, and we need to be more careful anyway. It could be a bug or the phone. I know Thomas had said there was an unusual clicking sound on his phone. Better to be cautious, as I think I have a plan,' Leo said with a grin. 'You won't like it and it is dangerous, but we need to get the sniper before he has another chance to catch us unawares. Who is the best long gun on your SRG?'

'Easy, Jake Russell, he was in special forces. Why?' But he knew she wouldn't like the answer.

'We need him to work out the best position for a long gun. I need him to base this on using me as the target.'

'What! Leo, are you mad? You must be kidding me.'

'Hear me out. So, I was thinking, reverse engineering. If we know where the shooter will be to take a shot, we just have to ensure that we lure him there. When he aims to take his shot, Jake can take him out, you can act as cover, should he be too slow.' He laughed as she punched him. 'With the gunman out of the way, we might be able to lure out whoever is organising this; but anyway, at least one threat will have been dealt with.'

'That's a fucking stupid plan, so much could go wrong,' she snapped, clearly concerned.

'Not if we plan it carefully. We already know that somehow he is aware of our plans, we just have to use whoever it is collaborating to feed them the information so that he turns up at the right place. You choose the location, somewhere we know that is suitable, so we can scope out every bit of the layout. Look, just speak to this guy and we will see what he says. But we need to get on as quickly as possible before we run out of luck.'

Julia knew that she would not convince him that the idea was impossible but felt sure that Jake would say the idea was ridiculous, so she reluctantly agreed to speak to him.

They went back inside, got their phones, and talked about going to lunch. Back outside, they drove to the SRG base. Jake was on a callout but they left a message to meet them at the MCA Café on George Street later that afternoon. It was after three pm when he arrived and listened intently to Leo's plan. His immediate reaction wasn't good. First off, he was not willing to kill the man, which had been Leo's ideal scenario. He said he would wing him, so Julia could arrest him. They talked about possible locations and he said he knew of a couple of possible places that he could go and scope out. He was clearly sceptical but having listened carefully to the problem they faced, he was willing to think about it.

Julia hoped that when they next spoke, he would say it was not possible. As Jake left, she sat down next to Leo. 'We'll go with what he says, right?' Leo kissed her but said nothing.

After that first meeting, Jake Russell had given Leo's plan further consideration. Much to Julia's surprise, he suggested a couple of changes but agreed to do it. They met again the next day to agree on the location Jake had selected. Having decided, they needed to ensure the message got out to the sniper.

Leo said, 'We need to spin a believable story to get the shooter to follow us.'

'I think we should make it known that we've had a call from someone who has information about the location of the stone and that they want to meet.'

'Sounds a bit of an obvious one to me, we don't want to make him suspicious.'

'What if we get someone to phone in an anonymous tip, saying they have some information about where the woman with the stone can be found.'

He grinned at her. 'That would work if we had someone with a Russian accent to do it, as they are clearly involved in this somewhere. Which reminds me, did you buy Remy's story about the Russian drugs gang?'

'No, I didn't and *net, no ya govoryu dostatochno, chtoby oboytis*, which loosely means, I can speak enough to get by. Don't look so surprised, Leo, my mother came from a town near the border with Finland,' as Leo looked quizzical. 'You have probably forgotten my last name was Savenkov.' He was surprised, as he suddenly realised that she was still using her married name, Tremaine.

As they worked out exactly what she should say, he smiled as he watched her as she wrote out a couple of lines. She looked up, 'what?'

'Nothing,' he kissed her and she laughed.

They decided a public phone was safer as it wouldn't be traced to them.

Getting up, pulling her cap down further to cover her face and putting on a jacket she'd grabbed from the back of a chair on her way out, she said, 'I won't be long.' After she had made the call, she came back giggling. 'My mother would be furious if she had heard my broken Russian accent.' She left the jacket on the ground by the chair and shook her hair from beneath the cap.

'Even if Jake doesn't come through, we might still be able to use it to pin down how, or who is leaking the info,' said Leo.

'Come on, we can talk that idea through but we better get back, we don't want to arouse attention just yet.' Julia got to her feet and they headed back to the station.

Chapter 32

After the device had been examined more closely, Thomas spoke to the bomb disposal people. They confirmed that the explosive charge although small, could have ignited the petrol tank, causing a much larger explosion. He thanked them, but was perplexed. Who had planted it? It seemed likely that the man Wes had spoken about was working alone. He recalled what he already knew about Remy's husband's death and thought it was highly unlikely that someone from or connected with those in the factory was the bomb maker.

Clearly, someone was watching them and feeding back intel about their movements. He did not know that he had come to the same conclusion as Leo.

Thomas was getting out of the lift when his phone rang. It was Andreas, who told him the team had looked at the hotel's surveillance system and although it picked up the grey car, there seemed to be nothing suspicious. There had been a lot of activity, so this could easily have masked someone moving between the cars, which possibly spooked him, so the device was primed but not set. He said they suspected the bomber either knew the shooter's plan or was receiving information from someone close to the team who did.

'Take care, it sounds like you've stirred up a real hornets' nest.' Thomas had to agree.

Meanwhile, Lissa, in the room she now shared with Thomas, was considering how Darius Shafiq might be involved and wondered whether he was still alive. She thought that either he was the one who had the ruby or knew where it was. Having contacted the Iranian paper, the *Khabar*, she was still waiting to hear back from them. Her mother hadn't contacted her yet either but that could just be the time difference. It was frustrating, not being able to be more proactive, but she knew they needed to ensure that the information they got would not lead them away from the truth.

When he returned, Thomas was preoccupied. The issue of Leo and his plan was firmly foremost in his mind, so he didn't initially speak to Lissa, who was also clearly deep in thought. He went to the fridge and grabbed a beer. While furious with Leo, he had finally agreed to meet him and listen to what he had to say. But he told him he did not agree with the idea and wanted to talk it over further. Leo said there wasn't time and that Julia had already made the call, and put down the phone. 'Fuck!' was all Thomas managed. Clearly furious, and frustrated, he paced the room. When he finally sat down, he told Lissa the plan. She agreed and said that without more information about the attack at the motel, they would not have time to build the idea.

Her phone rang, it was a reporter from the paper; however, the caller was quite curt and said they were unable to help. It was very clear either this person was afraid or had been told not to say anything. As she closed the call, she stopped as she heard a click and a buzz. She was aware Thomas had thought their phones were being monitored and she could imagine the reporter was probably being monitored too.

Within minutes, her phone rang again. She saw it was a different number.

'If you want the information, come alone, ten minutes, wait in the lobby.' The phone went dead. It was the same voice. This time, there was no click at the end. Lissa wondered what to do. Thomas was on the phone again. Clearly, he was talking to Leo and rather than interrupt him, she decided to do as the caller had said. So, she leant over, kissed him, and said she was going to speak to reception. He nodded without turning and she headed down in the lift. Who or what would be waiting for she didn't know. The receptionist saw her and called her over. 'This came for you.' She handed Lissa an envelope.

Lissa opened it. Inside was a typed letter.

My name is Darius Shafiq. I went to your mother and asked her to gather the pieces of the regalia. My intention was, and still is, to use these to help save my country. If we cannot stop the radicals and fundamentalists, there will be a war like no other.

You know that your friends and I are being hunted. I must speak with you.

Please, in one hour, be at the disused factory where you met Bizhan. You must come alone as the men are the target and you will be able to slip away unnoticed.

In case we do not meet, you must remember: HARIAH

Destroy this note. Trust no one.

Lissa checked her watch, 11 am. She went back to the receptionist and asked for the use of a shredder. The woman held her hand out. 'Sorry, can I do it myself please? It's really important.'

The woman shrugged and showed Lissa to the shredder.

Back in the lift, she began to plan but needn't have worried, as when she arrived at the room, Thomas was still focussed on the hair-brained scheme Leo had in mind, and heading for the door, he said he needed to speak to him again in person. He told her to lock and bolt the door and that Jem would be back soon having ensured Remy's safe arrival at the airport.

She nodded, said goodbye, kissed him and then settled down in front of the TV.

Having given Thomas a few minutes, she grabbed her bag and slipped out, using the stairs to go down to the lobby, keeping a careful lookout as she descended. Once outside, she walked two blocks before hailing a cab. She laughed. When did she get to be so cautious she asked herself. She gave the driver the address and he looked around as if concerned. 'It's okay, I am their social worker.' He shrugged and seemed to accept that. She got in, laughing to herself as she turned off her phone. Too many spy movies!

She arrived at 11.40, paid for the taxi, and walked around to the back entrance they had used before. Remembering the setup of the building, she pushed open the door. Climbing the first few steps, she was surprised to find the room was completely empty but full of rubbish. She carried on up the stairs, and here too, all the tents had gone and only remnants of the "houses" that had been pulled down were left. She had not expected them to have left so quickly. She headed over to the office. Nothing. All the equipment had gone, just the chairs and desk remained. She was still early, so decided the office was a good place to wait and hide if necessary.

Looking out of the grimy window, she could see the courtyard and the gate, but the door was hidden by a flat roof that ran around the building above the lower floor.

As she was deciding what to do, a car pulled up and three men got out. One of them seemed to be in charge, she couldn't see him properly, as his hat was pulled down, but there was something about him that looked familiar. They came towards the door and then she could hear them on the stairs. She panicked and pushed the door to the office but it wouldn't close all the way, so she hid under the table.

It was clear the men were nearby and then someone shouted something in Arabic. As she pulled back further under the table, she heard running, banging, and then a man's scream.

Then a man shouted a curse and there were the sounds of a scuffle. *The next voice,* she thought, *sounded familiar.*

'You scum, do you really think that bringing back a Shah will cure everything? You are wrong. Like me, they are after only one thing, money, because that is where the power is. These religious fanatics will not loosen their grip and will destroy you and all your treasures. Why? For the same things, money and power. Tell me where it is and give me the special word that will unite them and I will release you.'

Someone shouted, '*Allah Akbar.*' Then there was a cacophony of sounds; laughter, a gunshot, followed by a deep silence, which was broken only by the sound of people moving away across the room and out onto the stairs. Lissa waited. Finally, she crawled out from under the table, she could hear no one, but keeping low, she looked over the window ledge and saw the three men leaving. When she was sure they had gone and no one else was around, she opened the door. There was a body lying on the floor. She raced over to it. It was Bizhan and he was dead.

Lissa sat, uncertain of what to do. Her thoughts were abruptly broken by the realisation that she could smell smoke and it was beginning to sting her eyes. She got up and ran over to the stairs but was taken aback, as already there were flames blocking the exit.

She could smell petrol.

She knew the fire would spread quickly, the doors to each floor had been removed, so it wouldn't be long before the rubbish left by the refugees and the old dry wooden floor timbers caught light, and the draft would bring the flames up through the building; she needed to find a way out and quickly, or she would be trapped. She looked out of the window and while she realised opening a window might increase the flames and spread the fire more rapidly, but this was clearly her only way of escape. With the smoke stinging her eyes, she knew she didn't have much time.

The windows opened inwards and she pulled at the first one, but it was stuck fast and so was the second and the third. The fourth opened a bit and she used all her strength to make it budge further. Finally, with a creak, it opened wide enough for her to fit through. She got a chair from the office and stepping on it, she climbed up and out of the window, dropping down onto the roof below. She stepped out gingerly onto the rusty corrugated iron roof. Sticking close to the wall, she edged herself slowly along the building, aware of the sound of the fire getting closer. She moved as quickly as she could. At times, her foot slipped, threatening to slide her down the roof and crash to the ground. She stopped to regain control. Taking a deep breath, she looked up, almost there, she thought taking another step. But then she realised that she was confronted by a large hole in the roof. She was still too far off the ground to jump and there was rubbish below that could be more dangerous than the fall. She was really scared now, as going over it was out of the question, it was too big to step over and the roof too rusty to risk a jump. She had no alternative, so she sat down and inched her way along the edge nearest the wall, almost holding her breath. A rusty nail caught her trousers and bit into her leg, but despite the pain, she edged further along. By now, she could hear and feel the heat of the flames behind her and she worried that the windows might explode outwards; she moved as fast but as carefully as she could.

As she reached the end, she realised she was above the steps and the doorway but she was too high to jump down, There was a drainage pipe, which on testing it, she thought would hold her and she edged off the roof onto it, sort of sliding and slipping into a heap on the stairs.

Getting up dirty, scratched and scared, she moved quickly away from the building. Turning back, she looked up at it, seeing it was now well alight. She limped shakily over to the gate, wondering how she would get back to the hotel, to find Jem leaning on a car by the front gate.

'Next time, take the battery out!' He hissed as she looked quizzical. 'Of your phone. I tracked you! It's our business remember; ask Thomas sometime, when he's not furious with you! I take it he didn't know you were coming here.' She shook her head.

'How long? 'She asked.

'Have I been here? Long enough to see you pretend you were in a Bond movie.'

'You didn't think to help?'

'Nah, you were doing fine. I would 'ave but you didn't need it, you did well.'

'Will you tell him?'

Jem shook his head. 'Don't need to, he already knows, he was 'ere. He ain't happy…so watch out, Lissa.'

'Oh God! Where is he?'

'Following Rafik.'

'Rafik! My mother's friend. Yes, of course, I thought I knew him. That means he is part of this. He killed Bizhan.'

'Let's go. I phoned the police and fire brigade; we don't want to be here when they arrive.' Lissa got into the car; she was now shaking uncontrollably as the enormity of what she'd been through hit. As they left, she watched as part of the factory collapsed in the raging fire.

'You're bleeding,' Jem said, pointing to a first aid kit on the back seat. 'I'd make the most of that when you see him.' Jem laughed. Then his smile softened. 'You're okay,' he said gently touching her arm. 'It's the adrenalin, the shakes will pass,' and handed her an energy drink. 'This'll take the edge off.' He put the car in drive.

Chapter 33

Thomas had arrived back at the hotel to find Lissa had gone. Checking in with Jem, he said he hadn't seen her. Thomas cursed and phoned Julia and asked her to locate Lissa's phone. Calling back, she told him that it appeared her phone was en route to the factory that they had already been to.

'Thomas, you also need to know that we have a confirmed identification for Rafik Yazdi, I have sent you a picture.'

'Shit! That's him. Why didn't Remy just tell us he was after us, I am sure she has known for some time. No wonder she disappeared off to London!'

Thomas was now furious with both Remy and her daughter. Turning to Jem, he put that to one side and said, 'We need to get after her.'

In the lift, Jem thought about the team that had met together in London at the start, Cooper was in hospital, Spider was dead, and two others were now on their way to the UK. He needed to shuffle people around. He picked up his mobile. 'Leo, can you get Patch and Lori out to the coordinates I'm sending, Lissa's gone missing and the boss is spitting feathers.' These guys were now based in Australia but were part of the original team who he had worked with a few times, so knew they could be trusted.

They headed down to the carpark and using Jem's skills as a driver, always careful not to alert local cops, they arrived within sight of the factory, where Patch and Lori met them.

'A SUV with a driver is parked way over there and three men got out and went through the gate about ten minutes ago. Boss, I think one of them might have been the guy whose picture Jem sent us.' As he spoke, the three reappeared and got into their vehicle. At least, she was not with them, Thomas thought with a sigh, as the car moved off.

'Lissa's signal is still here and moving, boss.'

'Okay, Jem, you stay with her. I don't think I can speak to her right now.' As he spoke, the SUV with Rafik, Mahmoud, and two men turned up the road away from them. Thomas got into the car with Patch and Lori.

'All okay, boss?' One of the men said, but seeing Thomas' face, he didn't expect an answer, neither did he catch what Thomas muttered under his breath, as the car headed off, but he could well imagine. As his car moved away, Thomas did not see the smoke.

While Jem was taking Lissa back to the hotel, Thomas' car followed the SUV at a discrete distance. It headed out of the Weatherill Park Industrial Zone, along the A28 heading northeast, then picked up the M4 heading for the harbour bridge. Patch, the driver, was careful, never to get too close. He would sometimes overtake them, then let them overtake, while one or both men would lay flat out of sight. Eventually, the SUV turned onto the road towards Manly and then down a side road towards another industrial estate.

Thomas signalled to stop the car, as the SUV had stopped by an entranceway further ahead. A man got out and removed the barrier that closed the road. The SUV went in, and he put the board back, then got in, and it moved off up the road.

Thomas turned to Patch. 'You stay with the car.' Thomas and Lori got out. The area around the road was wooded. They crossed the road and headed down the side of a building. At the bottom, they then climbed over the low fence and headed into the wooded area, parallel to the road. Thomas could see the SUV; it had stopped up ahead. Two of Rafik's men were heading for the door of the largest building, while one remained outside.

Thomas whispered to Lori, 'Go around the side of the building to the back and just keep watch, I don't want to lose them sneaking out that way. Click the radio once if you see them, if not, wait till I call you.'

Lori nodded and set off through the trees. Thomas could clearly see the man at the front, so needed to be careful. He kept low as he headed through the trees towards the building. As he got closer, the trees gave way to bushes, so he had to virtually crawl to get near to where the SUV was parked. He used it to shield his approach and when he thought the man was more interested in his phone, he moved across the path behind it. Thomas was now close enough to jump the guy from the side, which he did easily, taking him down with a kick to the knee and then using the gun butt to ensure his silence. Thomas caught him as he fell and pulled him into the bushes, securing his hands and feet with zip-ties and gaffer tape across his mouth.

He stayed still for a minute to ensure no one came out, then moved to the door and crouching low looked through the window. The hall was empty, so he quietly opened the door and slipped inside. He stayed close to the wall in the shadows, which provided him with good cover as the main corridor was unlit. The only light was coming from an open office door at the end of the corridor. He heard raised voices and cautiously headed towards them. The door to the last room was open and the voices were coming from inside. Thomas' Arabic was basic, so he couldn't decipher exactly what was being said but by the tone, the man speaking was clearly furious.

Thomas crossed the corridor to an adjacent room, with an open door and slipped inside. This enabled him to see part of the office across from him. The two guys sitting on tables faced into the room, and were watching a third man, who he assumed was Rafik, shouting in English at someone tied to a chair.

'Where is he, old man? What has he done with the stone?' He hit the seated man across the face but he did not answer. It was clear to Thomas that he had been hit several times. Rafik hit him again and this time, the old man laughed and spat back at him.

'If you think this is bad,' Rafik declared, 'wait until the SAVAK catch up with you, and it won't just be you who suffers; you know they will eventually kill you, your family and your friends. Look, it is simple, tell me where Darius is and...' Rafik's phone buzzed and he tossed it to one of the seated men. '*Vozmite* (take it).' He spoke in Russian. *Mesto, gde mozhno nayti kamen.* "Place where you can find stone," the man said.

'Too late,' laughing, Rafik said to the man tied to the chair. 'You could have died quickly but now, I will leave you to face retribution for your treachery!' He turned, as Thomas pulled back into the darkness of the room, and told the one with the phone to call the number he gave him and then wait until someone came to collect the *kafir*. Then he left the room.

Thomas pulled further back into the shadows as Rafik and two men passed the room he was in, then watched as he entered another further up the corridor, the door slowly swinging shut. Thomas was unsure of the number of people in the building and knowing that the odds of being discovered were high, decided it was time to leave and get back to the cover of the trees. Clearly, there was nothing he could do right now for the old man in the chair. One of the men on the table got up but did not turn, then moved out of sight into the room. Thomas held his breath, sinking back into the shadows.

Putting all his training into action, he crept noiselessly past the occupied rooms, then moved quickly and quietly out of the building and back into the relative safety of the bushes; he clicked the radio. After a short while, the shape of a man emerged from the shadows. Lori said he had seen four men in the back room, plus the man in the chair and one in another room downstairs, but upstairs was clear.

As Thomas was explaining what they needed to do, Rafik and three others stood in the doorway. One called out for the guy that Thomas had taken out and when no one answered, he headed around the building. He came back and shrugged but no one seemed concerned, as Rafik gave orders and then got into the SUV. Someone went back inside, then returned, with two others and they got into the car, which reversed and then headed back down the road.

By Thomas' calculation, that left a guard and the old man tied to the chair inside. When he were sure it was safe, Thomas told Lori to keep watch outside and untie the unconscious man, then he re-entered the building, gun at the ready and headed for the end room. Through the door, he could see that the man who had been sitting on the table was still there, earbuds in and phone in hand. He did not hear or see Thomas before he was quickly taken out.

The man in the chair had clearly been badly beaten and appeared to have been tortured. He was unconscious and his head slumped on his chest. Thomas felt for a pulse and was relieved to find a faint one. He untied the man. On the floor was a bottle of water and he used some on his hand to swish across the old man's face. He didn't open his eyes, just faintly whispered, '*Maa*.'

Thomas knew *Maa* was Arabic for water. The man's eyes fluttered open and he raised his head, so Thomas could help him to drink. As he was untied, he almost collapsed forward onto the floor.

'*Shukran*, thank you,' then in a hoarse voice he said, 'I speak English.' At this point, he fainted.

Thomas knew they needed to move and shouted to Lori to get the driver to turn the car around. He carried the old man to the entrance and propped him up.

Thomas phoned Julia and gave her their location, the licence plate of the car and the tracker code. She said an ambulance would be with them shortly.

Thomas used more water to gently bring the man around again.

'What's your name?'

'That's not important, I am a friend of Darius Shafiq,' he whispered.

'Where is he? We have been looking for him. I think it was him we were supposed to meet today.'

'I am sorry. It was too dangerous for him here; he has gone to London. He said you must protect the woman, your friend, and her daughter. He will not stop and he will use them to get what he wants.' He had used up his strength and fainted again, just as they heard the sound of an ambulance and police sirens.

Lori had returned and Thomas told him to stay, 'I think they will want to speak to him.' He said pointing to the old man. He wanted to leave before the ambulance and police arrived. He had put a tracker on Rafik's car, so he knew they should have no problem locating them, but the old man was conscious again. 'Lori will stay with you, he will keep you safe.' Thomas whispered, 'If I can, I will come and see you and we can talk further. Until then, keep quiet.' The man nodded, then closed his eyes again.

Chapter 34

Arriving back at the hotel, Lissa and Jem met up with Leo and Julia in the bar.

'Oh boy, you're in deep shit, lady,' sniggered Julia. 'I've spoken to Thomas and he told me what you did. To say he was angry is an understatement.' She was clearly serious, ' Listen, they are trained for this, and so am I, you, however, are not, so stop playing spy.'

As they sat down Jem whispered, 'I didn't even tell her about the roof, 'spect you want me to keep that bit quiet when Thomas gets back.' he laughed.

'That would be great if you could please,' she said duly chastened.

'So, how did you get yourself involved in such a stupid and dangerous episode?' Leo said obviously angry.

Thinking quickly, she blurted out, 'I got a text to say Bizhan had something he wanted to give me. I knew where the factory was and I thought since I had been there, there seemed to be no problem.' She paused, still developing her story. 'You were all so busy, I thought I could help, and well, (sniffle) it might have been important.' She added a small sob and picked up her tissues, dabbing her eyes for effect. She heard Julia "huff", this sort of feminine behaviour made her choke.

'I'm sorry, so what happened?' Leo said, falling for it.

'When I got there, I just waited and when I saw the men arrive, I hid in the office. They sort of stood quietly in the middle of the floor and then Bizhan appeared. Rafik spoke quietly at first, then when he asked him to tell him where the stone was, he got angry and grabbed Bizhan. He asked him for the "word" but Bizhan refused and so Rafik shot him. I waited till they left, that's all.' She didn't tell him about the roof. She had not forgotten about Darius' note or the word "HARIAH", but as her mind was so filled with what had happened to her and what she had seen, it was the last thing on her mind. She sat back, dabbing at her eyes, this time for real.

'You didn't see Darius then?'

'No, no one else was there. I think maybe Bizhan was going to take me to him.'

Leo had been in contact with Thomas, who was also now aware that Rafik was clearly the most significant person of interest, but they were still unsure what his motive was. Leo thought that this was most likely money. He remembered Thomas saying that Remy had suggested money and power were important to him. Motive aside for the moment, he was just relieved to know that Thomas, Patch and Lori were okay and now following Rafik at a safe distance.

Julia relayed a message from her boss instructing her to go into the station. He wanted to know what was going on. Obviously with a device being found and a shooting, he was keen to hear the truth and their intentions. Leo thought the best thing was to contact Andreas. He knew that Wes and an MI5 operative were now liaising through the NATO task force, so it was now imperative that they should also fill in the Australian authorities. Andreas told him that this had been discussed at a government level and they would keep their story to "stolen jewellery" and an "international smuggling gang".

Chief Inspector Carmichael had been told this and he gave Leo a contact number for a secure line and told him that they should use this for any further communication, which he passed on to Thomas.

Leo wanted to speak to Wes to thank him for his help and use the secure line. Wes answered but seemed somewhat hurried. 'I am sorry not to have been more useful,' he said, 'but I am dealing with a situation here that we think might be connected. It's been clear for some time that a network of people, American citizens as well as Iranians and other Arab nationals, were spying in the US and on bases in the Middle East. Up until now, we haven't been able to put all the information together. This Rafik character could be the link we need. We know he was active a few years back and it appears that Madam Akbari's husband may have discovered something, which possibly got him killed. I will let you know if I get any more information.' He wished them good luck and rang off.

Leo remembered that Thomas had suspected there was something suspicious about Remy's husband's death, maybe he had been right. Until he heard more about this, he decided to keep it to himself, so as not to muddy the waters.

He phoned Andreas' number and instantly recognised the familiar soft tones of Andreas' voice.

'You have had a busy time,' he said.

Leo told him about Lissa's adventure, Darius, Rafik and the prisoner, but said that they had not been able to gather any further evidence and did not know where Darius was. Leo could almost see Andreas nodding, aware of the lack of interruption and questions, that he probably already knew as much as Leo. Andreas told him that the team had dispatched forensics experts and a member of his staff would be interviewing the prisoner. He told him that while the man they had found was being kept under sedation, doctors believed that he would make a full recovery.

Leo remembered what Thomas had said about the man's parting words, about Remy and the women and relayed the information to Andreas. It was clear that he was surprised that Rafik had left the man alive. He said, 'Perhaps the men who were sent to collect him had other plans for him.' He asked Leo to get Thomas to call him as he was keen to try and find out whether he had heard anything that might explain why Rafik had left so suddenly.

With that, the line went dead. Leo suggested Julia tell her boss that as the Australian authorities were involved in the case, she had been seconded to the task force, at which she smiled. 'Reassure him, we will be out of his hair soon.' They both laughed. 'When we have dispatched the "Arrow", we will need to head to London.' Jem said he was going to talk to one of the policemen outside Lissa's door. Once he was out of sight, he headed down to the carpark and, at Andreas' request, put a tracker on Leo's car. He then returned to the bar.

Lissa, with Jem in tow, headed for what had been her mother's room, which was now hers and Thomas.' Jem had been told that he was to stay with her. She realised she was hungry and asked Jem to order some food, while she had a shower and dressed the wound on her leg. He asked if pizza was okay and she nodded. Suitably refreshed, as the doorbell rang, she re-emerged and headed for the door. Jem's growl made her jump and then she laughed. He opened the door and she realised that there was a policeman standing outside, who handed Jem pizza boxes and colas.

'Can't stand hotel pizzas; Julia said order from a great joint down the road.' They ate, Jem managing two to Lissa's one.

The phone rang and Jem answered, saying nothing, just nodded, and then said, 'Good luck.' He didn't tell Lissa what Leo was about to do.

Chapter 35

Having agreed to the plan, Jake decided to see what information he could find out about the sniper and read the information on "The Arrow" Andreas had sent the team. Further research through police files online led him to the autopsy report on the dead Russian from the motel shooting. He was surprised that it had been carelessly misfiled with the multiple accidents that had happened the same day. Reading it, he found the bullet had come from high up, a similar angle to the shot at the hotel. He thought to himself, *Clearly the man likes to be up high, so the site needed to ensure he had that.* Jake didn't want a wooded site, so the man couldn't hide easily.

But he wanted him to feel comfortable, not too exposed, or he may choose not to try, or guess it was a trap. The location Jake selected was a factory, with two other buildings nearby, and a fence around it but with no low cover. There were other buildings but these were over eight hundred metres away.

Having agreed on the site in principle, Jake went and visited it. When he returned, he said that if Leo parked his car on the access road, just outside the perimeter fence, and walked in, there would be only two spots that provided a good angle.

When Julia heard this, she asked where Jake would be. On the map, he pointed first to the furthest building. 'I will wait here, as I will have a good view of the only two buildings that will allow him the necessary sight of the target. He will choose one, I will be on the other. The other buildings are too close for a guaranteed getaway and would only offer a rifle shot, not his weapon of choice.'

This did not calm her fears as the list of variables was growing. She was also concerned that, although Leo had told Thomas a little about what they had planned, he had not been totally honest and her list had begun to form a knot in her stomach. She was sure that if he knew the whole picture this would provide the opportunity, she really wanted, to stop the plan.

But she didn't say anything, as Leo was so animated. He had gone down to the carpark to meet Jake Russell. They double-checked the arrangements before Jake headed off. He would be at the location in good time and in a position that would allow him to see both possible sites, so he could see when the shooter arrived and where he set up; this would then allow him to move to the other site. Leo then went back to the room he was sharing with Julia, to find her uncharacteristically quiet.

'It's going to be okay; Thomas knows what we're doing,' which wasn't strictly true. He wrapped her in his arms and she hid her tears in his shoulder, the knot of fear almost overpowering her. She felt something was wrong but she could not voice it.

So instead, she headed to the police station as agreed, where she would put their plan into action. She told a colleague that she had heard that one of the refugees from the factory was willing to help them find Rafik. As they chatted, one of the uniformed constables came over and said that he had an informant who had told him the factory was empty and the people had moved on. He said he had asked the man where they had gone and he had given him their new location. This was almost word for word the same one Julia had given over the phone in her heavy Russian accent. She played into the narrative, thanking him, saying it was great info and they would head there once she had spoken to the chief.

The constable seemed a little agitated by this and she was not surprised when he said that they should go straight away.

Julia nodded. 'Okay, yes, time will be crucial, can you tell him where we're going?' He nodded. 'Leo will be here in a minute, I'll just get my body armour,' she said.

As she left, Julia said to herself, 'This might just work!' Leo had brought the car up from the carpark and met her outside the station. The constable came to the door to see them off.

'Is that him?' Leo said. Julia nodded. 'Yes, I recognised his voice.'

'When we get back, that little shit is in big trouble!' He snarled but forced a grin and waved at the man.

Jake had arrived at the site early and made some adjustments to try and ensure Leo's safety as much as possible. He had moved a large blue metal waste bin into position so it could provide cover if things went awry. He had plenty of time to ensure that his car was well hidden and his hideout provided a clear view of the entrance road. A couple of hours later, a car pulled onto the access road and drove up to the base of one of the buildings. Jake recognised that the man was clearly an experienced professional, allowing himself plenty of time to set up before his target arrived.

A man dressed in grey clothing got out. He carried a gun case over his shoulder and a bag in his hand. The man started to walk towards the factory, staying low to the fence line, checking out the factory and using his scope, focusing on the buildings surrounding it. He seemed satisfied and moved towards one of the disused buildings. At the door, he put his back to it and then kicked hard a couple of times till the door gave way. He waited but there was no alarm, so he went in and shut the door. Jake knew from his own experience what his routine would be; choose a site, check the angles, move to the chosen position, check everything again, etc.

Unsurprisingly, this was the building Jake would have chosen. The man reappeared, walked to his car, and reversed it out of sight behind the building he had chosen. Then he returned and disappeared inside.

Jake needed to get to the other building and then radio Leo to confirm his position and tell him that the game was on. He left the building nearly half a mile from the one where the shooter was setting up and headed to the second site. There was good cover on the road but to be on the safe side, he left the car and set off on foot to cover the last hundred metres. Having correctly selected the shooter's likely choice of site beforehand, he had already opened the door to the second site. He entered and climbed the stairs to the roof, ducking low behind the wall.

When he was in place, he used his scope to check out what the shooter was doing. He could see the man clearly, stretched out on the roof of the building. He picked up his radio and sent out a beep to alert Julia and Leo that he was in position. He set up his gun.

Julia knew the shooter could not be following them as he would already be in position, so it was clear that the only other person it could be was the policeman who had given her the "tip". She didn't want to lose him, concerned that if she did, he might warn the sniper. As they entered the Manly area, Leo's radio beeped. This meant that the location was now covered. Leo was buoyant, he seemed to think that the only thing left was for Julia to ensure that she arrested the "mole" after the sniper was down.

'Are we doing the right thing?' She asked. 'Didn't Thomas say to wait for him?'

'I know you are worried but you needn't be. Jake seemed really confident, 'all I need to do is walk, and if needed duck,' he laughed, patting the Kevlar vest under his shirt.

Arriving at the location, Leo drove to the spot that he had agreed with Jake. He told Julia to stay in the car.

'It's okay, Julia, we need to get this man.' He kissed her and she nodded, and he set off.

It had been agreed that he would play into the policeman's narrative that the "refugees" would be nervous, so he should therefore go in alone. Leo was glad Julia was safely in the car and pleased for once that she hadn't argued. Jake radioed to say he had the sniper in sight and when the man raised his head to shoot, he would take him out. So, Leo was not unduly concerned about walking towards the door of the building, which was the target point Jake said he would have chosen. At the last minute, he would run to his right, where Jake had positioned a large rubbish container. As he was ready to move, he heard a shot and Jake say, 'Target dow...' but Jake never finished the line.

Leo was about to react when the second shot came and was louder. Suddenly afraid, he started to dive to his side; the third took him off his feet. He did not hear the fourth or fifth.

The policeman walking away from the car, crumpled to the ground. There was silence. Jake lay on his front, over his gun, an unknown man was dead in the sniper's nest, and Leo lay on face down in the dusty courtyard. The "Arrow" stood up, dismantled his gun, and headed for his car.

He had been following Jake, ever since he first saw Leo talking to him. He had guessed his plan. He had been correct. His task completed, he left the site.

Chapter 36

Rafik was heading to the airport when his phone rang; he answered and said nothing but smirked. The call finished and then he said, 'One down,' and laughed out loud. The driver looked up at the mirror but said nothing, he knew what that meant.

Arriving at the Sydney private airport, he walked through to the lounge and poured himself a glass of champagne. He did not drink as a rule as it was frowned upon by his religion but generally accepted among the ruling elite. He hoped that in the not-too-distant future, he would have the finances to have whatever he wanted, and his grin broadened. As someone who had spent many years in America spying for the Ministry of Intelligence of the Islamic Republic of Iran, Rafik had learned to fit in with the ways of both countries.

As he settled back into one of the chairs, he thought that just two more men to get rid of and then nothing would stand in his way. Beckett, like his friend Tremaine, should be relatively simple for "The Arrow" to dispose of. While he had been furious that Andreas and Remy had eluded him, they would not escape a second time. First, the jewellery and then, he licked his lips, he would kill Andreas himself, and finally take his revenge on her. A cold flame had burned in him since she had rejected him and the voices of other perceived injustices were getting stronger. He shook himself. He had carried the bitterness in his heart ever since she settled for that insignificant traitor Farzad.

He had spent a great deal of time and money on her; did she not realise that he had disposed of him so that they could be together? Ah, but then duty called and had interrupted his plans, as it had often done so before.

His thoughts turned to his life. As a valued businessman, he had always been able to meet and get to know many important contractors and politicians, some of whom he had been able to set up, blackmail or threaten so that they provided vital information, which he could send to his masters in Tehran.

He knew that now the international authorities had him on a watch list, he needed to be more careful; but he had been devious and astute so that no evidence of spying was found, just some unauthorised dealings. However, the demands for information from his masters were becoming ever more difficult to supply and this meant organising increasingly risky actions.

Recent events had forced him to use his Russian friends to kidnap the son of one of the defence department's minor characters. This ensured he would be able to access certain documents. However, before he had been able to collect them, the man had told Farzad he was being blackmailed. It appeared that Farzad, far from being some lowly employee in the US State Department, as he had thought, was, in fact, a senior analyst, who had been gathering evidence to demonstrate that Rafik was spying. It seemed he might be close to bringing down Rafik's whole operation; so he decided he needed to find and destroy the documents that could prove his activities and remove Farzad, the man hunting him.

He had employed a man skilled in arranging "accidents" and once this had been successfully carried out, Rafik would return to Iran until he felt it was once again safe, as he had not been banned from travelling to America. The man in the defence department and his son were no longer useful, so were disposed of.

Thinking back to Remy, how he had loved her when they first met. He remembered that he had told her once, there would be a time for them, but stupidly he had never said more or made his intentions clear. But now, he was tired of waiting. She needed to wait no longer, it was time but maybe not for what she thought. His tastes and uses for women had grown with his mania. He mused, perhaps the pretty Lissa?

'Mr Yazdi? My name is Mayam.' He was roused from these thoughts by a beautiful, petite oriental woman, in a silk Kimono.

'I am here to provide massage.' Rafik smiled, then looked not at her but at the man behind her and nodded.

'Yes, my dear, this man will show you where to go.' The woman bowed and followed the man. Mayam was not taken to the private space provided for guests at this facility, instead she was smuggled on board the plane in a large box. The loader had been paid handsomely for his services. She was now sitting terrified in the main cabin of Rafik's plane. When later questioned about her disappearance, one of the girls said she had heard the manager talking about a plane, but like many others who were either trafficked or sold into houses to provide "personal services", there was no further information or evidence as to who she was, or of her whereabouts.

Rafik boarded his plane having cleared customs. Pre-flight checks were completed and the plane took off.

'Now, Mayam, it's time for that massage,' said Rafik, undoing her seat belt and roughly pulling her behind him through the curtain to the back of the plane.

Later, he emerged, and a man gave the female flight attendant a medical kit, as he said the girl had fallen. She took it and went to the back of the plane, where she found Mayam naked, curled in a ball, shaking uncontrollably. The woman dealt with the superficial cuts and bruises and then helped her to put on a dressing gown, as her silk kimono was torn. She gave the girl a bottle of water and then put a blanket over her, strapping her into her seat. 'Try to sleep,' she said. 'I'll come back later if I can.'

Rafik had too much work to do to worry about the woman he had taken so brutally. When they refuelled in Dubai, he knew she would be taken to a similar facility, probably along with the pretty attendant. There they would work or make similar trips until they were of no further use.

This and other similar facilities were part of the business empire which he had developed under the noses of his SAVAK masters. He had cultivated a chain of holding areas across Europe, each focusing on a particular clientele requirement. While he was in the UK, he intended to review the facility there as there had been complaints about the condition of the merchandise. He had decided to establish his daughter, Dilara, in London. She had already been successful in improving his business in Dubai and he felt confident that she would be able to do the same in London.

Personally, he had no taste for the simpering blonde blue-eyed girls that so many Middle Eastern men favoured. For him, the looks and sexual expertise of oriental women were far more to his taste, though sometimes even they could fail him, as the last girl had.

Now relaxed, Rafik enjoyed a meal. He knew that he needed to report the current situation regarding the regalia to the chief minister in the SAVAK, the secret police. Sipping his wine, he made the call. The minister was unavailable but the man he spoke to asked him to explain the plan, so he could relay his message correctly. At the end of the call, Rafik smiled and his mind turned to his plans for the future. He settled down to sleep happy, that when they arrived in

Dubai, he would be meeting up with his daughter. He would take her to London with him on a shopping trip and then discuss his plans for her future.

However, Rafik's conversation with Tehran had been intercepted. The person he had spoken to was an Iranian-speaking member of the task force that were focused on bringing an end to his business operations and spying. At this point, it wasn't totally clear to the team what was going to happen, but it appeared Rafik had just heard from a sniper he had employed, that the trap was set. Andreas knew Remy was on her way to London and he had just spoken to Thomas, who had told him about Lissa's escapade. Therefore, it must relate to Leo's plan, which meant that Leo and Julia were the ones in danger. Andreas put in a call to Lissa and asked her if she knew where Leo had gone; she said she didn't know and passed the phone on to Jem.

His face did not betray the information he was receiving as he didn't want to frighten Lissa. He said he would get in touch and let Andreas know.

'Is there a problem?'

'No,' said Jem. 'Just need to get some info to Leo, seems he's out of range.'

He stood up and, without another word, grabbed his jumper and headed for the door.

'Where are you going?' Lissa called after him.

'Might be gone a bit. This time, do not leave this room. I will tell the policeman outside he can put you in a cell if you try,' and with that, he was gone. Lissa's face clouded; she knew he was worried and he wasn't telling her something. Now she was angry as she knew she was being sidelined again. She picked up her phone to call Thomas, having decided he needed to be straight with her but got a voicemail.

Thomas was on the line to Jem.

When Thomas heard the news, he immediately told the driver to turn off and head for the location he knew Leo intended to use. It wasn't far, fortunately. As they sped along the motorway, he called Julia's boss and told him what he knew so far. Carmicheal told him that he'd had a call from Jem and had already dispatched police and medical personnel to the location.

Thomas arrived within five minutes of the services. Three bodies were being put into the back of a coroner's van. He got out of the car and headed to the van.

Chapter 37

Lissa finally got through to Thomas, who was in the first of the ambulances as it arrived at the hospital. He had told her he was busy but didn't say how or why but just that Patch would pick her up, so she should stay put until he knocked on the door; then the line went dead. He knew she was already suspicious and that she was no doubt angry at being kept in the dark but he told himself it was for her own good.

Meanwhile, he had spoken to Leo's father, Remy, Andreas, and again to Chief Inspector Carmichael, so that everyone was clear about what he knew so far about what had happened. Following their shock at the news, each then had their own idea about the stupidity of the actions that had cost three lives but none voiced their feelings. For some, they struggled with the fact that they had not stopped it from happening. It was especially difficult for Thomas, as he knew how reckless Leo could be. He hadn't agreed with the plan but cursed himself for not having done more to stop him.

In the days that followed, Andreas relayed to him the information that had been gathered. From what he had seen and knew of the situation, he guessed that the sniper had taken three shots, Jake one and the policeman one. It was clear from looking into the policeman's bank account that he had received a large sum of money. This proved Leo's suspicions that someone on the inside was passing information. As it turned out, this was a decision that had cost the policeman his life.

They found an unidentified man dead in the sniper's nest. Seeing his picture, Thomas recognised him as one of the men he had seen outside the building where they had found the prisoner. Somehow, this man had either already been in the building when Jake arrived or had somehow slipped in unseen and replaced the sniper. Clearly, this meant the sniper had either known or guessed at Jake's plan and had done this with the intention of drawing Jake's fire. Andreas wondered whether the man knew he was a "sitting duck".

Jake, having seen his movement, had fired, killing him but then had himself been killed by The Arrow, who, evidence showed, was about two hundred metres behind Jake, which made his second shot an extremely long one of nearly eight hundred metres. It appeared that when Jake moved to shoot, it gave the sniper a clear target. Next, he rapidly targeted Leo, as he moved, then finally, when he heard the policeman fire, he took him out. The only evidence that he had left behind this time, were some tyre tracks.

Karimi, turning onto the main road, wasn't worried about the tyre tracks as the car was a rental and would be returned to the hotel and then the depot. He drove back to the Novotel near the airport, smiling and humming as he listened to the radio. He allowed himself a moment of satisfaction before he phoned the client. He had hoped both his targets would be there, but at least he had eliminated two. Sadly, he felt the woman had been necessary and had instructed the policeman to do this, as he always hated killing women. But then Karimi had killed him as he had outlived his usefulness. The client had said the women were to be captured, not killed, but as she was not on his original list, he allowed himself forgiveness. Tonight, as ever after a kill, he would pray for their souls.

He called the client. 'One man down. It was also necessary to dispose of my informant and a woman who was not on your list. I apologise for my lack of accuracy.' The phone clicked and the line went dead. He was unaware that his message was heard and passed on to Andreas, who took immediate action and activated a line tap and trace.

In his room, Karimi carefully packed up the rifle he had just cleaned so meticulously. *The CheyTac M200 Intervention sniper rifle was the longest-range sniper rifle in the world,* and he thought, *One of the best sniper weapons ever created.* This gun was his prized possession and had helped him through many encounters and kills in Afghanistan, Russia and America.

He liked these places, they were easy to get around and as his appearance had changed over time, he had been difficult to capture. He had already decided that soon it would be time for further plastic surgery.

Humming to himself, he cleaned the case with the same care as the gun. There was a knock at the door. He was not startled as he was expecting the packers to arrive. Opening the door, two men entered carrying a large box. The gun was big, so the container needed to be much bigger. The box carried the medical insignia and would be loaded on the plane's manifest as medical equipment. He chuckled, a nice thought. With plenty of shielding, it would appear on scanners to be an "Ultrasonic Surgical Equipment Cleaning System" bound for a UK hospital.

Once they had left, he finished packing up his few belongings, wiped down the last of the surfaces, and using a cloth, opened the room door. He went down to reception and asked them to return the car, then he paid and headed out to the front door, asking the doorman for a taxi to the airport. Getting in, his mind was already considering how he would tackle the next part of the contract, so he paid no notice to the driver, or the car that pulled out, which was driven by a large black man crammed into the driver's seat.

Jem had followed the loan car and was now waiting outside the Novotel in Wolli Creek; he was not going to let this man out of his sight. He had had very little time to process the events of the last hour and, what had happened kept rolling through his brain like a movie.

As he had waited outside, he remembered how thankful he was for Andreas' foresight in insisting a tracker had been put on Leo's car. This had helped him follow Leo to locate the meeting point. Arriving he could see that Leo's car further up over the road. He was of two minds about what to do; as he was slowly rolling forward, he saw another car. It was parked behind a building and he was immediately suspicious. He got out and checked the car's rental number plate and phoned the secure line, giving the man the rental number for it to be tracked. As he waited for confirmation, he got back in his own car, and that was when he heard the first shot. He told the man on the line that his team needed help, dropped the phone, and jammed his foot on the accelerator.

Unfortunately, he was too far away to stop any of what happened next. However, thinking fast, his quick action ensured a medical helicopter was immediately despatched, which, because of the incident's closeness to its station at the airport, arrived within minutes. To ensure they didn't lose the shooter, Jem also gave the team the car's rental number. Then he ran in the direction of the shots, already fearing the worst.

'Too many shots, too many shots,' he kept mumbling through the tears. He stopped sharply, as he saw the first body.

Later, despite replaying the scene over and over as he waited outside the hotel, Jem knew there was nothing else he could have done. He had followed the loan car with the tracker, there was no way that he was going to lose it. Sitting outside the hotel, he had contacted both Thomas and Andreas and together, they agreed the sniper could not be allowed to leave the country. Andreas wanted him alive; the others made no comment.

Jem waited and watched. They were certain that when Karimi left the hotel, he would be heading for the airport. So, with the agreement of the hotel, they had arranged for a taxi, driven by a plain clothes policeman to be placed outside ready. Jem wanted to do this but it was pointed out that he may have been seen by Karimi as he was really quite memorable. Instead of driving to the airport, they would for safety's sake, drive him just a few blocks to a quiet part of Cahill Park, where the taxi would be surrounded and Karimi arrested.

Karimi was too deep in thought to notice the taxi turning away from the airport and heading instead around the block. Once there, the policeman driving the taxi stopped, and other officers arrived and dragged Karimi out of the car. Jem, pushing his way through the throng, managed to grab Karimi around the neck and slam his head against the car. The man crumpled and Jem stood back and turned away. For those who knew him, they would not be surprised to see the tears brushed roughly from his face. He walked back to his car, his shoulders heaving.

Imram Karimi, The Arrow, was arrested. But thanks to Jem, he was on his way to the hospital, not prison, under a heavy police guard.

Thomas, meanwhile, was leaving the hospital and heading back to the hotel. He was met by Patch, who told him that Karimi had been arrested. Relieved, he told Patch and Lori to get some food and then hang around until he knew what their next steps would be. He left them and headed upstairs. He wasn't quite sure yet what he was going to say to Lissa. He knew that she had been against Leo's plan and he felt responsible for having talked her around. The policeman was still at the door and moved to open it for him as he arrived.

Lissa was not in the room. Thomas swore.

Chapter 38

After Jem had left so suddenly, and the abrupt phone call with Thomas, Lissa decided she'd had enough of being couped up, ignored and lied to. She knew the policeman outside had been instructed not to let her leave, so she knew she could not get out that way. Looking around, it was clear that the window was a non-starter. She decided that the only possibility, therefore, was through the inter-connecting door. Trying it, although she could undo it from her side, the other side was locked. Quick thinking suggested an alternative. Picking up the phone, she called housekeeping.

'Oh hi,' she said in her best winning voice. 'I wonder if you can help me. We are getting a surprise visit from our son and I have asked if he could be put next door. The connecting door is locked now. Please would you be kind enough to unlock it from the other side for me as he will be here soon. You can? Thank you so much.' She put the phone down with a look of surprise. To her amazement, it seemed this worked as within five minutes, the door opened and a maid popped her head around and asked if there was anything else she needed. She shook her head and thanked her.

Without further thought, especially not to what Thomas might say when he found her gone, she grabbed her bag and slipped next door, shutting and locking the connecting door. Fortunately, the room was unoccupied, something she had not considered. Now she needed to find a way to get past the policeman in the corridor. Clearly, she needed to make herself less obvious to anyone outside; so gathering up all the towels and bathmats in a bundle, holding these in front of her, she hoped that if he looked her way, he would think she was a maid. The lifts were to the left but that meant going past him. There were stairs to the right, so leaving the room, she turned right and fortunately the policeman ignored her.

When later Thomas asked him about how she had got out, he said that all he had seen that afternoon was the maid leaving next door. Thomas found himself smiling, even though he was angry, she was nothing if not resourceful!

Once she got downstairs, Lissa got a taxi to the police station. There was nobody on the front desk and when she managed to attract a woman's attention, it was clear that the place was in a state of turmoil. She asked to speak to either Julia or Chief Inspector Carmichael and was surprised when the woman seemed to be on the verge of tears. A uniformed officer stepped in and asked her to wait. About twenty minutes later, she was escorted upstairs and into a side room. Now she knew something terrible had happened. The chief inspector opened the door, his face was grave, his voice thick with emotion.

'I am sorry to keep you waiting, there have been several difficult incidents that we are dealing with.' His phone rang.

'Yes, send him up.'

Thomas knocked on the door and entered. Lissa looked up, at first relieved and then angry.

'I think I'll give you a few minutes to catch up,' said a relieved Carmichael, quickly leaving the room.

Lissa sat with arms folded across her chest, ready for whatever Thomas had to say. She did not get up.

'Well done for getting out of the hotel,' Thomas said.

Lissa said nothing.

'Look, I know you are angry but you need to listen to me.' There was something in his voice and the situation that cleared her anger and made her look at him. She saw his face was such a mixture of emotions. He had clearly been worried about her but what else?

'You know that Leo was determined to catch or kill the shooter.' She nodded. 'Unfortunately, things didn't go to plan. Jake, the marksman, has been killed. Leo's plan was leaked by one of the policemen, who was also killed.' Her eyes widened and her hand went to her mouth as if she was fearful of what was to come. 'Julia and Leo were both shot.'

Before he could finish, she stood up and rushed to him. 'What, are they...' She didn't finish.

'They are alive.' He couldn't manage another word, he just took her into his arms and they clung together. After what seemed an eternity, he held her away from him and gave her the box of tissues from the table.

Then he said, 'Leo has dislocated his shoulder; it appears to have happened when he threw himself to one side when he heard the first shot. As he was moving, he was struck in the chest by a bullet but the vest saved his life, although he has several bruised ribs. He banged his head on the bin as he fell and was knocked out, so he appeared to be dead. Julia wasn't quite as lucky. She had gotten out of the car after the first shot but it appears the policeman came up behind her and shot her in the back. The sniper then took him out and disappeared.' Thomas paused.

'It was only thanks to Jem, and the speed with which he acted that she is alive. The medivac helicopter got her to the hospital quickly and they operated immediately. She is in an induced coma now; they aren't sure of the prognosis.' While they had only been together for a short time, the team had already really bonded with Julia. This news had saddened and shaken them all. Lissa's eyes were again filled with tears.

'Look, I think we should go to the hospital as Leo will probably be discharged soon. We can check up on Julia at the same time. Okay?' Lissa, drying her eyes, nodded. 'While I do some sorting out, can you please stay here? Oh, and before we go, you had better phone your mother. It appears she knows what has happened and has been trying to contact you.'

'I left my phone at the hotel as that was how Jem found me before.' Thomas laughed.

She took Thomas' phone and called her mother in London. It was clear from the conversation that Remy had been terrified, so was happy to speak to her, but angry for what she called "Alessia's childish behaviour". For once, she felt her mother was actually right. Finishing the call, she stayed put and waited for Thomas. When he returned, she was more composed, and they headed for his car.

They travelled to the hospital in silence, both with their own thoughts and still too shocked by the turn of events to express them. Thomas' phone buzzed and he was told that the police had arrested Karimi. Somehow, that did little to lighten their mood. At the hospital, they were greeted by armed police outside both Julia and Leo's rooms. Thomas went to the nurses' station to find out the latest on Julia as they were not allowed in to see her, while Lissa went into Leo's room. She was surprised to see him sitting on the edge of the bed, fully clothed; a sling holding his arm, and a bandage on his head.

She moved to put her arms around him but he moved back, cautiously holding his arm. He grimaced, 'Perhaps we can save the hug till later, it took them three attempts to get my shoulder back in, I don't want a fourth round!'

Lissa laughed with relief, holding her arms wide. She did, however, plant a kiss on his bandaged head. 'I am so pleased to see you,' she said. 'Have you any news about Julia?'

'No! No one is saying anything. Where's Thomas?'

'Asking for an update.' At that point, he came into the room.

'Hi, mate, you look better than the last time I saw you. Apparently, there has been some improvement in Julia's condition and they are going to lift the sedation they have her under and let her come around. Are you ready to go?'

'Yes,' he said removing the bandage, revealing six neat stitches along his brow line. 'I just want a minute.' He got up and limped to the door, then went to Julia's room, despite the nurse's objection. After about five minutes, he returned.

He surprised everyone by saying, 'She was so excited about going to London with us.' He looked away, clearly dejected, he was not coping as well as he was pretending.

Thomas didn't question, as this had not been mentioned, he just said, 'Next time,' as they headed for the exit.

In the car, Thomas tried to keep the conversation light. He spoke about Jem's journey and how he had been so quick off the mark. He rattled on about Lissa's escape and she added in the detail about how she got out of the room. Leo listened and nodded in all the right places but was uncharacteristically quiet.

Chapter 39

Back at the hotel, the mood was still sombre. They had each been interviewed by the police and members of the task force. Later in the afternoon, Andreas appeared and asked to speak to them.

'I am not going to ask you how you are doing, I can only imagine. However, we need to talk about the reason you are here. I have had Remy on the phone almost endlessly since this happened. She threatened to get on the next plane out here but I have promised her that as soon as I can, I will get you on a plane to her in London.'

The next thing he said surprised them all, as he suggested that, although some things had to change, the task force needed them to continue as if nothing had happened. At this point, everyone seemed to start talking all at once.

He held up his hand. 'I know that the last thing you want to do right now is to continue but it is now a matter of international importance that you locate the stone. It appears that only Alessia can do that and without the stone, the regalia will not be completed.' The others looked to Lissa.

'I don't know what you mean,' she said.

'Okay, let me go back a little. You know now that it was Darius Shafiq who asked your mother to find some valuable items that he said had been stolen from his family years before. This, was only partly true, as we now know, this was the regalia. Years before the Shah's abdication and the revolution, the Shafiq family were given the responsibility of ensuring its safety. Shahtiar Shafiq, had sworn to protect it and as a result of refusing to give up its location, he was killed in Paris. However, before he died, having feared something might happen he split the items up and gave the pieces to the people or families that you have now collected them from.'

'Following his death, many people have tried to locate them. Rafik Yazdi was just the latest in a long line. Some like Yazdi have wanted it for themselves, no matter the lies and lives it costs. Some wanted it to support a cause, some to stop one. Not for many years has it been so close to being complete again. The final part is the ruby. Alessia, why did you know to go to the factory alone that day?'

'I got a message from Darius. He said I should go there alone as he had something for me.'

'Did the note say anything else?'

'Just one thing, he told me to remember a word.'

'Well,' said Andreas. 'This is significant as only you, he and the person with the ruby and sash that completes the regalia know the word. Only when it is spoken to the person who has the ruby will it be given. What this will mean, we have still to find out.'

'So, what now? We hear what you say but one of our group is critically injured and we have no idea of how this will impact her life in the future.'

'I know and believe me, I am truly sorry.' He looked at Leo. 'We will ensure she gets the best possible treatment but for now, you must focus on completing the task.'

Leo was about to speak but Lissa gently touched his arm. 'I know you will want to stay, Leo, and we wouldn't blame you. But you know her, she wouldn't want you to just sit at her bedside. We have to finish this.'

He was quiet for a minute. 'You're right, we have to finish this and finish him. I want Rafik Yazdi dead,' he said and hobbled out. Lissa moved to go after him but Jem beat her to it.

'I'll go, he may need to hit something.' He laughed as he left to follow Leo.

Andreas nodded. 'I know how he feels. Look, this man Darius is now in London, and I believe that he will be able to get the stone and the sash to complete the regalia. He has a boat on the Thames near Erith, so we should focus on that.'

'Not just that,' added Thomas. 'There is Rafik to consider also.' Andreas nodded but said nothing.

'We have you booked on an Emirates flight tomorrow evening,' Andreas said as he got up. 'We will arrange transport to the airport, I suggest you all get some rest.'

Jem came back and said that Leo was heading back to the hospital, so he would go with him.

Thomas and Lissa headed back to their room. They packed up what they could for everyone and then ordered room service. Getting into bed that night, they clung together and fell asleep in each other's arms, totally exhausted.

Chapter 40

Leo slept on the chair by Julia's bed until her hand touched his arm. He took it and held it tightly. When Jem crept in later in the early morning, he found them both asleep; Leo having somehow climbed onto the bed beside Julia and had curled up protectively around her. Jem returned to his chair outside the door. He did not sleep.

As the hospital became busier the next morning, Jem insisted that Leo go back to the hotel to shower and change. He only agreed as the police would remain and Julia was now fully awake and clearly more alert.

Jem was still unusually quiet. Even seeing Julia smile at Leo hadn't lightened his mood. It was clear he was taking the shooting of Julia personally. When much later, he talked about it with her, she finally got him to accept that it was not his fault; even if he had been a little closer, he might still not have been able to stop the policeman and could have been killed or injured too. That morning, this fact was furthest from his mind and he almost hit the side of a passing truck. 'Sorry,' he said but Leo didn't complain, as he was suffering similar "what if" scenarios himself.

Leo, of course, was the one who was suffering the most. It had been his plan. Jake had died and Julia had been seriously injured because of it. He did not include the death of the policeman. Leo thought that this man's part in the tragedy almost seemed to have been disregarded by the police. Although he didn't know it, that was far from the truth, but the whole incident was under wraps. The authorities were looking carefully at everything that had happened to ensure that they interviewed and arrested everyone responsible. This included arresting key members of the Russian gang, with the cross symbol on their hands, who had been involved throughout. It appeared the policeman was associated with them and had been a key player.

Arriving back at the hotel, both Leo and Jem headed for their rooms. Having showered and packed, they arrived at Thomas' door. Opening it, Lissa saw that Leo was a little brighter than he had been but Jem looked exhausted.

'Long night?' Thomas said quietly to Jem. He nodded.

There was little else to do. Leo said he was going back to the hospital and would then meet them on the plane. Thomas thanked the local guys, Patch and Lori, who took their luggage to the airport. He and Lissa then headed to the police station.

They were surprised when the chief inspector said, 'Considering the fact that one of the men under my watch was, well…' He didn't finish as he was obviously finding it difficult to select an appropriate word. 'An investigation is still ongoing. Look, what the hell is going on? I don't want any more bullshit about a jewellery robbery. I think you owe me the truth.'

'I will tell you what I think I can. I agree, you have been more than fair with us,' said Thomas and told him a slightly abridged version of events to date. Carmichael listened intently, nodded occasionally, and did not ask any questions, and when Thomas spread his hands, indicating the end of his story, Carmichael's look said volumes. Finally, he spoke but only to say that he was more than pleased to see the back of them. That evening, they were accompanied to the airport by a police team.

The police escort was useful when it came to getting quickly through the embarkation processes, so that all four were soon in the first-class lounge, which had been at Remy's request. There were smiles all round as they boarded the plane and were shown to their seats, but particularly at the look of pure childish glee on Jem's face, when he found out that he had been included. They were soon settled, and after take-off, asleep, totally exhausted by the last few days.

After a stop in Dubai, the plane flew on to London Gatwick Airport, the home of Emirates. Arriving, they cleared customs and headed for the exit, where a uniformed chauffeur Leo knew well walked over to meet them.

'Hi,' said Leo.

'It's good to have you home, Sir,' the man said as he took Leo's bag and the luggage cart. Thomas and the others followed in procession out of the airport.

'I gather we are not going home, Sir,' he said.

'No, for the time being, we are heading to The Frances Hotel in Kensington.' This was a hotel that was near Remy's house. On arrival, they agreed to meet for dinner and then headed to their rooms. As Thomas opened the door of the room he would share with Lissa, his phone rang. It was Remy.

Chapter 41

Rafik had been in London for two days by the time Thomas and the others arrived. He was unaware of what had happened in Sydney. He was settled in the new apartment he had bought in Canary Wharf, chosen because of its views out over the river Thames. It was edgy, modern, stark even, and contained few personal possessions. As he swung lazily in his one luxury purchase for the room, his Eames lounge chair, his phone rang. He received the news about what had happened in Sydney and exploded, picking up the footstool and smashing it against the glass table which shattered.

Angrily, he considered his next move as he took the bottle of pills from his pocket and swallowed a few. Trying to think, he watched the boats, barges and some yachts making their way up towards Tower Bridge. He felt like them, he needed to manoeuvre, remove obstacles and keep a steady course. He was reminded of the games of chess he used to play with Farzad and how he never managed to beat him, and screamed for Mahmoud. Focusing his mind, when his confidante arrived, he told him his plan. The man smiled and said he thought it was a good one.

That evening, he sent a coded email to his SAVAK masters telling them that he had now made the necessary arrangements and that he was confident they would be successful. Their reply was clear. He needed to ensure there were no further problems, loose ends or hold-ups as there would be consequences.

He took a breath. Part of his plan was already in motion, as he had made arrangements to ensure the shooter did not spend too long in police custody. Now he just needed to finalise his plans for Andreas and Remy. He had not discounted the man who accompanied her but he would be dealt with in time also.

In Sydney's Long Bay Prison, Rafik's plans were in place. Karimi, having left the hospital, had been placed in protective custody and only allowed out of his cell alone for a short period of exercise. He was still being treated for the head wound and some broken ribs he had sustained on his way into custody; but now he had developed a chest infection and needed to be taken to the prison's hospital facility, where he was hooked up to fluids and antibiotics.

That evening, an alarm in the nurses' station sent staff rushing to Karimi's room. Despite several attempts being made to revive him, it was too late, he was dead. When viewing the CCTV, Chief Inspector Carmichael identified a person dressed in hospital scrubs who had been in the room just before the alarm had sounded and it appeared that they had injected something into Karimi's fluid line. An autopsy identified that the introduction of air into this tube, had been the cause of Karimi's death. The person's back remained turned to the camera, so they had no idea who this was.

The nurse who should have been on duty was found dead in her apartment and later, the body of an unidentified woman was found in a car in the staff carpark. It seemed likely that the nurse's pass had been taken and used to gain access to the prison, and then when Karimi was dead, the killer themselves had been disposed of.

Rafik allowed himself a sigh of satisfaction on receiving the news, that this problem, had been successfully dealt with. The other important news Rafik received was the whereabouts of the regalia, and although pleased, now increasingly more important to him, Remy. He had forgotten his hatred it seemed and now had decided that the time was right for Remy and Alessia to be with him as a family. His mind was now constantly fluxing between love and hate. As his behaviour and appetites had grown, he was exhibiting more and more traits of a psychopathic, narcissistic personality disorder. One moment, he wanted to seek revenge for Remy's perceived slight in marrying Farzad; the next, he felt he couldn't live without her.

Today, he thought that once this was all over, he would take her to the island in the Philippines he had purchased. They would be away from the world and so could be a happy family. He would, of course, still need distractions, but the country was full of beautiful young girls he could enjoy. Then his thoughts turned to Lissa and as his desire rose, his face contorted and he licked his lips.

At this thought, he called to one of the guards to bring in the "escort" they had arranged for him. The door opened and she sashayed in. She was beautiful, young and dark-haired, just as he had asked for; just like Alessia. As she came in, she slipped out of her coat, turned, and bent down at the waist displaying the minutest, sheer black underwear. His face was a mixture of anticipation and loathing but also a growing need, as he reached out for her. Once he had used her, she would know that like all women, she was a slut and should be treated as such, just like his wife, and before her, his mother.

He stood up as his mind clouded, grabbed her hand, and pulled her roughly into the bedroom. The door closed and the men outside just looked at each other. This was the third girl in two days. So, they knew the routine.

Later, lying naked on the bed, the girl discarded on the floor, Rafik's thoughts were not about the pleasures of the last hour, but of the first time he had met Remy. She had been the most beautiful thing he had ever seen and he fell in love with her instantly. However, she barely noticed him, she only had eyes for Farzad. He tried to find ways to woo her but each time she shook her head, gently stroked his cheek, and then laughed. *How dare she laugh at him,* he thought. When she married Farzad, he was beside himself. It was then his hatred of this woman but women in general began to grow.

His sexual appetite, which was always only self-satisfying, changed. The night of their wedding, he had driven away from their stupid party blinded by hatred. He had almost killed a woman crossing the road and getting out of his car, he heaved her into the boot and stuffed her in. Driving away, he had stopped in a wooded area and dragged her into the bushes and raped her, then left her for dead. That night, afraid he would be caught, he decided to leave America and return to Iran.

In Iran, he married and focussed on the opportunities and positions provided by his father-in-law. These allowed him to gain more power. He also accrued a considerable fortune as he was an astute businessman; he had built an empire, both legal and illegal, beyond the control of his Iranian masters. At times, he even managed to gleefully thwart or manipulate deals that negatively impacted her company. For a time, this seemed to satisfy his lust for revenge on Remy and Farzad. When he eventually returned to America, he flaunted his riches and bountifully shared his wealth with them, giving each a beautiful, inscribed diamond ring. Deep down, he still had hope that this would curry favour with her that she would leave Farzad.

Once, at his house on Great Neck, he arranged for them to be alone. She had smiled alluringly, hugged and teased him, so he decided that now was the time to consummate their union. He had kissed her passionately and she had laughed, pushing him away but he was not to be denied as his body burned to have her. He forced her back onto the bed and used his weight to subdue her. He enjoyed the look of shock on her face but then she did not respond as he had hoped. When he explored her beautiful body, she just lay there and when he pushed her legs apart and entered her, she showed no enjoyment in their union.

Taking her did not provide the pleasure he had hoped for and he felt the desire for her leave him. It was replaced by frustration and anger at her lack of response. He stood up and with a look of hate, told her, 'There will come a time when you will regret this.' Then left without turning back.

He didn't care that he had left a bruised and shocked Remy spreadeagled on the bed, unable to react, asking herself, was she to blame? Had she let him believe that their playful banter was more than it was? Had he really thought she would leave Farzad? She didn't know what to do. She felt so ashamed.

He knew she would tell no one. He was right. As she had told herself it was her fault, how could she? So she cried, as she headed for the shower, to clean the scent of him from her body; then gathered her torn dress and panties that lay on the floor. Picking them up, she did the best she could with the straps of her dress and stuffed her underwear in her bag. Still shaking, she had headed for the stairs.

Mahmoud had seen Rafik stumble from the room and his eyes hardened. Then he heard her leave the room and stood by the door waiting with her coat. He helped her on with it, his face clearly reflecting the horror he felt. He whispered, 'I will make him pay,' but she barely heard him. It was clear now that this would not happen unless he found a way to make it so.

As she left the house, she stopped and took a deep breath. In her mind, the events of that afternoon were placed in a box, hidden deep, but not forgotten. She dried her eyes and made herself a promise. Then got into the waiting car and went home.

Rafik chose to return to Iran, as an expedience, but also to gain greater power in one of the more extremist political groups. This gave him the opportunity to have more involvement in the political machinations and direction of his country. Eventually this led again to an increased number of trips to America. He did not contact Remy on his return. He had convinced himself that she was playing a game and what had happened was done to tease him. He would give her time.

He was good at playing business "games" too. He was quick to pick out weak individuals who he could threaten, blackmail, or hurt in other ways in order to get the information he needed. This was well received in Iran and he was rewarded by becoming involved with the SAVAK, the secret police; but they demanded more and more information and at top of their list was the return of the royal regalia.

All the time, he planned and plotted his revenge on people who had hurt or slighted him. He remembered only too well how his mother had beaten and rejected him; so she had been the first to receive his vengeance. She had said he was evil and had disposed of him, sending him to a boarding school, where he was bullied and sexually assaulted. So, in retribution, he had her confined to a psychiatric hospital. He had shown her, as he would with all the women in his life, how little he valued them. The thoughts of their pain aroused him, as he rubbed and pulled at himself, until he climaxed; something he had been unable to do earlier.

With a groan of satisfaction, his mind floated to the days after he had returned to America and bought a house in Great Neck, across Long Island Sound from New York, where Farzad and Remy lived with their daughter. He contrived to have an accidental meeting with a man that he knew worked with Farzad. Used carefully, this would give him access to some interesting opportunities useful to the Iranian government. He could also use this to plant evidence to suggest it was Farzad who was the spy. Unfortunately, it seemed that Farzad was becoming suspicious and had to be stopped.

Rafik sat up and ran another line of white powder onto the small glass bedside table, snorted it, and recalled how stupidly he had thought that this would give him the opportunity to possess something he had so longed for, Remy. He lay back as the drug and pills swirled into his system.

Finally, an invitation to the home of an old friend offered a convenient opportunity, as he knew they would be there too. Using his contacts, he met a professional who had an excellent reputation for organising "accidents", and had great experience in this line of work. The man did not share details and Rafik didn't care as he knew that the whole scenario would be well-planned and timed. However, he had been given clear instructions to firstly, remain in the house, and second, to ensure that the man would be in the car alone. The first was easy, he feigned illness, but he had puzzled over the second. Then he saw the present on the table.

As he was considering what to do, he was surprised by Farzad picking it up and putting it in the cupboard drawer. His immediate thought was that with the parcel out of sight, and in the rush, they would leave the parcel behind. He was sure the gallant Farzad would drive back to get it. As he smiled to himself, Farzad looked directly at him. 'I'll be back, and then we need to talk. Don't use that surprised expression, Rafik, you know what I mean.' And with that, he called up to Remy that they were late and he was going out to the car.

At that moment, Rafik had known that he had made the right decision.

A soon as they had gone, he searched the house, found the file he was looking for and left.

Now, lying on the bed, he shivered remembering that evening far too vividly.

He was aware she would hate him then, but believed time was a great healer and she would forgive him; but when they met again, she barely spoke to him. He had apologised and explained he had left because elections had been called, so it had been imperative that he returned to Iran. He did not mention the incident at his house. He again promised her that there would come a time for them but she had turned away.

Now his rival was dead, it was necessary to dispose of one more obstacle to his happiness, namely his wife. He had never loved her; she was just a means to an end, and she despised him as much as he hated her. She took every opportunity to belittle his lowly background, but he had dealt with her.

He got off the bed, ignoring the blood on the sheets, or the girl on the floor but was suddenly aware of the blood on his body and shuddered. He went into the bathroom and was confronted by his image, he was horrified and immediately headed for the shower. As the scalding water burned away the hatred and self-loathing, it also hid the tears of the boy in the boarding school shower where the man had held and used him.

The Rafik who emerged was different. He dried himself, and looked in the mirror then smiled; at nearly sixty, he was still handsome and fit. He didn't need her and decided that he would take his revenge on her. He had loved her once but she had played games and rejected him. Now he would seek retribution. She should have considered herself lucky to have him offer his love, so he would make her suffer. Spinning round and round, he was thrilled at the thoughts that rolled through his mind. He dressed and prepared to put the next phase of his plan into operation.

He left the room ignoring the naked girl, whimpering in a corner, and told Mahmoud to, 'Get rid of her!'

Chapter 42

Rafik's men had followed one of the cases and had found the location of the safe house. They were surveilling it but had been warned not to attempt to enter the premises. However, they had been unable to find any information or plans of the site and therefore did not know about its complexity, and assumed that it was an extremely well-guarded shipping point. When they notified Rafik, he carried out further online checks through his sources but got nothing further.

This made him wary as he had also received information regarding the various government agencies who were interested in his activities, and he realised that he would need to be extremely careful with regards the regalia. Remy was a different matter.

He had been thinking about ways to secure her but realised that it would be too dangerous to try and make a forthright attempt to take her, or her daughter, at the present time. That would have to come later. The people in Iran were beginning to get worried and wanted to see the whole thing concluded. He knew what the consequences of failure would be; if he was unable to complete his task, and for that eventuality, he needed to plan an escape. Reluctantly, he decided, that he needed to get the regalia first, and to do that, would need to force her hand.

He believed that taking something she so obviously valued would be sufficient. Lissa was not yet in the country, so it would be Andreas. He laughed a perfect opportunity to dispose of him at the same time.

Considering this man, however, he had been amazed by what he had heard both from his men and from other intel sources. Despite knowing that Andreas had spent time in the Navy, he, like Remy, had dismissed this. Rafik had always assumed that Andreas was a bit of a weakling, an artistic type with no backbone. Now it appeared he might have been wrong. Although he did not fully understand the man's naval career, the information made him cautious. His mind spun and all he could think about was how much he would enjoy the idea of breaking this man, especially as it seemed that Remy was fond of him.

An image of a spider with Remy's head came to mind, a black widow. His anger was growing and he took a breath, realising he needed to keep his control and focus on the task at hand. He reached into his pocket for the vial of pills, swallowing three or four, he didn't count. He sat down and breathed deeply.

Calmer now, his plan was simple. Considerable intelligence gathered by his network told him that Andreas regularly ran through Battersea Park and came out of an entrance onto Prince of Wales Drive, then returned home. The men who had been watching him would probably not find it difficult to pick him up. He could then be used as an excellent bargaining chip, ensuring that Remy would give up the keys, and then Andreas would be of no further use.

Little did Rafik know that this was one of the scenarios that Andreas, and the task force team, were preparing for, thanks to their informant. It had been agreed that Andreas would play the part of a compliant hostage. Once taken, he would reveal he was the one who had the keys but would only deliver them to Rafik in return for a promise that he would leave the country and leave Remy and Lissa alone. He would offer to take Rafik to the keys and that was when the task force would be able to take him. Remy and Lissa would no longer be in danger and the task force would deal with Rafik.

Remy was horrified when Andreas told her about their plan and his decision. She was so angry about not having been consulted that she threatened to call Rafik herself and meet him. It took all the arguments he could muster to make sure that she knew that would not be sensible or wise. Finally, Andreas managed to convince her that their plan was the best way to stop and catch him.

'What will happen to the regalia?' She asked.

'That is complicated; a decision will be made in good time.' His answer was evasive, which Remy did not like. She knew that Darius Shafiq was waiting on a boat near Erith and that he knew where the central stone was and wanted to take the regalia back to Iran. Yesterday she had spoken to Darius about what would happen when he had the regalia and had asked many questions, but Darius was as vague as Andreas. He finally told her that if he could smuggle it in, then it could provide a symbol for people to embrace, a rallying point for the many disparate groups to come together. If the task force had it, however, it would mean that rather than serving the hopes and dreams of the people, political decisions and expediencies would be served, and so stop the fight for freedom.

' If we have it, a leader will come forward and save our country.' She was about to ask how he could be so sure but he just said, 'We have faith.' And the line went dead.

Now, she felt as if everyone was ignoring the danger Rafik posed. Andreas picked up his phone, kissed her forehead, and then turned to leave. At the time, he did not recognise that her acquiescence was simply uncharacteristic; if he had, he might have found out she had a plan.

'When do you plan to do this?' She asked quietly.

'It will be another day. Don't worry, it will be fine.' She nodded as he left.

'That's what Leo thought,' she whispered quietly.

Remy did indeed have her own idea and she felt confident that her plan was more likely to succeed. Now, having spoken to Andreas, she knew she needed to act immediately and picked up her phone.

Andreas returned to his apartment near Battersea Park to finalise arrangements. His living room was now filled with equipment and people on phones, the internet and trolling through paperwork. A British Army Captain and one of the Intelligence Analysts looked up from their conversation.

'Okay, so she knows and is obviously upset but I think she will stay out of the way.' However, he was already beginning to wonder if he had been too hasty. The captain fired a number of questions at him and as the discussion took his attention, his fears melted away.

The next morning was cool as Andreas crossed into the park. Despite being part of many covert operations, it had been a while since he had been out in the field. Most of his time now was directing operations, so he couldn't help feeling edgy, he had not slept well. He was glad, therefore, to get going, both to warm himself up but also to be doing something concrete at last. As he ran, he enjoyed the peace and was able to think. He was about to be taken by men on the instructions of a "friend". Somehow, despite all he now knew, he was still having problems matching the Rafik of their early years to the man whose file was thick and full of despicable acts.

Did Remy suspect that Rafik had killed Farzad? Or had she, like him, been completely fooled into believing that this man was still their friend and could not be the one who could do that? And now, even more importantly, did she love him? He shook the thoughts from his mind and tried to focus on the task at hand.

He always enjoyed this part of his run as it took him past the Thames, where he could see early morning rowers heading downstream on the ebbing tide.

Today as he watched them, an unwanted shiver ran through his body. He knew that there was still time to pull out, they had said that it would be all right as they had another plan which could be instigated. But he had agreed with the team that by taking him, Rafik would see this as his best option for getting the keys and then the cases stored in the safe house in Peckham. The plan surmised that by using him, Rafik thought he could force Remy to give up the keys.

Andreas had to persuade him that he, in fact, had them and prevent any attempt on the house or to take Remy. There was a possibility that Rafik might demand she went with them, perhaps in exchange for letting Andreas go. But he knew that if it came to this, rather than risking her, he would kill Rafik.

Remy however, full of steely determination was setting her own plan in motion. She was not prepared to let anyone else die on account of some Iranian, Russian, Saudi or American plan to gain control of the regalia and the supposed power it might wield. For her, there was another driving force; the chance to ask Rafik one burning question, which she wanted to do face to face, before she killed him.

Remy's plan didn't involve the safe house, a place that had been suggested to her some time ago by one of her less reputable friends, to store "valuables". On the outside, this was a renovated Georgian detached property in a part of Peckham that was undergoing gentrification. It was humorously named "Sunshine Villa" and it was registered as being owned by a Mr E. Morcombe, which caused amusement to those of a certain age at the land registry. The man who owned the property and provided the service was Terry Wise, no relation to the comedy duo, but he had named the house thus as he thought it was a fitting tribute to a pair of comedians he loved.

Although it was not obvious, this property had several surprising secrets. Both outside and inside, it appeared to be the home of an average suburban couple. Terry's son and his wife lived in the house rent-free for "keeping up appearances". Outside in the garden, an ordinary looking home office was protected by an intricate locking system. Inside, Terry's team were responsible for protecting the entrance and stairs that led down to an old Cold War nuclear bunker. This was one of a number developed in the late 60s and 70s to protect important citizens should a nuclear attack occur.

Underground, a maze of tunnels stretched back and down under the gardens and this was where items of importance, among other things, were now stored.

The doors on all levels were extremely thick, so any unauthorised entry was unlikely to succeed.

The day before Andreas left on his morning run, Remy had contacted Parsons, one of Jem's men, who was also watching the safe house, to finalise her plans. He said all was ready.

Then she phoned Thomas and spoke briefly to him and then Alessia and asked them to meet her at the London house in Kensington. She didn't tell them what Andreas had said or the task force plan as she wanted them to help her with her own plan.

As Thomas and the others got into the car Remy had arranged, Andreas was heading out of the park gate onto Prince of Wales Drive. To anyone watching, they would have been unable to say more than a man had been taken by some men who jumped out of a van. It all happened so quickly and efficiently. The man was bundled into a white van, so common that no one took any notice of them. But the task force did, as they were watching every movement, satisfied that the first part of the plan had taken place much as they had expected.

Inside the van, Andreas was totally calm but struggled a bit as would be expected as they tied his arms. They took photos of him to send to the boss and then covered his mouth and put a hood over his head. He was confident that these men would not harm him. He was, after all, going to be Rafik's bargaining chip and so he would not want him marked. He was right as the men in the van were cautious, clearly only too aware that Rafik could be an extremely violent and unforgiving boss.

The van travelled slowly as it navigated its way southeast through the traffic, heading for a flat on an estate in Camberwell, where he would be kept until Remy had been taken; then, and only then, would he be disposed of.

The estate was quiet when the van arrived, but it would have made no difference if they had been seen as no one would do or say anything. This was not the place that shared secrets. So, a hooded and tied man bundled out of the van meant backs were turned and curtains closed. He was pushed into the building and then a lift, which stank of urine and creaked as the men got in. He counted four floors, then they marched him to a flat and he heard the door being kicked open. The smell inside was only marginally better than the lift.

He was pushed up some stairs and into a room, where someone took off his hood and removed the tape on his mouth. The one clearly in charge said in a strongly accented voice, 'You cause us no trouble, you will be well treated.' He cut the zip-tie. Andreas nodded. Reluctantly, he sat down on the filthy, stained mattress as the bed was the only piece of furniture in the room. Condoms on the floor suggested what this room was generally used for.

'You will stay in here. The windows are locked.' With that, he handed Andreas a bottle of water, and left the room, locking the door. Andreas thought, *Stage one complete.* He went over to the window, moving the tattered curtain to one side, and saw the flash of a car's headlights, signifying that the team was in place.

Chapter 43

Thomas and the others arrived at Remy's house, where Tiana, her assistant, opened the door and showed them into the study. Thomas was initially shocked; here was a totally different Remy. She was dressed casually in jeans and a sweatshirt, her hair tied back and she had no makeup on. To him, she looked even more beautiful than when he had seen her that first day on the ship. Her eyes were extremely bright and her skin seemed to have a warmer glow. Lissa rushed into her mother's arms and they clung together, Remy whispering into her daughter's ear.

Eventually, Remy pulled free and moved to Thomas, who she hugged and kissed, then Leo, who she was careful not to hug. Jem, however, decided to take it upon himself to pick Remy up in his arms, whirling her around, to thank her for his unexpected ride home. She laughed as he put her down.

'You're welcome,' she said touching his face and then hugging him. Thomas thought Jem might burst.

'So, what's happening? Has Andreas told you yet what the task force is going to do?' Thomas asked.

'Not exactly,' she lied, 'but I do know that it involves allowing Rafik's men to take Andreas, as a way of forcing me to give up the keys.' There was a gasp from Lissa, the men said nothing. 'Rather than wait for him or the task force to dictate my actions, I have started to put in place a plan that will ensure Rafik will no longer be a threat.'

'Be careful. Remember the last time I had an idea, it didn't work out too well,' said Leo sadly. Lissa gently touched his hand.

She nodded then continued, Rafik thinks the keys are the only things stopping him from getting the cases. He has no idea how secure the cases are in the house in Peckham; however, rather than waiting for him to hatch some plan to attack the place with goodness knows what consequences, I propose we go on the offensive. It is the least obvious scenario.'

'Remy,' Thomas spoke softly and using her first name, 'don't you think that the task force will have considered this?'

'Whatever their plan, it will be too careful, they want to try and take him alive, use him and or imprison him.' To everyone's surprise, her voice rising, she said, 'I don't want to capture him, I want to kill him. Alessia, don't look so shocked, this man is pure evil. He is a psychopath and he killed your father. It is only as a result of seeking the regalia that I have finally been able to see him for who he really is and face the truth.'

She stopped, clearly emotional. Regaining her composure, she explained she had learned the truth as a result of a private investigation into her husband's accident and it had become clear that it was Rafik who had arranged for the truck to hit Farzad's car that night. It appeared that a colleague of Farzad had been involved in stealing defence information. It seemed that for some reason, he was passing this on to Rafik. Farzad had discovered the link and realised that Rafik was sending valuable information back to the Iranian government. In order to avoid being discovered, Rafik had arranged Farzad's death.

She grasped Lissa's hands. 'All this time, I thought it was about me, that he wanted me, but it was all just a pretence to him to ensure I didn't know or dig any deeper. How blind I have been to so many things. He deserves to die.'

The room was silent.

Finally, Leo spoke, 'What do you want us to do?'

Remy brought over a map. 'He has an apartment here,' she pointed to Canary Wharf. 'He believes he is safe there. I plan to set up an early morning meeting with him to give him the keys.'

'You can't!' Lissa said aghast. 'What did the task force say about this?'

'Nothing, they don't know; they have not involved me, so I have not told them. Look, can't you see that if they take him, he will disappear forever.'

'But that's good, isn't it?' Leo asked.

'It's not enough!' Remy was clearly becoming angry.

Taking a minute to calm herself, she went on to explain her plan. 'I will suggest that the meeting takes place near his apartment.' She explained she would wait completely alone in the middle of an empty carpark, near the O2, which early morning would be quiet and generally quite empty. He would be able to see her and know that she was alone. She was certain that he would not be able to contain himself as he was so self-obsessed and arrogant, that he would not miss this opportunity to meet her and gloat.

'Remy, this is too dangerous,' Thomas started to say.

She stopped him. 'This is the only way, there are no alternatives. Right now, the task force has played right into his hands. They think once he has the keys, that he will release Andreas and then go to the safe house. Their way would ensure Andreas would be killed, whatever happened. I must do this to save him. It is not up for debate. You either help me or leave now.'

Everyone started talking at once, then at a pause, she said, 'I know where they will take Andreas, Parsons has that in hand. When we have disposed of Rafik, Parsons or the men from the task force will free him.'

Leo sighed. 'There is obviously much you aren't telling us but go on.'

'When Rafik arrives, he will no doubt have a gun pointed at me. I am sure that he will tell me that if I give him the keys and go with him to the safe house, he will release both Andreas and me. But I know if I were to agree, he would probably phone the people who were holding him, giving them the sign to kill him. I intend it to go differently. He does not know that the central stone is missing from the regalia and that will be my bargaining chip. I will tell him I will give him the keys and take him to the safe house but only if I see that Andreas has been released to some of my people. Then, and only then, will I take him to collect the final pieces, the ruby and the sash.' She raised her hand as others moved to protest.

'You need to know that my people have spent time gathering information to develop and support this plan. Crucially, we needed to get access to Rafik's car. We found that his chauffeur regularly attended a mosque on the Old Kent Road. So, we ensured that more than once he overheard conversations about a "Kafir", someone who couldn't be a true believer, as they beat up and stole young women. The men said they were scared for their wives and daughters. Leaving the mosque, they always headed for a local coffee shop. The chauffeur followed and they soon started chatting.'

'After meeting a few times, talk turned to protecting their families. One man, a minicab driver, told how he had picked up a badly beaten girl from apartments in Canary Wharf and from the description of the marks on the girl, the chauffeur knew that she had been one of Rafik's escorts. Listening to the men, he felt responsible for having taken and left her there, especially as he had a daughter the same age as the girl. He had finally heard enough and had spoken up.'

'He said he thought he knew who the "Kafir" responsible was, and it was clear that he was very angry. He went on to explain what he had seen. As they left the café, one of the men introduced him to a friend who he said could help.'

Thomas looked puzzled. Then he realised, 'Wes, but I thought the FBI was part of the task force.'

'Not really, when the task force took over, he was sidelined. He is very loyal to you, Thomas, and he'd said if I needed any help with anything, he would do whatever he could.'

'Do you think you can trust the driver?' Lissa asked.

'To ensure his compliance, Wes has taken his family somewhere safe,' Remy responded.

'So how are you planning to capture him?' Leo asked.

'Rafik is so proud of his Rolls, that he will come to the carpark in it. The chauffeur does not know this but he has ensured that we had access to the car. A device has been attached that can be deployed remotely, so when a cyclist pulls out from a side road at an agreed location, it is brought to a safe stop, although apparently hitting the man. An ambulance will be parked nearby and appear to be taking a patient to hospital, the paramedics will arrive and…' Leo interrupted.

'And Rafik will shoot you and then them. It won't work as long as he has a gun.'

Thomas was thinking and said, 'It might but we need to simplify it. Forget the cyclist, find some way to incapacitate the people in the car, then they can be picked up by the ambulance.' Taking out his phone, he stood up and called Wes.

Remy responded, 'However he is captured, there will be only one ending. Once I have him, I intend to exact an appropriate punishment.'

'That is revenge, mother, this isn't you.'

'In this case, my darling, it is, there is much you do not know. Well, what do you think?'

No one spoke.

Chapter 44

Rafik reluctantly answered the phone; although, looking at the nubile figure, fighting the bonds that tied her tightly spreadeagled on the bed, he would rather be doing other things.

He was expecting further information about how his plan was progressing but the voice on the other end was not the one he was expecting.

'My darling Remy, how unexpectedly good to hear from you.'

'This is not a social call. I believe you plan to capture Andreas.'

'Really? But my darling why would I?' His glee almost slid down the phone. She ignored his comment.

'I will make this offer once only. You want the keys to the cases, I have them, and I will trade them for his life. When I know he is safe, I will then take you to the safe house. If you refuse, then I will go to the authorities and give them the keys.'

'But, my darling, surely that would be very reckless.'

'Which is why I am making you this offer. I will be waiting tomorrow at midday, by the entrance to All Saints church car park on Bazely Street. I will be alone and you will be able to see that there is no one else there. One last thing. The main stone of the belt that locks the regalia and the sash are missing but I know where they are. So, we will need to collect them first, giving you time to arrange Andreas' release. If you try anything, you will never complete the belt. Those you are working for will be unhappy to pay you. Unless the regalia is complete, I am sure the consequences for you will not be pleasant.'

'Touche! It seems as if I have no alternative and a surprisingly worthy opponent.' As he spoke, his mind whirled with possible scenarios. She was right, without the complete ensemble, he would not be paid. He was sure there must be some sort of catch. Would she really risk her own safety for that idiot Andreas? Unless, he mused, she really wants to be with me. 'I have one condition, my love, that you will come with me willingly. We have so many experiences, we can explore together.'

She shuddered. 'Yes, you know I have waited so long for you.' She tried to make her voice as soft and throaty as possible to mimic emotion and longing.

'Then I will see you tomorrow. I trust you will be alone, as will I. Goodbye, my love.'

The call ended and Leo, despite a sharp pain in his shoulder, broke the tension with loud applause.

'Do you think he bought it?' Lissa wondered.

'I could almost hear him salivating,' said Leo.

He was almost right, as Rafik's mood changed and he called for someone to remove the girl.

This had been an unexpected offer, one he knew he should be wary of, but he thought, *she sounded sincere.* If this meant she would really go with him willingly, he felt his desire building; he would finally win. The years of longing for her dispelled his caution as he told himself that she had never remarried, or had an affair, so that, he reasoned, showed she really had waited for him. After Farzad had died, she had always ensured that they kept in contact and was always pleased to see him. There were times when he thought about moving forward with her, a kiss here, a touch there, but somehow, it had not been the right time.

Maybe now, that he was on the brink of such a coup, it was finally the right time, and she would deliver this prize to him, along with herself. He shuddered in delight. They could go to Iran, where he would be well rewarded and then, if she wanted, they could go anywhere in the world, or to his island in the Philippines. She would be the dutiful wife, while he would still be able to enjoy his other pleasures.

He knew the task force would let his men take Andreas to lure him out. He laughed; this way he would not need to worry about them, he could shift his focus instead to retrieving the last pieces. Once he had the keys, the cases would be his. He could take her and then have Andreas disposed of. The thought of finally owning her and the pleasure he would have in taking her, made him shudder and as a result, he finally dismissed any negative thoughts that might have warned him of the dangers.

Rafik lay naked on the bed and called Mahmoud. He trusted this man. He was the one who would lead the raid on the safe house. They went over the plans;

it built his appetite and not for the first time, he patted the bed next to him and lazily stroked the man's face.

'Are there any changes?' Rafik asked.

'No, at the safe house, only the change of personnel every twelve hours, there is no evidence of any others. It is clear from the plans that the office at the end of the garden is the location of the vault. The drone has seen people regularly coming and going and we watched a consignment of three boxes of some sort arrive yesterday. They were moved through the house and into the office. The house, whose garden backs onto the office, has been taken; the occupants have been removed. This will be our point of entry.'

'Well done. When do you propose this will be done?'

'Tomorrow, just before the lunchtime change; people tend to be slower when they are hungry and tired.' Rafik nodded.

'Good. I will have the keys by then and then we can finish our plan,' and he turned and smiled in a way that made the man shudder. He knew what was coming next.

Chapter 45

Leaving Rafik asleep, Mahmoud spat in his direction. Soon he would kill this man, he would seek revenge for so many. On behalf of Darius and his people, he had endured nearly two years of working for this *al-kafer* (infidel), gaining the man's confidence; but in the process, he feared he had lost his soul.

The sands of time were running out for the evil *alqatil* (murderer), finally, it would be time to act. When he did, he would ensure that Rafik would pay for every indignity and depravity that he had forced on people. Disgusted, he left him sprawled asleep on the bed, muttering curses under his breath. He had wanted to kill him, and it would have already been done, if they hadn't needed him to get the prize.

Mahmoud had been placed in the US by the dissident group Darius led to watch Iranians who they suspected of being spies, or who worked to support the hardline government. He had been assigned Rafik Yazdi. Initially he had just watched and gathered evidence, but eventually he made contact with Farzad Akbari, a government analyst, who was researching Yazdi having grown suspicious of his various activities, including people smuggling. It was clear that Yazdi's activities were becoming of increasing concern. To further his cause, Mahmoud had arranged for an introduction, as someone loyal to the Regime, so that he could infiltrate Rafik's organisation.

Mahmoud was the only person who knew about the incident at the house in Great Neck which had left Remy so distressed. It was following the attack on her that Rafik's treatment of women seemed to escalate. He knew that along with the regalia, Yazdi's eyes were fixed on another prize also, Remy Akbari, he would not let that happen. When Farzad was killed, Mahmoud suspected Yazdi was responsible, although he had no proof.

When Mahmoud heard rumours that the royal regalia had resurfaced, he felt this was a sign. A plan had begun to grow in his mind and he had taken it to Darius. He knew the man would be sympathetic as his father had been assassinated by the Revolutionary Guards. Mahmoud was surprised to discover that Darius' family had been responsible for the safeguarding of the regalia, following the fall of the Shah. To avoid suspicion, Darius arranged for families, seemingly unconnected to the items or the country, should keep and protect them. He believed that when the time was right, they would be brought back together, as he, like others, whispered that the regalia had some sort of mystical power.

Darius suggested that the regalia could be used to unite the various factions who opposed the Islamic Republic. Together, they hoped it would be possible, to remove the oppressive authorities. One way or another, he would ensure that his beloved country was returned to the Iranian people, who lacked something to unite behind. For years, the clerics had depicted their opponents as divided and lacking in credibility. Exiled groups and personality cults, that had launched intermittent attacks on Iranian military targets, but overall, they remained estranged from the Persian-speaking Shia majority.

Khatami, a previous reformist president, had brought some hope and the possibility of political relaxation; but then people's hopes were dashed as the unelected ultra-religious clerics replaced him with a hardliner. For many young professionals and students who might have been able to form an effective internal opposition, this was too much, and they left Iran and so the clerics tightened their grip.

When an airliner carrying Canadian Iranians, including Mahmoud's wife and their daughter was shot down by the Revolutionary Guards, he became part of an association of victims' families, and other Iranian expatriates, demanding the abolition of the Islamic Republic. This was well received abroad but their extended families within Iran suffered the consequences and were forced to flee or go into hiding.

Mahmoud knew the time was right to further their cause, they just needed the spark to light the flame of hope and he believed that this could be the royal regalia. Following his discussion with Darius, it was agreed that he would find someone he trusted to bring the pieces of the regalia together. Sometime later at the house of a friend, he met Remy Akbari. He told her that he had met her husband and was sorry for her loss. They had talked for a while and he was convinced he had found the right person to carry out the task. He told her his friend was looking for a courier company to collect some items, and she said that she might be interested as she had completed similar tasks for others.

He was careful about what he said and suggested only that they had been stolen, which she accepted. When she finally agreed to complete the commission, he felt the task might be possible.

Rafik had returned to Iran and Mahmoud went with him, all the time watching and biding his time. That time had now come. So, he encouraged and supported Rafik's plans, aware that he would either fall into the trap laid by the task force Mahmoud was liaising with, or the one he was sure Remy had set.

Chapter 46

Remy stood alone. The road was almost completely empty; her only companions, some paper, leaves and a can that rattled and danced as it was caught by the wind. She pulled her coat closer. She thought, *God, please let this work*.

The team had ignored Remy's claim that she had already explored all avenues and following discussions, they had put in place some changes and safeguards. Jem had called Tyrone, who they had first met in Sydney and who he knew was extremely capable, both as a driver and quick thinker. He asked him to park up beyond the carpark entrance and wait for instructions, but he knew that if needed, he would not need directions to act. Lissa and Jem were in an ambulance at the destination, ready for their part. Leo had ensured that hidden on the roof of the church a sniper was positioned. Meanwhile, Thomas and Tyrone waited out of sight to follow Rafik.

At midday exactly, Rafik's new silver Rolls came into view. Thomas almost held his breath. Was her plan really going to work? Had his driver kept silent? Would she be safe? The car stopped by Remy and the door opened, after what seemed like an hour, she got in and the car set off on the pre-arranged route.

Settling back in the car, Rafik smiled like a Cheshire cat. 'Well, my dear, you look wonderful. So where is this magical mystery trip taking us?' He asked.

'We are heading for a boat moored off the Eastly Yacht Club near Erith. The person who has the jewel does not wish to set foot in the country and will be leaving as soon as your business is complete.' Undoing her coat, she was about to remove the keys now on a single chain around her neck.

His hand stopped her. 'You can keep these safe for now, it will give me great pleasure to remove them later,' he said, stroking her chin, then sliding a finger down her chest, across her breast. Then suddenly stopped abruptly.

'Do not worry, my dear,' he said leaning close to her ear. 'I am just checking for any communication devices. Please give me your phone.' She suppressed a shudder and opened her bag, holding her breath as he leant over and looked inside. He took out her phone and removed the chip and battery.

'There,' he hissed. 'Now hopefully, we will have no interruptions. Please give my driver the postcode.'

Remy leant forward and spoke to the driver, who input it into the satnav system.

'I know your men were at the carpark but please do not try and alert them or have them follow us. I do not want to hurt them, you or the beautiful Alessia. Where is she by the way?'

'Somewhere safe where you will never be able to find her. I know that stealing precious jewels isn't your only business. Stay away from her or…' Was all she could manage as she hoped to God this was true, as Thomas had refused to tell her where she was going to be.

'My other businesses…?' he laughed and raised a quizzical eyebrow.

'Yes, I know that you are an Iranian agent for the SAVAK.' She paused and without thought to the consequences, went on, 'And I know you have murdered people. But do they know about your other business, that you have women taken and delivered to men or placed in prostitution houses and…' He put his hand on her arm and she stopped breathless, trying to keep both her emotions and temper under control.

He laughed. 'Oh Remy, Remy, Remy, such a narrow view of the world! Let me open your eyes.' He sneered and tightened his grip on her arm, twisting it. 'We are not so unalike as you might think, you and I, despite what you say. You move consignments in sealed containers across the globe, with little or no real idea of what is inside them, and you do it to make money. Do you care? I do the same thing, only I don't care and am unconcerned about who or what is inside them if there is a profit.' He glared at her, and it was clear that he was becoming angry.

Remy, fearing she had gone too far, recognised that she needed to try and calm the situation, so she turned to him and with tears in her eyes, she whispered, 'But, I care for you, my dear sweet Rafik. Do you remember those days of our youth and the times we spent together? Can we not recapture them?'

'My darling, do not worry,' he said, and she felt his grip on her arm loosen and his shoulders relaxed. He turned to her and she could see his look had softened. 'I have such fond memories of those days.' He kissed her forehead tenderly, stroked her hair, and then closed his eyes.

Breathing a sigh of relief, she leant in closer and whispered, 'And so I too. Do you remember that afternoon in Great Neck, at your beautiful house?' He smiled.

Her memory, was clearly different from the one the smile on his lips suggested he recalled. For so long, she had hidden the truth of that day, telling herself it had been her fault. But with all that she now knew, the truth of that afternoon had resurfaced. He had raped her and the release she had felt, saying those words out loud, was indescribable. It had become the catalyst for her plan. He would feel the depth of her pent up pain and anger, at what he had done to her and to Farzad, in the punishment she would exact.

'So, my darling,' his voice was silky. 'We have waited so long, a little longer will make our union so much sweeter.' He laughed, pulling her to him, he whispered, 'Remember, I always promised there would come a time.' And with that, he kissed her passionately, smiled and stroked her face, but then moved away and lay back, his eyes closed. Her relief was almost palpable, and she brushed a tear away.

The journey was tense. She looked out of the window at the houses and shops, wishing and hoping that when this was all over, Rafik would be dead. This helped her survive the almost forty silent minutes before they turned off the main road and onto Manor Road, where a sign showed the way to the yacht club. About halfway along, the car shuddered and smoke appeared.

'What happened?' Rafik shouted, leaning forward. As he did, Remy quickly removed the perfume spray Thomas had given her from her handbag and as Rafik turned his face contorted, she sprayed him full in the face as instructed, then quickly opened the car door and got out. The result was almost immediate. There was a momentary flicker of understanding in his eyes and even the ghost of a smile before he became unconscious.

The ambulance, with its siren blaring, quickly arrived on the scene. Alessia and Jem dressed as paramedics knew they had only minutes to secure Rafik before the effects of the spray provided by Wes wore off. To anyone observing the scene, it may have seemed somewhat inappropriate that a paramedic, despite the size of the patient, would pull and carry them to the waiting ambulance. Lissa was waiting inside to administer a longer-lasting sedative injection. Remy and the driver got out of the car and got into the ambulance. Leo arrived and opened the bonnet of the Rolls and removed the connector to the remote control so that the car could be moved. Then he got into the driving seat of the ambulance.

Once it had pulled away and was clear, two men, one dressed as a chauffeur arrived, got in, and drove the car away. The men left the car near Dover and removed any possible fingerprints and the remains of the remote-control mechanisms. Later, they reported the vehicle stolen.

The ambulance now headed for the agreed meeting spot on the Mayfield Industrial Estate, where they would leave the ambulance and be picked up by a white van. Then they headed back to the yacht club, where the boat that Darius Shafiq was on, was moored.

Remy, Lissa, and Jem were quiet, each had their own thoughts as to what should happen next. The driver just looked bewildered and a little afraid. At the yacht club, Thomas and Leo waited for their arrival. Tyrone had brought a car for them to use and had arranged for the driver to be taken to his family. The ambulance would be returned to the "props" department of the friend he had borrowed it from.

The previous day, Leo had arrived at the yacht club and had given the manager an official-looking document and showed a badge that clearly identified him as MI5. He told him that the site was needed for the discrete arrival of a head of state and therefore they would be appropriating it for at least the next forty-eight hours, so he should alert all boat holders. He gave the man a number to call to confirm this information. This, of course, went through to Lissa and then Thomas, who confirmed this was the case.

Darius' boat had arrived earlier and moored. It was a large, clearly expensive, sea-going cruiser and therefore moored further out in the Thames Estuary. When the group arrived, they did not go into the clubhouse but straight down to where a small motorboat was waiting at the jetty. Remy and Lissa were to go alone over to the boat to meet Darius. Thomas and Leo were initially unhappy about this, as previous experience made them wary, but having scoped the surrounding area, they felt sure they were alone. Jem was left to keep watch on Rafik, who was now under a blanket, tied up, with his mouth taped. The men, still watchful headed in opposite directions along the bank.

Climbing onboard the boat, Remy and Lissa were shown into the main salon of the boat where Darius was seated. Mahmoud stood beside him.

'Thank you for all you are doing,' he said. 'You can leave the man with me now.' He did not use Rafik's name. 'He will be dealt with.'

'I can't do that,' replied Remy. 'I only came to give you these.' She showed him the keys. 'Alessia will go with you to the safe house; however, you are no doubt aware by now that there is considerable "other" interest in the cases; so, I am unsure how you will be received. What you do with the pieces from now on is up to you. I have what I want.' She turned to leave.

'I understand, believe me, I have given up as much as you, perhaps more, but I also know that what you intend is not possible, surely you must see that. You cannot and must not ever think that what you propose to do is right. I am sorry that this will not be possible.' Darius was adamant. There was silence and then he continued, 'I have agreed with the British Government that, as we are in their territorial waters, I would give them Rafik and his extended network for the return of the regalia. We have had a man working undercover in his employ for some time and have many secrets to provide.' Mahmoud bowed and nodded.

With that, he produced a pouch. 'I want you to have these,' and he handed Lissa a large envelope and a pouch and, without even opening it, she knew exactly what it contained.

Darius could see the look of surprise on her face and added, 'I was able to collect these. Your father died to protect his country and I now pass this on to you and your family to protect. You will ensure that without it, the regalia will remain incomplete, so no one will be able to use it for power, reward, or seek its secrets, until the right time. You will know when it is. Do you remember the word I gave you in the note?'

She nodded. "HARIAH."

'Yes, freedom. It has six letters and the regalia has six parts. The dagger, the sheath, the belt, the clasp, and those you hold in your hands, the sash and the stone, make six. Woven into the sash is, *'Al-haria lelnas'* (freedom for the people).

Remy couldn't speak, she had been so focused on this moment that she had not really considered anything beyond her hatred of Rafik and desire for retribution.

Holding the pouch, Lissa turned to her. 'Mother, you know he is right. I hate Rafik as much as you do for what he has done to our family but there is more here than just our hatred, there is the hatred of "people" for their oppressors. If we can help them, surely, we must. Part of my heritage demands it!' Lissa broke down sobbing.

'What will happen to him?' Remy responded after what seemed an age, clearly broken by Lissa's plea.

'You need not worry; you will not see or hear from him again. I have already been informed that Andreas is free, without our help, and some of Rafik's men have already been arrested.'

With a small sad nod, Remy phoned Thomas and asked him to bring Rafik to the boat. She sat down and Lissa quickly wrapped her mother tightly in her arms. Remy sobbed into her daughter's shoulder.

Finally, she spoke through her tears. 'Your father would have been so proud of you.'

A while later, Thomas and Leo arrived, supporting a clearly still groggy Rafik between them.

'We meet again,' Rafik said focusing on Darius.

Then seeing Mahmoud, his face contorted in rage, and he screamed, 'Do you really think they will let you get away with this? The SAVAK will seek you out.' He laughed. 'They are probably here right now, and they hunt and kill dissidents and their supporters.' He laughed looking around at the people in the cabin. 'We are all dead already; you just don't know it yet.' Leo had had enough and despite his shoulder, landed a resounding blow to Rafik's chin. The man staggered back then dazed, pulled forward, but Thomas held him tight. He spat out blood at Leo's feet and swore in Arabic.

'Bloody shoulder, I must be losing my touch, that should have shut him up,' he said shaking and rubbing his hand.

Darius spoke, 'And what do you think the SAVAK will do with you? You are a traitor in both countries. I suspect you will have a better chance here of surviving than you ever would in Iran.' He laughed.

'Where are your people now, who will help you?' Mahmoud sneered. 'They have gone and you are alone. It is your turn to take the punishment that you have so keenly enjoyed. We will have your secrets and then maybe you will beg and wish that the gentle arms of Madame Akbari had killed you.'

Two men took hold of Rafik, who was screaming obscenities and pulled him towards the cabin door.

'Mahmoud, where are they taking him?'

'We'll go across the river tonight, then tomorrow to a small airport near Upminster, where he will be flown to a secure location.' He bowed slightly and then they left.

As Remy's group prepared to leave, all was silent. Darius joined them on deck. Only the lapping of the waves slapping against the side of the boat could be heard as the tide turned. Remy and Alessia huddled together watching as the lights began to come on along the riverbanks, lost in their own thoughts. A small boat was untied from the cruiser and as the darkness crept in, the sky reflected the oranges and purples of the setting sun in the river's dark depths.

The sound of an explosion was heard all the way to Woolwich. Flames rose high above the surrounding buildings and reflected in the dark waters of the Thames.

Chapter 47

Andreas, at the flat in Camberwell, waited a while before attempting to escape. As it turned out, this was unnecessary as security, either by design or laziness, was weak. He had been left untied, so had no problem dealing with the locked door; a simple one to "pick". He opened it slightly and listened. There were a couple of muffled voices, he thought it sounded as if the TV was on but he saw no one. He moved quietly down the stairs and although they creaked, neither of the men sitting at the table responded.

As he reached them, he realised why; the table was strewn with drug paraphernalia. They were high and so would not have been able to stop him, even if they could stand, which he doubted. Ignoring them, he picked up his phone and wallet and called the response car to pick him up. Leaving the building, he found it difficult to get the smell of the place out of his nostrils and the room out of his mind.

Getting in the car, Andreas received a message briefly explaining what Remy and her friends had been up to. He cursed himself for ever believing she did not intend to act. He was about to tell the driver to head to Peckham when a message over the police radio said there had been an explosion in Erith. Without giving it a second thought, he knew where she would be and he leant forward and told the driver to use his siren and head for Erith at speed. It took another twenty-five minutes weaving through the traffic before they arrived at the Eastley Yacht Club.

The scene was chaotic and crowded. They had to pick their way through a large group of locals, police, fire, ambulance, and military uniforms. Showing his credentials, he was taken to a van parked behind the clubhouse. The building itself had suffered some minor damage and had clearly lost all the glass in the windows facing the river.

Sitting at the back of the van was Jem. He had a bandage around his arm, where blood was just beginning to seep through and various less serious cuts, some of which were being stitched.

'Jem, what the hell happened?'

'I don't know,' he said. 'One minute I was walking down the jetty and the next, I was on my back. My ears were ringing, the dust and smoke were awful.'

'Where are the others?' Jem shook his head and it dropped to his chest. A sob-like sound was just audible. He tried to rise but looked really dizzy and sat down again.

'Stay here,' instructed Andreas. 'I'll see what I can find out.'

Andreas walked over to a group of people from the task force gathered at the side of the river. Out on the river, he could see what remained of a large boat was still smouldering. There were other boats around it representing Fire, a lifeboat, and the River Police. Above, a rescue helicopter had arrived and its light was scanning the water.

He approached Commander Fisher, head of the UK side of the task force. 'What do we know?' He did not ask about survivors as he was too afraid to hear the answer.

'The boat we believe belonged to Darius Shafiq. As far as we know, there were at least eleven people on board. Jem told us that Madam Akbari, her daughter, Thomas Beckett, Leo Tremaine, Rafik Yazdi, and a number of crew, as yet unnamed. We don't know yet if any of them survived. I am so sorry; I know you were close to Madame Akbari. The coast guard has said that as the tide is ebbing, they could have been washed upriver. They are widening their search now that the bomb squad are sure that the river is safe. Excuse me, I must talk to them before they leave.'

At that moment, a shout came up from the river and they could see a boat heading towards the jetty. In it was an RNLI crew and an extremely shaken and tired Leo wrapped in a silver foil blanket. He had clearly been in the river and apart from being wet and grimy, his clothes were torn, he had several cuts and was covered in what looked like oil. However, he was able to climb out of the dinghy onto the jetty unaided, so clearly, he was otherwise unhurt. A growl was heard from the bank and then all six-foot-six of Jem hurtled down the jetty to pick up the six-foot Leo in a bear hug.

Leo didn't move, just took in the warmth of his friend's body. When Jem finally put him down, Andreas stepped forward.

'I know what you are going to ask.' He shook his head. 'But I just don't know. I think that Rafik had already left the boat with Mahmoud and his men. We had just set off in the dinghy when the explosion happened. The next thing I knew I was in the water, and upstream from where the boat was in flames. I looked around but as it was getting dark, I couldn't see anyone. I'm a strong swimmer but I couldn't do anything as my shoulder had popped again. Next thing I know, I am bumping up against a boat and a hand reaches out and grabs me.

'They saved my life and pulling me in, my shoulder went back. The guy said I was lucky as it was a slack tide, or I would have been halfway to London Bridge.'

'Andreas,' Commander Fisher shouted. 'They have found someone else. Now they know a possible direction of the tide, they are looking towards Erith Pier.'

The sound of an approaching boat and shouts from the shore made everyone scramble down to the jetty, where a police boat was pulling alongside. Crouched in the bottom were the two women. It was clear from the bandages that both had been injured. Andreas rushed to help them out. Lissa, first, was clearly in pain, her arm was in a sling.

She only managed a brief, 'I think it's broken,' before she was picked up by Jem, who carried her to the ambulance, while a very relieved Andreas helped Remy out of the boat. She was clearly disorientated and had a gash on her head. He picked her up and she gasped.

'I must have hit something in the water, I'm fine,' she said. Despite her protests, he took her to the ambulance as well.

When they were settled in the ambulance and Lissa had some emergency pain relief, she was able to tell Andreas that they had been in the dinghy when the explosion had flung them out of it. Somehow Thomas had managed to hold onto it and had scooped up Remy and then Lissa, who were clinging to a rope dangling off the side. He had tied their dinghy to the barge before setting off to find Leo and Darius.

It was a good half an hour before a body was found. He was later identified as one of the boat's crew.

People were waiting in silence on the jetty, hoping for the sound of an approaching boat. All the time, Darius' boat continued to burn, lighting the scene. A fire tender, now alongside continued to spray the wreck till the last flames died and only smoke and steam curled into the night sky. Commander Fisher was on the phone to the military salvage team and asked them to tow what was left of the boat, which was still miraculously afloat, to the shore. They agreed they would attempt to bring it out of the water the following day and search it for any bodies.

There was still no word about the whereabouts of Thomas, Darius, Rafik, Mahmoud, his men, or the other crew members.

The search continued into the darkness.

Chapter 48

As the team pieced together what had happened, it was clear that having just got into the dinghy, the force of the explosion had knocked the four passengers into the water. Surfacing, Thomas had acted without thought, grabbing the dinghy. He realised that Remy was in the water next to him and he told her to take hold of the rope. Moving around it, he saw that Lissa was trying to hold onto it too but was clearly having problems. 'I think my arm is broken,' she said. He didn't wait till she finished the sentence and ignoring her scream of pain, he hoisted her into the dinghy and then helped Remy in.

He pushed the dinghy into the growing darkness, away from the flames, following the flow of the current. He then pulled it over to a nearby barge and tied the small craft to it.

Lissa said, 'The last thing he said was "I'm going to find Leo" and set off into the darkness. Mother shouted that she could see something by one of the barges and the last we saw of him was that he was clearly heading in that direction.' She began to shiver uncontrollably as if recalling the memory had brought her back to the cold waters of the Thames.

The search continued and eventually, the following morning, a body was found wedged between two of the barges. Much of the body had been badly burned, so it was not possible to make a definitive identification. Leo asked to see it and said he knew, by what was left of the clothing, it wasn't Thomas. As no trace of Darius or Mahmood had been found, it was presumed this could be either them or a missing crew member.

Andreas had spent time talking to each of the survivors and the picture that he built up suggested it was possible that there had been enough time between Mahmoud and his men taking Rafik off the boat for them to be out of reach of the explosion.

Remy, Lissa, and Leo had all been taken to the hospital in Woolwich and were currently under police protection. Leo had indeed dislocated his shoulder again, but it had popped back in when the RNLI crew had hauled him out onto their boat. He was now dressed and his arm was tightly strapped to his body.

Lissa's broken arm, fortunately, a straightforward break, had been set and her various cuts either glued or stitched, so she too was dressed. They both sat at Remy's bedside, who was under observation as she had a nasty head cut.

Later that day, Andreas received news that two more bodies had been found on the north bank of the Thames. Leo's immediate fear was that one of them would be Thomas, but it was the two men who had been with Mahmoud. They had been shot.

'This puts a totally different light on matters,' Andreas said to a colleague.

Commander Fisher came into the temporary HQ they had set up in the yacht club building. He said, 'We now think apart from Mr Beckett, Yazdi, Darius and Mahmoud, all the others have been accounted for. Now that the boat has been hauled up, the forensic team hope to be able to give us some information about where and how the explosion was set off.'

'Are we hazarding any guesses yet as to who is responsible for the explosion? I presume there are several different possibilities.' Andreas left the thought hanging.

Fisher said, 'You are right, we are not speculating. We need more evidence. But suffice it to say, we have been told that a private jet from Tehran landed at the airport near Upminster the day before yesterday. It appears that there were three "businessmen" on board here to meet a distribution company in Purfleet. Which seems like a remarkable coincidence. Perhaps the team looking at the remains of the boat will find something that will help us; we will have to wait. For the moment, we have, however, made sure that surveillance teams are monitoring the group's every movement.'

Jem had been sitting quietly in the corner listening to the conversation. It was painfully clear to him from what he knew of the goings on in Iran, that the one group that all Iranians were afraid of were the SAVAK. He reasoned that since the regalia might become a crucial factor in uniting groups to fight for freedom, stopping this from happening would be important to them. Rafik was a loose cannon and therefore a hindrance, getting rid of him would be useful, as would disposing of the so-called traitor Mahmoud. So "Boom", all problems solved. But it hadn't quite gone like that, there had been survivors and there would be questions, which would make getting the regalia even more difficult.

Suddenly fearful, Jem raced over to Andreas and Fisher. 'If Yazdi is alive, he will still want to get to Remy,' he said. 'He needs the regalia, and she has the keys to the cases. It's so fucking simple. Where are they?' In his effort to make them see the danger, he was becoming almost incoherent and was shouting at Fisher.

'Hey, dial it down. I don't know who has them and you are assuming something we have no proof of,' he replied.

'Fuck proof, you know damn well it's the Iranians. Do you need a confession before you bloody well act? In the meantime, they could be at that hospital now.' With that, he turned and headed back to the carpark where Tyrone had been patiently waiting.

'Woolwich Hospital,' yelled Jem as he threw himself into the car. Wheels spinning, Tyrone didn't ask, he just put his foot down and set off, calling on all his years of experience. He left the yacht club and after a hair-raising drive, they arrived at the hospital. Tyrone thought they had probably collected a number of speeding tickets, although the police escort they picked up along the way would help.

Remy's head hurt but she wanted to know what had happened since she was put in the back of the ambulance at the yacht club, after which things were very hazy. Lissa stood up. 'Leave it, mother, you have six or seven stitches.' She gently touched her mother's hand.

Remy looked at her daughter. 'You look as if you have one or two yourself, and your arm. Oh, Leo, I see your shoulder must have come out again.' She stroked his face. He dreaded what was coming next.

Remy said, 'Where's Thomas? I want to thank him.'

Before he could speak, Jem barged into the room. 'I think we need to get you all the fuck out of here. He'll come for 'er and when he does, they will be there and there'll be one hell of a bloodbath.'

They all looked at him, trying to make sense of what he had just said.

Chapter 49

Thomas had started to swim towards the other barge in the direction Remy had pointed. When he got there, he found that the body was probably one of the crew. Although he hated to just leave it, he knew he had to move on, but was uncertain what to do next.

The cold and exertion were clearly beginning to sap his strength and his clothes weighed him down. He shook off his shoes but had no strength to remove his jacket. He knew that he couldn't stay in the water much longer, so looked around desperately for a boat or somewhere to haul himself out. He knew that he was running out of time.

He had almost given up and with his strength ebbing, he tried to swim towards the shore, but the current was getting stronger and pushed him into the middle of the river. He knew his strength had gone and had resigned himself to this being the end when he felt something hard hit him and it seemed to catch his jacket. Then he felt himself being pulled backwards until he hit the side of a boat. The last thing he remembered was being pulled out of the water. Exhaustion overtook him and he passed out.

When he came around, he found he was in a dark room and tied to a chair. Wherever he was, it was quiet and cold, and he realised that he was still wet. He started to shiver and felt sick. He had swallowed a lot of Thames water, not a pleasant experience, and it now threatened to escape him; however, throwing up did not make him feel better. In the darkness, a voice called out, startling him.

'You're awake then. Who are you? It's so dark in here, I can't see you.'

Thomas knew the voice; he did not reply.

'Suit yourself. They will be back soon and they will make you talk,' said Rafik.

Time passed. Thomas was sick again and the stench permeated the darkness. As his clothes dripped, gradually his shivering lessened. He could hear the muffled sound of voices to his left and the clinking of metal somewhere to his right, which created an eerie atmosphere, that made his skin crawl. He was concerned that Rafik would suddenly appear and shuddered, but as time passed and he did not, so Thomas presumed he was also held captive in some way.

In the darkness, the silence was deep, and it was hard to tell whether five minutes or an hour had passed. As he felt stronger, he decided it was time to try to loosen what he presumed were zip-ties. He had learned strategies in the army but he needed to get his arms over the back of the chair. Fortunately, he found that although his legs were secured to the chair, he could stand up. Then it was just a case of bending and pushing against his body until the tie broke. As he was about to tackle his legs, he heard a noise. He sat down and put his arms behind him, as he had been, then dropped his head down on his chest as if he was still unconscious.

Suddenly, light flooded into the room. Thomas remained still and did not look up, just listened. Someone walked in and away from him; then came the sound of someone being hit with something, followed by a scream, then silence. Thomas heard a chain being undone and someone grunted as if lifting something heavy. He very slowly raised his head a little and opened his eyes. In the dim light of the corner, he saw that a man, with a body over his shoulder, moving away from a small cage, like one that some dogs were kept in. As the man left, Thomas chanced a quick look around, he saw that the room was large, like an empty hanger. He located a camera above the cage, but apart from that the room was featureless. The man returned and walked towards him.

Thomas was conflicted did he have the strength to tackle this man, while his legs were still tied, or should he wait? The decision was made for him, as the man returned and threw a blanket and bottle of water onto his lap.

'You can stop pretending to be unconscious, we are watching.' The man had a strong Russian accent. He bent down and cut the ties on Thomas' legs. As he did, Thomas saw that he had the cross symbol on his hand and remembered the man in Los Angeles who had tried to kill him had the same one. Whoever these people were, this was clearly no small-scale operation. 'We have no interest in you. Don't cause us any problems, understand?' Thomas nodded and with that, the man left the room, he shut the door and the darkness returned.

Thomas stood up and checked his pockets but they were empty, either in the river or with the man. He stripped off his jacket and wrapped the blanket around him, then jumped up and down to get the blood flowing in his legs and warm himself up. He used the water to wash his mouth out and then drank the rest. Still feeling weak from his time in the river, he sat down again, considering what he should do. He had no idea if there were more men outside or where they were. Whatever he decided, it would have an impact; either he would be able to free himself, or he would be killed.

He decided that when the man returned, if he returned, he would need to try and escape, and would need to disable him at the very least. So, he needed a weapon and decided that there might be something useful in the cage he had seen Rafik in. His training had helped him establish key points in the room when the door had been open, so he knew the rough location of the cage. His eyes had again grown accustomed to the darkness but looking around, he could only make out the vaguest of features. However, he saw the blinking red light of the camera high on one wall and hoped the man was not watching. He calculated that it would be about seven steps, so counted as he stepped, with arms outstretched.

Bending down, he felt for the cage and touching it, he felt elated. Feeling around he found a chain and traced it back by feeling along the bars, until he found the door. Reaching inside, he felt how the chain was attached and realised it had been looped through itself, so with some difficulty, he threaded it through and undid it. He thought this would be both a weapon and a way to secure the man if he came back. He remained still, listening, and was both surprised and grateful that no one came to the room.

He knew the orientation to the chair from the cage and started to inch his way back to it. Then he took three steps to the wall, and moved along it till he located the door. He was amazed that no one had come to find out what he was doing. He was about to turn the door handle when he heard three loud popping sounds. He instantly flattened himself against the wall, winding the chain round his hand in readiness, as he recognised the sounds. He held his breath. He waited and, when the door didn't open, he breathed a sigh of relief.

There were no other sounds but still, he waited. When he thought enough time had elapsed, he turned the handle and opened the door.

Chapter 50

As Thomas was trying to escape, Remy was trying to deal with the news that he was probably dead. She hadn't known him that long but she was aware that she felt his loss deeply. She was both confused and troubled by this, especially as she was also aware of the growing relationship between Thomas and her daughter.

For the moment, there was nothing she could do to make things better, as the group were bruised and battered, she knew they needed time to heal. Andreas arrived and greeted the walking wounded and then bent and kissed Remy.

'Chérie, I have seen you looking better,' he declared. She gave him a weak slap on the wrist.

'You wouldn't be too well either I suspect having swallowed half the Thames. What news?'

'I am sorry, I have no news of Thomas to give you, but that just as easily could be positive. Fortunately, the remains of the boat were hauled up onto the slipway before it disappeared into the depths. The team worked overnight; the only things they found of note were these,' and he held up a small plastic bag. Inside, among what was obviously part of what could have been a timer, was a lighter with "Love ♥ NY on it" 'I can see by your face you recognised this. It was found in the remains of the boat, carefully protected but near to where the explosion took place and ignited the fuel tank, making the fire more intense.'

'I remember, that's what Wes said about the one they had found in the car in Sydney,' observed Leo.

'I have the one they found in my father's car. I thought it was his. We know that "The Arrow" is dead, so it can't have been him,' Lissa concluded.

Andreas became even more serious as he explained the situation as it appeared to his team now. He said they were now certain that the SAVAK, or Iranian Secret Police, were involved and this meant everyone needed to be on their guard. The bomb had clearly been set by the same man who killed Farzad in New York and the bomb in Sydney. Having checked the inclusion of the lighter against the database of arsonists, they had a clear suspect, but unfortunately, despite being prolific, he had never been caught.

The task force was unsure whether the man, who had presumably commissioned the bombing of the boat, was aware that while most of the regalia were safe, the keystone and sash had presumably gone into the river with the keys to the boxes.

'No, they haven't,' said Lissa, pulling out from her pocket the keys and a pouch. 'They maybe got a little soggy but they are safe. I put the pouch on the chain with the keys round my neck when we left the boat.' She opened the pouch and extracted first the stone, then the sash, which she unrolled. Fortunately, it seemed to have remained remarkably unmarked.

Andreas beamed. 'Excellent! So, Jem, your heroic dash across to the hospital made the team reassess the protection. Now with this news, you will get your wish. You will all be taken into protective custody.'

A chorus of objections was halted by Andreas. 'We suggest that Remy will be more comfortable at home anyway, so we will ask you all to stay with her at the house in Kensington.' The grumbling died away, although Jem still looked as if he was going to explode. Only Lissa's gentle touch on his arm seemed to calm him.

Chapter 51

To Thomas' surprise, the door wasn't locked. Staying low, he cracked it open just a little further, trying to peer outside. It was quiet, so he opened it a little further.

Lying on the floor, clearly dead, was the man who had come into the room and taken Rafik. Thomas opened the door a little more and saw two other men sitting at the table, who were also dead. He stood listening; silence. He decided it was relatively safe and stepped into the light, immediately shielding his eyes from the sudden brilliance. Looking at the men, they all appeared to have died from a single shot, execution style. In the corner of the room was the surveillance system but it appeared that the recording disk had been taken as the draw was open. Thomas thought that whoever had killed the men and presumably taken Rafik, did not know or care that he was there.

Looking at the table, he saw an array of pictures of young blonde women, in various stages of undress, and a list of distinctly Arab men's names; it was clearly a manifest. A sheet attached headed "Export", gave basic information about the girls, the locations where the girls had been picked up, and various statistics about each and who they were going to.

Next was a list headed "Imports". Inadvertently, he made a mental note of the crest, as he didn't recognise it.

There was no heading on the paperwork, just a phone number, dock location and a name to contact. Next, he checked the men's pockets. There were no signs of their phones or wallets; in fact, nothing at all personal. Thomas swore. On the back of one of the chairs, one man's jacket was the only one not marked by any blood.

He took it and put it on and despite the scene, the warmth immediately made him feel better, although he still had a deep coldness that was difficult to shake off. He picked up the papers and stuffed them in his pocket. Looking around, he opened the cupboards, and found a few tools, several large boxes of water bottles, and packets of sandwiches. A door led to a bathroom with a shower. He drank some water and grabbed a sandwich but didn't eat it; he wasn't generally squeamish but he was increasingly aware of a really unpleasant smell.

There were two doors besides the one he had come in through and the bathroom and he headed to the first. It opened into what he thought was a large room, not unlike the one he had been kept in. The light from the room didn't stretch far, but this room appeared empty. He couldn't see another door, although there may have been one. He went to the other door and opened it, immediately stepping back, as the smell of urine and excrement was unbelievable. Holding the jacket across his face, he stepped in, feeling the wall for a light switch. As light filled the room, the scene he was greeted by was like a picture of hell.

There must have been about four cages, each filled with what he first assumed were piles of rags, then seeing a slight movement, he thought *Oh God, they're bodies*. Having seen the pictures he thought these were probably the women. At first, he wasn't sure whether they were alive or dead as they were curled up and the single bulb made almost everything a shade of grey. Then he saw one shape move and sit up.

'Hello,' was the only thing he could think to say.

The woman who had moved whispered, 'Please help us!' Her accent was clearly British.

Thomas moved to her "cage" and saw the padlock. 'I'm going to get something to break the locks, I will come back.' She nodded.

He went back to the room where the dead men were and picked up a hammer and chisel from the cupboard, then returned, smashing, the locks of each of the cages and opening the doors. Gradually, the women crawled out and stood up shakily, holding each other up, unsure what to do next. The woman who spoke to him first said, 'Thank you.'

'How long have you been here?'

'What day is it?' She asked.

He realised he wasn't sure himself but thought it might have been Wednesday. Her voice trembled as she said she thought they had been there since Friday. The women had now gathered in a silent group, he counted fifteen in all. Looking round, he realised the scale of the operation, as there were actually ten cages, each showing the remnants of previous occupants. He told the women to follow him and he took them to the door of the room where the dead men were.

'Look, the men in there are all dead. I didn't kill them. I don't think anyone else is around but I will go and check, then I will go and get help. You should stay here. Do the others speak English?' She nodded. Thomas told her that there was a shower next door and food and water. He opened the door fully and the women initially stepped back, like Thomas had, as they were blinded by the light. The woman he had spoken to and another went through into the bathroom.

Thomas went back to the room he had been kept in and felt inside for a light switch. The lights came on and he could see a large roller door at the end and a small door to the side. He had the hammer and chisel with him and headed across the floor of the warehouse to the door. He turned the handle and the door opened. He was greeted by a blast of cool air and he breathed it in deeply. Looking around cautiously, he dropped the tools, and stepped out. He could see the river behind the warehouse but had no idea where he was.

He went back to where the women were gathered, ravenously eating the sandwiches.

One said, 'There's no water in the shower, we just used the bottles in the boxes.' She started to cry. One of the other girls put her arm around her.

'Come on, it'll soon be over, he will get help.'

In the light, he could see that they were all about the same age, between fifteen and twenty-ish, blonde and probably blue-eyed, although filthy and scared, likely the ones in the pictures. He knew from what he had seen on the table what this meant; people trafficking didn't just go one way.

'There is no one around, so stay here, you should be safe. I am going to get help,' he promised. Realising he had no shoes; he looked at the men and found one had feet about the same size. He hurriedly took off the man's shoes and put them on. They were a little tight but would have to do.

He headed back to the door and out into the daylight. The sun had come out, and he shielded his eyes from the sudden brightness. Ignoring the pathway that led to the river, he saw that the other one led away from the warehouse towards a road. As he headed up the road, he began to hear the sounds of traffic. It didn't take long till he arrived at a small roundabout that gave access to two other warehouses, but all seemed quiet, and he presumed empty. Summoning the strength, he pushed himself to walk on and came to the main road.

It was clear that this was not a busy stretch as standing there, no cars passed. Walking along it, he saw that what traffic there was ran along a dual carriageway further over. He was about to head that way but was increasingly beginning to feel really unwell and his energy levels were rapidly decreasing. He again forced himself on. Fortunately, a lorry having turned onto the side road he was on, passed him and headed down a side turning just ahead. Thomas followed and found himself outside a busy area, full of lorries.

He had no idea later how he managed to cross the road but staggered into the carpark, where a man, focusing on his paperwork, came out from the factory. He looked up and saw a totally filthy, bedraggled man heading towards him. The man thought, *Oh fuck, a bloody tramp*, and took a step back.

But there was something about this man that made him say, 'Shit, are you all right, mate?'

Thomas shook his head and collapsed onto his knees. The man got his phone out and the last thing Thomas heard was him asking for the police.

He came around in the ambulance, with a policeman sitting opposite, and he realised he was handcuffed to the trolley. 'Take it easy, mate,' the man warned.

Thomas used the last of his energy to tell the policeman about the warehouse and the women. At first, the man thought he was delusional but when he gave his name, things immediately changed. The policeman alerted HQ.

'Mate, the entire world's been looking for you. I'm Andy, you're okay now,' he said as he undid the handcuffs.

As the ambulance arrived at the hospital, the door was thrown open and a tall, heavily built man squeezed himself into the ambulance. He introduced himself but Thomas couldn't respond. The man had a fearsome look and eyes which Thomas thought almost burned into his very soul.

'You've been a busy boy. Three bodies and a whole bunch of women caged like animals,' he almost spat the last words. The policeman stood up and got between Thomas and the inspector.

'Sir, please,' he said as he tried to stop the man pushing past him. Then, the door of the ambulance opened again and Thomas looked from the inspector, whose face was getting dangerously close, to the one who looked both pleased and shocked all at once.

'Sir,' the policeman begged. 'This is Thomas Beckett, who everyone has been looking for.' The inspector stopped and stood up and silently glared at the constable and Thomas, then turned and pushed past Andreas.

'Looks like I got here just in time,' he laughed.

Outside, Andreas showed the inspector his badge and they walked away talking quietly. As they left the ambulance, Leo appeared and jumped in and despite the warnings of a slightly bemused doctor who was hurrying forward to treat Thomas, Leo helped Thomas to stand and climb out of the ambulance. Immediately, Jem literally picked him up and carried him over to a private one. Not a word was spoken but the grins on everyone's faces said it all. Andreas shook hands with the inspector and then walked over to the ambulance and climbed in.

Inside, a nurse was hooking Thomas up to a drip and as they set off, Leo finally said, 'Bloody typical, leave you alone for five fucking minutes and you manage to not only save two women from the Thames but then upset a people smuggling racket to boot!' Thomas closed his eyes; it had been such a very long few days.

Chapter 52

The fever hit Thomas like a ton of bricks. The Thames water, although much cleaner now, was still not a pleasant place to take a drink, and Thomas had drunk a lot. Epidemiological analysis had detected Weil's disease and he was placed on high doses of antibiotics. The doctors suggested that it was thanks to his strong physique that he began to improve on his second day in hospital, but he was still very weak. Lissa had been at his side, but he didn't know that until the fever broke and he woke feeling better, to find her sitting in a chair next to him.

Leo and Jem arrived, as did their escort. Andreas suggested, however, that he thought that they were out of immediate danger but should still stay at Remy's house in Kensington, as soon as Thomas was able to leave. Between the three of them, they brought him up-to-date with what had happened to each of them after the explosion. Finally, Thomas asked, 'Where's Remy?'

Lissa said, 'When you are feeling up to it, we'll go to the house. She has been rather busy.' He just nodded. Despite the fears and advice to the contrary of the medical staff, the next day, Thomas said he was ready to go.

He was still attached to a drip, linked to a stand, and while Leo passed a dressing gown around his shoulders, he added for effect, 'Don't want you displaying your bum to everyone and scaring the nurses!' Thomas laughed and started to cough, holding his chest. Lissa looked concerned but he indicated he was okay. With Jem's support, they headed out of the room and along the corridor and then into an ambulance.

When they arrived at her house, Remy was on the phone but ended the call immediately as they arrived. They made a motley crew with Leo, his shoulder in a sling, a black eye, and stitches to his forehead; Thomas with cuts, stitches and bruises, pulling a drip, and Lissa, who looked fresh-faced but had two bruised ribs, a broken arm, and stitches to a wound in her side. The group was being herded like a flock of sheep, by sheepdog Jem, arms akimbo driving them into the room.

'My goodness me, what a sight. Thomas, I am so pleased to see that you are alive.' Remy rushed to then him hugged and kissed him. 'I have a lot to thank you for,' she added.

'Thanks, good to see you too. How are you feeling?' He said.

'Better than you it seems, although I won't be running any marathons for a while. You?'

'The same but forget the marathon.' Their exchange broke the tension and everyone laughed. He sat down heavily on the sofa and she started to ask him questions about what had happened. As they talked, the others gradually withdrew until only the two and Lissa remained. She watched them and saw the deep affection that had grown between them, and for a moment, she was jealous; then shook this off and quietly slipped from the room.

Andreas came by briefly as Thomas had asked him to tell him what had happened to the women he had found in the warehouse. He told him that the site had been used by a group of Middle Eastern origin as a safe house to hold items such as cars and women before they were shipped out of the country to various Arab states, where blonde women were particularly enjoyed. The men who had been killed were Russians and were probably only there to guard the women. He thought Yazdi had been held there, only until the Iranians arrived at the airport to take him back to Iran. Thomas thought that all made sense but asked why they had left him alive.

'I suspect you weren't of high enough value to risk them being caught.'

'Oh thanks,' he laughed.

'They would probably have come back for you with the women and tried to ransom you off sometime later,' he confessed, which mollified Thomas.

It wasn't until the next day that the whole team was reunited at Remy's house. Tiana and Grace had flown in from New York together. Remy, having declared they needed a holiday too, had sent them first-class tickets. They then spent a considerable time organising arrangements for the group.

They had just finished a delicious lunch, that even Thomas had managed to eat some of, and were just about to raise glasses of elderflower fizz, as most of the group was still on antibiotics or painkillers when Remy stood up.

'I have some news,' said Remy. 'The pieces of the regalia have been reunited and are currently held at the house in Peckham until their future can be determined. In all likelihood, it would seem from what Andreas has been able to tell me, they will remain there until free and fair elections are held.'

'Cat in hell's chance,' Leo chortled.

'Then what?' Lissa fumed. 'The whole point was that the regalia should be given to the people to decide!'

Her mother interrupted, 'What, and start a war? It is not as simple as just giving it to someone. Who would you give it to, and who would decide if they were the right ones? What if this decision turned out badly? What then? This is not something for us to debate, we do not have all the facts. We have done our job; our part is over!'

'No, it isn't,' interrupted Thomas. 'We were all nearly killed and I, for one, want the man who was responsible. If it wasn't for Yazdi, a lot of people, including Julia, would never have been hurt or killed.'

The silence that followed, was broken by the doorbell. 'Tiana, can you get the door please, it's probably Andreas.'

'So, what are you suggesting?' Remy said. 'If the SAVAK took him, he may well be dead already.'

'I…we need to know that for sure or we need to bring him to justice,' Leo replied.

There were silent nods from the group. But although there was agreement, it was as if no one dared say anything more.

Jem was thinking about what this revenge might look like when he almost felt that he was having a vision, as a bruised and battered Rafik Yazdi stood in the doorway, holding Tiana by the arm, clearly for support. Behind him stood three men, all with semi-automatic weapons.

'Please don't get up,' the man behind Yazdi almost whispered as he saw Jem attempt to try. 'I would hate to have to make you sit down permanently.' He raised the muzzle of the gun.

'Mrs Akbari, I am sorry to intrude.' His voice was smooth and mid-Atlantic, although he looked to be of Arab origin. He sort of bowed. 'We haven't been introduced; my name is Omid Hakimi. I am here because it appears that you have managed to collect some valuable pieces of jewellery that belong to my country, and I will happily return them for you, to their rightful place. To ensure that this happens, I propose a trade to facilitate this. You want this man,' he indicated Yazdi, still propped up by Tiana, 'as I know he has committed many crimes that you want him to answer for. We have no further use for him, so I propose we give him to you to do with what you will.'

233

'Having heard your comments on the way in, I am sure that it will please you and the group. It is really quite simple; in return, you will give me the regalia. I should add, refusal would place the lives of you, your friends and your family in grave peril.'

Thomas started to rise. 'Please, Mr Beckett, your life was saved due to our grace. If my colleague here, had not seen and pulled you half-dead from the water well, I implore do not to waste it fruitlessly now.' Thomas sat down.

Chapter 53

Hakimi walked over to the sofa and sat down opposite Remy, his gun resting in his lap. Leo was clearly weighing up how to manage the situation.

'I would not bother, Mr Tremaine, besides these two men, there are a number of others around the building to ensure we are not disturbed. They will let Mr Metaxas' men go once we leave. Let me please explain what I want from you.'

He took out a gold cigarette box and lighter, opened it, and taking one out, lit it. The air was instantly filled with the sweet aroma of Middle Eastern tobacco. Taking a long breath in and then exhaling the smoke, he told Remy that she would accompany him to the house in Peckham. When Thomas and Leo started to object, he waited and then continued. Yazdi would remain here with them, as would the men around the house. If everyone stayed calm and Remy retrieved the boxes, no one would be harmed and on receipt of confirmation, his men would withdraw.

'Please be so kind as to ask your daughter to give the keys to my friend.' One of the two men stepped forward and standing in front of her, held out his hand.

'I do not have them,' Lissa said quietly. For a brief moment, she was fearful of the consequences for everyone.

'Please explain as I know that you did.'

'I gave them to Mr Metaxas. He has them and the regalia now, you are too late.'

'Ah yes, I see. So, Mrs Akbari, I would ask you therefore to accompany us,' and then smiling, he stood up and caught Grace's arm. 'Perhaps you can come with her as further surety.' His tone was not pleasant and she pulled her arm free. He went on, 'I am sure that there might be some way of persuading him to release the cases and their contents to you. Once again, I am sorry for the intrusion; comply with my requests, and this will soon be over. Please give your phones to my colleague. The landline and internet have been disabled. Please make yourselves comfortable, this might take a while.'

With that, he indicated to both Remy and Grace that they should do the same. Both did so, without comment. Thomas, Leo and Jem were clearly eager to rise and it was only Remy's slight shake of the head that stopped them.

Hakimi cautioned, 'Please do not worry, we will take great care of them.' he said. ' Oh and yes, I just remembered,' he said with a smirk, 'I wouldn't go outside if I were you,' then he followed the women out through the door. The two men left, never turning their backs to the room.

The door closed.

The next few minutes were almost chaotic. Tiana had been standing with Yazdi, who was clutching her arm, as neither had dared move. Now, Tiana pushed him off and he crumpled to the floor. Leo and Jem were arguing over who should go after him and Thomas was trying to stop an almost hysterical Lissa from wanting to kick and punch the man, who now lay curled in a ball on the floor.

He caught her in his arms and hugged her tightly, and shouted, 'Look, stop!!' then wheezing said, 'We all need to calm down. Jem, you go upstairs and see if you can spot any of Hakimi's guards. Leo, you do downstairs and, Lissa, see if you can find something to stop Rafik bleeding on your mother's carpet. Tiana, see how badly he is hurt.' Then he said he would go and see if he could find the jamming device, although silently he thought it was unlikely, he needed time to think.

When the men returned, Yazdi was no longer on the floor but sitting on the settee. It appeared that Lissa and Tiana had helped him to his feet and were now trying to determine how seriously hurt he was.

'I think he is lucky to be alive, I am sure from what he has told me, that he probably has quite serious internal injuries. He needs a hospital,' Tiana said and stood up, 'I have some nursing training but we need to keep him alive as we may still need his help.' Thomas nodded.

Jem hugged Tiana and kissed her forehead, which did not go unnoticed by Leo and he smiled.

Neither he, Thomas or Jem had seen any men but that did not mean they were not there.

'So, what do we do?' Lissa stammered. '' We wait,' replied Thomas.

Chapter 54

Outside, Tyrone watched and waited.

Having noticed one of Hakimi's men at the hospital, he had shadowed him as the man followed Thomas and Leo to Remy's house, as he became more and more convinced that this, and not the house in Peckham, would be the target.

He did not know at this point, that this man was the arsonist that they had been seeking and who, now out of sight, was hurriedly setting up explosives.

When Hakimi arrived, Tyrone had caught sight of the man again and when Hakimi left with Remy and Grace, Tyrone saw the man move forward and bend down by the door. His years of experience had taught him that this man's actions presented a real threat and, although still unsure of what the man was up to, he acted.

The sound of the first shot, like the backfire of a car, had made everyone in the house jump, the second and third were quieter, but Leo said, 'It looks like help is on its way.'

Once the man by the door and the others he had seen were down, Tyrone quickly moved to investigate what he had been doing. He did not touch the device but examining it carefully, he quickly appreciated that the bomb was far too complex for him to tackle.

Inside the house, on hearing the shots, Thomas immediately told everyone to sit down. 'Whatever is happening outside will not be helped by us barging in. They will tell us when it is okay.' Jem and Leo both nodded, everyone sat down.

Recognising the danger, Tyrone had immediately contacted Andreas, who said his team were already on their way. It was only minutes before they and the bomb disposal people arrived.

They immediately set about disarming the devices. Tyrone knew that the gunfire had alerted those inside, and that the men would have ensured no one moved. Now he focussed on warning them not to open any doors or windows downstairs till they had the all clear.

Thomas heard what he thought was a drone and went to the window. He could see Tyrone indicating that he should not open it, instead he was pointing upwards. The drone rose, and Thomas moved towards the stairs. As he felt sure that Tyrone was trying to indicate that they should not to open either the window or door. Upstairs, Thomas looked out the window and saw Tyrone giving a thumbs-up.

He opened the window and shouted, 'Good to see you, Tyrone,' as Leo and Jem joined him. Tyrone told them that he was convinced that Remy would be taken to the house in Peckham to collect the cases.

He explained about the device on front door and that they needed to check downstairs windows and any other doors, before they cleared the house.

'So she can disarm the bombs with everyone out of the way, we will get you all out from upstairs just in case.' Tyrone said.

Five minutes later, a ladder appeared at the window and everyone, including Lissa, carried fireman's style by Jem, and then Yazdi, managed to climb safely down it.

Leo grinned at Thomas. 'Great instincts, Thomas.'

Thomas just nodded.

Once everyone was down, Tyrone immediately reassured them that Andreas and his team were in complete control of the situation at the house in Peckham. An ambulance took Yazdi, under guard to a private hospital in Kent, where he would undergo emergency surgery.

Tyrone said they should stay together but somewhere no one would find them. Initially there were protests but then Thomas, held up his hand and said he agreed, as their being there would only complicate things. Tyrone said he would arrange transport and Thomas suggested they should go to his old house in Deptford as no one knew that he owned it. After some further concerns, they finally, even Lissa agreed. As they were all getting into cars, Thomas caught Tyrone's shoulder. 'Thank you, man, I think we'll need time to talk later.' Tyrone nodded, then got into the driving seat and set off towards Deptford.

After his mother died, Thomas decided to keep the house for sentimental as well as practical reasons. After years of renting to the same family, they had finally left, allowing him to complete a total refurbishment. He had considered both selling and renting it and had an estate agent appraise its value, which at over £800K he found staggering, as he had her original bill of sale which showed she had paid £101K. It was now furnished to show as it would soon go on the market; returning there, although it looked very different, would make him extremely nostalgic.

Sitting in the back of the car with Lissa curled up asleep against him, made him realise how important she was becoming to him, and he gently stroked her hair. He just needed to focus a little longer to ensure that everyone came through this in one piece.

The new phone that he had been given buzzed and he answered it; it was Andreas.

'My God, I am so pleased to hear your voice,' he said, 'Remy was so worried.'

'What's happening?' Thomas asked.

'It's quiet in Peckham, no sign of anyone yet. Tyrone called me when he saw the men arriving. That was about an hour ago. We are following the tracker he placed on the vehicle, it's still moving in this direction but traffic is slow.'

'Will you stop them before they get to the house or wait?'

'No, we'll wait. We don't want them to do anything rash and risk more lives. We have a nice little welcoming committee for them. Remy and I had talked about this scenario but expected it to be Yazdi who would come, but it makes no difference. I must go, they are on the move again and getting closer. Stay inside, we'll come to you when this is over.'

He rang off. Thomas found it hard to be powerless but as the car turned down Friendly Street, he knew he had to just sit tight for once.

Chapter 55

At the house in Peckham, everyone was ready, not that they thought there would be much of a problem as it was clear that of the original team that had landed at Upminster, only Hakimi and one other remained, thanks to Tyrone. However, the team watching Remy's house reported that there seemed to be another two in the Range Rover but no one else was seen in the street. The task force had found and "removed" two men from the house behind "Sunshine Villa" and released the neighbours, who were now recovering. So, if Hakimi had been relying on them to bolster his team, he was in for a surprise.

Andreas was now watching the house via surveillance cameras and tracking the SUV on screen. As it turned into the road and came to a stop outside the house, he almost held his breath. The first person out was next to the driver, and having checked out all appeared quiet, he opened the door on the kerbside. Another man got out, who Andreas could see from the picture and information he had received was Hakimi. He extended a hand into the vehicle but this was ignored as Remy got out. Andreas breathed a sigh of relief.

It was clear she was determined, despite the team's numerous protestations, saying this was something she had to finish. Slowly, she moved forward. She knew what to do; he just hoped she would be careful.

Andreas thought the next man he saw get out of the vehicle might be the bomb maker, but as he had only seen some blurred images, he remained focussed on Hakimi and Remy. It wasn't until later that he was told that the bomb maker had already been killed by Tyrone.

It seemed that Grace and the driver were to remain in the vehicle. Hakimi indicated to Remy that she should go through the gate and then he and one of the men fell in step behind. The third man was on the radio and walked to the path leading around the side of the house. Andreas presumed his team in the house behind would remove him. Remy limped slowly and somewhat dramatically up the path towards the house.

In the SUV, the man sat pointing his gun at Grace, who having been at the same briefing as the others, knew she just needed to remain calm. Then two things happened quickly. First, Remy slumped to the ground, and Hakimi bent to pick her up;; secondly, a thud behind him made him pull her sharply to her feet in front of him. A quick glance told him the man behind him was clearly dead. Pulling Remy backwards towards the SUV, Hakimi held his gun to her head.

Andreas knew this was the critical moment. If the task force marksman fired now, he could hit Remy but if he didn't and they managed to get back to the van, they may lose their advantage and either a hostage situation or a chase could develop.

The situation was taken out of everyone's hands as the man holding Grace in the SUV decided for them. He turned, put his foot down, and with a squeal of rubber the vehicle set off up the road. As it swerved down the road, the door slammed shut, trapping Grace inside, as she had fallen backwards as a result of their rapid departure. Hakimi, holding Remy, was now alone in the middle of the pavement. With limited options, he made the only sensible choice; letting go of Remy, he put his gun down, went down on his knees and put his hands behind his head and waited.

Andreas leapt out of the van, ran past the men, who were picking up the gun and marching Hakimi off, to where a startled Remy was standing. He swept her up into his arms and as their eyes met, his kiss, so full of meaning, dispelled any lingering doubts she had. She knew that finally, she could accept the love of this man, who had waited for her for so long, as she was no longer ashamed, or afraid to return it.

'I must go,' he said, passing her into the arms of a paramedic.

'It's quite all right, I am unhurt,' she said.

The woman smiled as she held Remy's elbow and pushed her firmly towards the ambulance. 'Shock has a nasty way of catching up with you, we'll just check you out,' she said, not listening to Remy's protestations, still holding her arm a little too tightly as she steered her towards the ambulance at the end of the road.

Chapter 56

The paramedic pushed Remy up the stairs into the ambulance. Then towards the bed.

'You don't remember me, do you? I know, we only met a couple of times. I am Dilara, Rafik's daughter.' Remy realised that she had a gun and sat down as indicated. The ambulance doors closed and it moved off.

Chapter 57

Climbing into the ops van, Andreas was focussed on following the departing SUV and the traffic nightmare that ensued, so did not notice the woman forcefully pushing Remy into the ambulance. He watched as the SUV careered through the cars, completely blocking the busy lunchtime traffic. After a short "escape", police cars caught up, and armed men immediately surrounded the vehicle, while others moved to unravel the chaotic scene. Eyewitnesses confirmed that having stopped, the SUV seemed to rock crazily, the side door opened and a dishevelled, young blonde woman had climbed out. Inside, they could see the driver, who appeared to be unconscious. The woman staggered a little but seemed otherwise unhurt and then sat down on the kerb.

Grace had to tell and re-tell her story. First to the police, then to the task force, and finally when she met up with them, Leo and Thomas. Once the driver saw what was going on, he muttered something about not being paid enough and shot off, taking her totally by surprise. Realising the traffic on the main road would not allow a fast getaway, he turned and sped up a side road with humps, meaning she was thrown all over the place. He ended up turning back into the main road and she took the opportunity to grab him around the neck and hang on.

While he was trying to shake her off, he missed seeing the island, which stopped the vehicle. As it mounted the kerb, she banged his head down on the steering wheel and he stayed down, giving her enough time to get out. The police arrived and quickly arrested the disorientated man.

One of the policemen had laughed that London was not a place to try for a quick getaway on a busy Friday lunchtime.

As to the ambulance with Remy and Rafik's daughter onboard, they had a similar problem, exacerbated by the SUV tying up the traffic. Despite using the siren, it was now stuck in the mayhem. The driver called back to Dilara that he could see two men approaching, one in uniform. Dilara, clearly angry, screamed at the man in Arabic, but he had already made his decision and had jumped out of the ambulance and was running between the cars, chased by a man in uniform.

'This isn't over,' Dilara hissed at Remy. 'Remember what my father said to you, "There will come a time",' and with that, she also jumped out of the vehicle and disappeared into the traffic.

As she watched her go, Remy muttered under her breath, 'Yes, and yours too.'

Tyrone reached the van just as she disappeared. He turned to chase her.

'No, let her go,' called Remy grabbing his arm. Tyrone stopped. He could see the look of total determination on her face, so he didn't argue, even though he thought this was a mistake that he feared would come back to haunt them.

He helped Remy out of the ambulance and together, they walked back towards "Sunshine Villa".

There were no further sightings of Dilara Yazdi, although a small plane had left from the airfield in Upminster the following day, destination Dubai. Andreas had been extremely concerned when he learned from Tyrone what had happened, especially when Remy later told him about the threat she had made. As there was nothing that they could do, Dilara was presumed to have left the country, and her name was added to the international database.

Remy already knew what she must do.

Chapter 58

Now the police, task force, reporters, and curious neighbours had gone, the house in Kensington was quiet. Remy sat with her phone in hand having just received news that Rafik Yazdi, who had been beaten and tortured by Hakimi, had initially survived surgery but had died of complications. Both she and Thomas had doubts, however, as to the truth of this. The task force had always intended to learn as much as they could from Yazdi, so they wondered about the veracity of this claim.

Thinking about him always brought such mixed emotions. She was aware that from their very first meeting he had loved her. She was flattered by his attention; he could be so charming. However, he had taken their playful banter as a sign of her acquiescence and suddenly, things got out of hand, even her shock did not prevent him. She shuddered at the memory. Ashamed, she told herself it was her fault, she had been responsible for what had happened that afternoon, he had misunderstood her; the guilt was hers to carry.

She knew she could tell no one, especially not Farzad, so, she hid her shame in the deepest corners of her mind, where it lay shielded, so she could get on with her life. After Farzad died, she had even started to convince herself that as a penance, she should be with him. But now finally, she had faced the truth of what had happened that afternoon. It wasn't her fault. The man she had trusted had raped her.

Holding a picture of the three men, for the first time, her tears were not those of shame but acceptance of the truth, she was not to blame. As she packed up the Kensington house for the last time, she looked again at the picture, seeing the handsome, laughing face of Rafik, and wondered what could have happened to the engaging young man she once knew to turn him into a monster, capable of such despicable acts. Now, one man was dead, another in her mind was missing, and the third, who had waited for her for so long, must wait no longer. She put the picture face down on the desk; that was the past. She walked to the door and into the future in arms of Andreas.

Chapter 59

Remy had invited the whole team to her house in Crete to recuperate. Once they had all arrived, they were finally able to spend a magical evening together, eating, drinking and reminiscing.

For the whole of the next week together, they enjoyed her hospitality. The weather was beautiful, the azure water of the bay cooling, so everyone relaxed and had fun. But eventually, people started to drift away. Some had further holiday plans, while Jem and Tiana, were off to see her parents, with some exciting news.

Soon the house was almost empty.

Late one night, lying safe in Andreas' arms, Remy told him about what had happened the afternoon at Great Neck and through her tears, she told him the whole truth. The words were difficult at first, but then they tumbled out. He let her finish and when she was calm, he whispered that she had nothing to forgive herself for and that he loved her. They made love and it was the most magically experience she had ever had.

In the morning, he brought her coffee and sitting on the edge of the bed he said, 'We should remember him only as the bright young man of our youth.'

She reached up and kissed him. Finally, she could leave the past behind, it was time to move on.

'What was that for?' He smiled and wrapped her in his arms.

'Just because,' she replied enigmatically and lay back, beckoning to him. Their love consumed them.

Chapter 60

It was just after dawn at a small private airport where a small group gathered, huddled together against the cold dampness in the air. A woman with her arm in a sling and a man carrying a case walked over to a figure standing alone by the side of a plane. The man handed him the case and then left. The woman offered him a small pouch but he shook his head, he seemed to almost bow. Then he pulled her into his arms and gently kissed her forehead, whispering something to her.

They clung together for a short time and then he picked up the case again and limped towards the steps of the plane. Briefly, as he turned, his other injuries were clear. 'HARIAH!' Darius shouted, and his breath caught the air like smoke.

Lissa shouted, *"AINTISAR" (Victory)*.

As Darius Shafiq ducked and entered the plane, the sun broke through the clouds.

Epilogue

Sitting in the warm sunshine, on the balcony of the Queen Mary as it headed for New York, she was glad to be returning home, after once again having been consumed by complex family matters. This time, it wasn't a problem with her cousin, Sophia, there had been enough of those over the years, but now it was with one of her two children, Stream. She had spoken about the issues with Leo's father, Lord Gordan, as he knew the family and hoped that they had reached a successful resolution, although she had her doubts. Anyway, she'd deal with that later, if necessary, she was not going to let it dampen her spirits.

She sipped her wine and let her mind drift through the events of the last few months.

The items that made up the regalia were together again and safe for the time being in a beautifully embossed ebony box. She smiled as she recalled how the Regalia had been certified as authentic, placed in its box and then locked in a crate. It had then been taken from the house in Peckham; the security had been elaborate. As he watched the crate being loaded onto the lorry, Terry smiled to himself, as he noticed some familiar faces. It was taken to an undisclosed location. The only thing missing, was the central stone, the ruby *i qalb bilad faris* (the heart of Persia). It would remain hidden and carefully guarded by its new protector, waiting for "Al-qādim" (the one to come).

She remembered how in the months that followed, various claims were made in court as to who were the rightful owners of the regalia items. The decision was that as stolen property, they could only be returned to their rightful owner, but having been stolen so many times, the court suggested that this might take many years to unravel and therefore, in the meantime, they would remain in a place of safety until their rightful owners could be determined.

Unsurprisingly, she thought, *the Iranian Government saw this as an antagonistic move, which led to a further deterioration in relationships between*

Iran and the UK. However, significant events intervened, resulting in the west being increasingly unwilling to negotiate with a regime that supplied drones to Moscow and weapons to dissident groups to attack others or crush civil unrest at home.

As she pondered these events, she no longer twisted a diamond ring; instead, a simple gold band had replaced it. Thinking of Andreas, she was reminded of how he had finally uncovered the depth of Rafik's betrayal. This also revealed that Farzad's death originally declared an "accident", was, in fact, an execution ordered by Iran, further escalating and sustaining tensions. There were strong denials, counterclaims, and protests from the Iranian Government, followed by threats of retribution. Still, those in power had their own battles to fight at home.

Remy sighed, aware of the issues and restrictions women in Iran faced. Recently, some had been appearing on the street without their hijab (scarf). Although the "Woman, Life, Freedom" protests had been crushed, many women were still refusing to wear hijab in public. Clearly, hardliners needed to find ways to reverse this enduring defiance. Crowds now gathered and cheered when women burned their hijabs, which inevitably led to the greater involvement of hardline forces until the inescapable happened, a woman protester was shot dead by security forces. Her death initially escalated the protests but this resulted in brutal repercussions, beatings, imprisonments, and deaths. The protests had again failed as no one could unite the groups. Remy hoped that one day, the *"Al-qādim"* would come.

Always there were angry debates amongst hardliners but there was a growing awareness of the depth of the challenge these protests posed to the Islamic Republic. While leaders fell back on rhetoric, saying the women's defiance played into the hands of Iran's enemies who they said wanted "to rob the people of the rule of religion". Critics of the government still hoped that the younger generation would be brave enough to change things, although they recognised that this might take time. It was clear that to be successful, a charismatic leader was needed to bring the disparate groups together. With elections being held a new reformer had come forward, many asked could he be the one?

Remy had read a newspaper article where a researcher had suggested that the "fire" for change was still alight, just under the ashes and could be ignited by the smallest breath. People who had become aware would not go back so easily, as one who has experienced freedom cannot go back. It concluded that if there was no hope of change, why would so many people risk their lives for it?

This made her think again about Rafik and those halcyon days at university. How he had argued for the need to recognise and uphold women's rights and freedoms in his country. She remembered that there had been real passion in his words. "There will come a time" might have once been prophetic but these words, like his mind, had become twisted. She asked herself which had been the catalyst that had changed him, was it money, or power, and sighed. Both!

Her thoughts now turned to the team. Once all the questioning and debriefing had happened, they were all finally told that they were free to go and that there would be no further action against them. They were, however, asked to sign secrecy documents relating to the whole episode as a condition of this.

This morning, lying in the sun, with a gentle sea breeze and the long rolling rise and fall of the mid-Atlantic waves, she recalled the days after they were all cleared to go. She had opened her home in Crete and jetted the whole team there for rest and recuperation in the sunshine.

She remembered how thrilled Leo was to find that Julia was able to join the group. She had been lucky as the bullet had grazed her spine in such a way that after weeks of rehabilitation, she had been able to start a progressive fitness regime, which Leo could continue to help her with. She was on extended disability leave and while she loved her job, so much had happened, that she was undecided what she might do next when the time came to decide. Any decision would prove especially hard now as the two were once again close and it was clear they made a great team. Leo had confided in Remy one afternoon that he had no idea where this would take them but like Thomas and Lissa, they were open to see what time would bring.

After a wonderful restful time together, Remy, Andreas, and some of the others were returning to New York on the Queen Mary. Thomas, speaking about the trip later, said that he had seen a very different Remy from the one that he had met that first day on the ship. Although the poise and elegance she displayed remained, he now saw a sense of peace and calmness that he had not seen or felt from her before.

Following Remy and Andreas into dinner on their first night on the ship, Thomas had noted the admiring looks as the couple walked to their table. As ever, she was an elegant and intriguing figure, but now seemed more relaxed and therefore, even more beautiful. She looked radiant as she held Andreas' arm and he dashing figure in a beautifully cut dress suit, his white hair tied with a red ribbon to match her black trimmed, red evening dress. As much as he was happy for her, he couldn't dispel a deep sense of sadness and loss.

Remy, thinking of that evening now, smiled at the memory; that had been a wonderful evening.

Getting up, she picked up her robe and went inside as she knew she should get ready as they would be in New York tomorrow and she still had things to organise for the agency. Casting a final look at the deep blues and greens of the ocean, she blew it a kiss. 'Till the next time,' she whispered.

Having changed, she opened her computer and looked at the current plans for the next few months. While they had been away, both organisations had received several requests for their services, which had gone unanswered. Some opportunities were no longer viable but a few contacts still wanted to talk. It was clear that she needed more staff and Thomas' team would benefit from her wider organisation and the increased marketplace her business offered. There had been a lot of discussions between them, about their options and a possible merger. While there were still things to resolve, the way forward was becoming clearer. Grace was preparing a proposal which she hoped would satisfy both sides.

Remy knew there had been several significant changes to Thomas and Leo's team and was pleased to hear that Tyrone had been offered full-time employment, on a similar basis to Jem. Clearly, they owed him a great deal as it was due to his understanding of the situation, and quick reactions at the house in Kensington, that had identified the true potential of the threat. He had eliminated the bomber and averted a tragedy. It was only when the bomb was being carefully disarmed that at the centre of its complex mechanism, they found a small lighter with "Love ♥ NY" on it. The bomber, who so many had searched for, had set his last device.

Tomorrow, the QM2 would arrive in New York, then later that month, Thomas and Lissa would head to the office to meet Remy. What had been her office and apartment had now become an office they all shared, as she and Andreas had moved out of the city. There was a space for Tiana and Grace to work and a variety of other working spaces. Jem was on paternity leave, so Tiana was now working full-time alongside Grace, helping to organise the new team.

Arriving at the Office, Lissa was excited to catch up with her mother and find out exactly what she and Andreas had planned for their new house. Remy kissed Thomas, then laughed as she rubbed the lipstick from his cheek. She went around the team, chatting to those who had arrived. As the staff began to gather,

Thomas sat back and smiled, remembering the first time he had sat here and how much his life had changed. Not for the first time, he was at a crossroads, unsure of what to do. Did he do what he had often done before, sabotage his, or another's happiness? This time, however, he knew he needed to face the future, whatever that might be.

Andreas arrived and Remy rushed to him and was caught up in his arms. They kissed oblivious of the smiles and whistles from the group. She had missed him so much as he had been engaged in finalising so many things to do with the task force and the end of his naval career, that she had hardly seen him.

Thomas was suddenly reminded of a beautiful evening, sitting on the veranda of Remy's house on Crete. Lissa was asleep and he was just finishing his wine and was gazing out at the stars, when he caught sight of someone, as they walked down to the sea. He realised it was Andreas, who stood alone, skimming stones, as the sky darkened, clearly deep in thought.

Andreas was worried, as the days on Crete had been magical, he didn't want to lose that feeling. He knew that he and Remy had finally arrived at the same point in time and space, and found great joy in each other's arms, but he was concerned that she still harboured some regrets.

Their first night together, had been magical; they had made love, and he had whispered as she slept, 'I love you and I always have.' He did not see her smile. But despite spending every day together, she said nothing. The night Thomas saw him, Andreas had gone down to the shoreline to think, suddenly unsure of himself. He didn't hear her approaching, just felt her arms encircle him and hold him close.

'I love you. ' she whispered. He turned to her and asked the question in his heart.

Thomas had not meant to watch and he didn't hear the words they exchanged, but he knew that these two had finally found each other. He got up and went inside, wishing he could be as sure.

A week later, he and Lissa were the only witnesses at the small hilltop church where Andreas and Remy were married.

Thomas smiled as he remembered how this had remained their secret.

People had started to leave, so he stood up, pulled Lissa to her feet and kissed her. 'Come on, we've a party to go to.' They headed off to Andreas' favourite Greek restaurant, where tonight they would celebrate not just a new business venture but also a union.